## Drusilla was entranced.

Devenish kissed her lightly, not on her mouth but on her eyelids, for her eyes had closed at the moment that he had touched her.

He said, or rather breathed, 'You have no notion how much I wish to make love to you, here, in the library.'

Drusilla opened her eyes and said as softly as he, 'Make love—or make lust, m'lord? Which?'

His answer was a short laugh. 'Pray, madam, what's the difference?'

**Paula Marshall**, married with three children, has had a varied life. She began her career in a large library and ended it as a senior academic in charge of history in a polytechnic. She has travelled widely, has been a swimming coach, and has appeared on *University Challenge* and *Mastermind*. She has always wanted to write, and likes her novels to be full of adventure and humour.

**Recent titles by the same author:**

THE WAYWARD HEART
REBECCA'S ROGUE
THE DESERTED BRIDE

# THE DEVIL AND DRUSILLA

BY

Paula Marshall

MILLS & BOON®

*First published in Great Britain 1998
Large Print edition 1999
Harlequin Mills & Boon Limited,
Eton House, 18-24 Paradise Road,
Richmond, Surrey TW9 1SR*

© Paula Marshall 1998

ISBN 0 263 16036 X

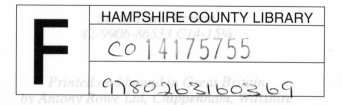

## Chapter One

'It's true what they say about you, you have no heart at all, Devenish. None. They rightly nickname you devilish. You fleeced that poor boy at Watier's last night as cold-bloodedly as though you were shearing a sheep!'

The subject of this tirade, Henry Devenish, Fourth Earl of Devenish and Innescourt, raised his fine black brows and said in a voice indicating total indifference, 'The boy of whom you speak is twenty-two years old. He was gambling with money which he does not possess and he needed to learn a quick lesson before he became a gambling wastrel for life.'

'But did you need to ruin him? I had thought better of you, Devenish.'

'Oh, never do that, George. Most unwise. You should know by now that I have no better self.'

George Hampden, who sometimes (wrongly) thought that he was Devenish's only friend in the world, gazed at his distant cousin hoping to see some softening in his coldly handsome face. He found none. Devenish might have the golden good looks of an archangel in a Renaissance painting, but they were those of an avenging one, all mercy lacking.

'So you intend to call in his IOUs. Including the last one when he bet the family home—and lost.'

'He took that risk, not I.' Devenish's tone was almost indifferent.

'And if you can ruin someone so easily, do you expect me still to remain your friend?'

'I never expect anything of anyone, least of all one of my relatives. And the choice is, of course, yours, not mine.'

How to move him? George said impulsively, 'I don't believe that even you will do such a thing. You don't need the lad's money, he's not your enemy—'

'And it's not your business what I do with my winnings—or how I gained them. Forgive me if I decline to pursue this matter further. I am due at the Lords this afternoon: they are debating this matter of the Midlands frame-breakers and I mean to put my oar in.'

George sank into the nearest chair. They were in the library at Innescourt House, off Piccadilly. It was a noble room, lined not only with books, but also with beautifully framed naval maps. An earlier Devenish had been a sailor before he had inherited the title.

His great-grandson was standing before a massive oak desk on which lay the pile of IOUs which young Jack Allinson had scrawled the night before.

'I shall never understand you, Devenish, never. How you can be so heartless to that poor lad and in the next breath dash off to the Lords to speak on behalf of a pack of murdering Luddites is beyond me.'

'Then don't try, dear fellow. Much better not. You'll only give yourself the megrims. Come to the Lords with me, instead, and enjoy the cut and thrust of debate.'

'Sorry, Devenish, I've had my fill of cut and thrust with you today. I'll see you at the Leominsters this evening, I suppose. They say that the Banbury beauty will be there. The *on dit* is that she's about to accept young Orville. Everyone thought that you were ready to make her a Countess yourself.'

Devenish laughed. He picked up the pile of IOUs and riffled carelessly through them before he spoke.

'Never believe *on dits* about me, George, they are invariably wrong. Besides, I could never marry a woman who has no conversation, and the Beauty is singularly lacking in *that*. Unfortunately in my experience the beauties have no conversation, and the conversationalists have no beauty, so I suppose that I am doomed to bachelorhood.'

'My experience, too,' returned George gloomily. 'Look, Devenish,' he added as he turned to leave, 'you will think of what I said about young Allinson, won't you? It cannot profit you to ruin him: your reputation is bad enough already without his committing suicide. He was threatening to shoot himself after you had left this morning.'

'Oh, as to that,' riposted Devenish, raising one quizzical eyebrow, 'it is also my experience that those who talk loudly and dramatically in public of such an extreme measure rarely put it into practice. No, he'll go and get drunk first and when his head's cleared he'll visit me to beg for mercy.'

'Which you will grant him?' said George eagerly.

'Who knows? It depends on whether my chef is on form at dinner that day. I really do have more to do than think about young Allinson, you know. My speech, for instance. Do be off with you, George. Go and visit the Turkish baths or lose a few hundred yourself somewhere.'

'Oh, I never gamble.'

'Yes, I know. It's a weakness of yours not to have any weaknesses!'

George's shout of 'Devenish, you're impossible,' floated through the double doors as he left.

Devenish raised his eyebrows again and laughed. However much he grumbled, George would be back again to reproach and chivvy him. He threw the IOUs on to his desk, and debated whether to send for his secretary, Thorpe.

At least *he* wouldn't have the impudence to complain about his non-existent moral sense as George always did. He noted idly that Thorpe had been in earlier and had left a small pile of correspondence on his desk for him to deal with.

Devenish picked up the first letter. It was from his agent, Robert Stammers, who ran Tresham Hall, on the edge of Tresham Magna village in Surrey, and the estate around it. He had never been back there since he had succeeded to the title ten years earlier when he had just turned twenty-three. He had preferred to go instead on a belated Grand Tour of Europe, even though Great Britain was in the middle of the war against Napoleon.

Robert had accompanied him as his secretary, and twice a year he visited Innescourt House as a favoured guest, somewhat to George Hampden's bemusement.

That the Grand Tour had turned into something more exciting and important was known to few—and certainly not to George. Even after that, when he had returned to England Devenish had never revisited Tresham Hall: it held too many memories which he had no wish to awaken.

And now Robert was urging him to go there. 'Your presence is needed at Tresham, m'lord,' he had written, 'and for more reasons than I care to commit to paper.'

Now that was a remarkable statement from an underling, was it not? Calculated to rouse a man's curiosity—which was doubtless why Robert had so worded it! If anyone else had written him such a letter Devenish would have dismissed it, but he had appointed Robert to be his agent because he had the best of reasons to trust him.

Devenish sighed. He sighed because Robert was one of the few people in the world who had a right to make a claim on him, so he must agree to what Robert wished. He did not call Thorpe in to dictate the letter to him but began to write it himself.

'Damn you, Rob,' he began without preamble. 'You, of all people, must understand how little I wish to return to Tresham and therefore I have to agree to what you ask, if only because, knowing you, I must believe that you have good reasons for making such a request of me—'

He got no further. There was the sound of voices in the corridor outside, the door was flung open, and Tresidder, his butler, entered, but not in his usual decorous fashion. He was being pushed in backwards by, of all people, young Allinson. He was not only shouting in Tresidder's face but was also threatening him with a pistol.

'M'lord,' gasped Tresidder, made voluble by fright, 'I dare not stop him. He insisted on seeing you, even when I told him that you had given orders not to be disturbed, and then he pulled out a pistol and threatened me with it if I did not do as he wished.'

'Quite right,' raved Allinson, releasing him. 'And now I am here, you may go.' He waved his pistol at Devenish who had risen, had walked round his desk and was advancing on him.

'Tell him to leave us, damn you, Devenish. My quarrel is with you, not with him. And if you come a step further I'll shoot you.'

Devenish retreated and leaned back against the desk, his arms folded, the picture of undisturbed indolence.

'Yes, do leave us, Tresidder,' he drawled. 'I am sure that you have no wish to take part in this unseemly farce which Allinson thinks is a tragedy! Really, you young fool, you should be writing this fustian for Drury Lane, not trying to live it!'

'Damn you, Devenish,' shrieked Allinson, waving the pistol dangerously about. 'First you ruin me, and then you mock me. I came here to make you give me back my IOUs, but I've a mind to kill you out of hand if you don't mend your manners to me! You've ruined me, so I've nothing to lose.'

If he had thought to frighten the man before him by threatening his life, he was much mistaken. However dangerous the situation in which he found himself, Devenish was determined not to allow the young fool to intimidate him.

'Oh, I might take you seriously, Allinson, if you were prepared to admit that you ruined yourself. Do stop waving that firearm about. Did no one ever teach you that it's bad form to point a loaded pistol at people? I suppose it is loaded—or did you forget before you embarked on these histrionics?'

Devenish's insults set Allinson choking with rage. He recovered himself with difficulty and ground out, 'Of course it's loaded—something you'd do well to remember. So, do as I ask, hand over my IOUs and I'll not shoot you, although it's all you deserve—'

'Oh, very well. Anything to oblige a man who's threatening my life. I've no desire to bleed to death on my best Persian carpet. It came from Constantinople, you know. It's supposed to be nearly five hundred years old. My heir—God knows who he might be, I've never taken the trouble to find out—wouldn't like it to be ruined,' Devenish remarked chattily, making no move to do as he was bid. 'It's one of the house's greatest treasures, you know.'

His frivolity nearly had Allinson gibbering. 'Stow that nonsense at once, and give me my IOUs. I mean it.'

Still waving his pistol about, he advanced on his enemy until they were almost face to face.

Devenish said with a weary smile, which merely served to enrage Allinson the more, 'Bound and determined to swing for me, are you?'

To which Allinson made no answer: only bared his teeth at him, and waved the pistol about threateningly.

'Oh, very well,' Devenish drawled, 'I see that I shall have to oblige you. Needs must—if only to save the carpet.'

He slowly turned toward his desk as if to pick up the IOUs lying there. And then, like lightning—or a snake striking—he swung round with the heavy glass paperweight he had snatched up in his hand, and struck Allinson full in the face with it before his tormentor could grasp what he was doing.

Startled, and letting out a shriek of pain as he threw his arms up in an instinctive gesture to ward off what had already hit him, young Allinson's finger tightened on the trigger so that he fired his pistol into the air.

The ball made a neat hole in the face of a bad portrait of the Third Earl which had been hung considerately high.

Between fright and pain Allinson dropped the pistol before falling to his knees, and protecting his damaged face by clasping his hands over it; blood was running from his nose.

Devenish picked up the pistol and laid it carefully on his desk before pulling him roughly to his feet.

'You incompetent young fool,' he said, still chatty. 'You are as inconsiderate as I might have expected. I don't object to you ruining a damned bad painting, but I don't want your blood all over the carpet. Here.'

He handed the moaning boy a spotless handkerchief, just as the library door burst open and a posse of footmen entered led by his chief groom, Jowett.

'A bit slow, lads, weren't you?' was his only remark. 'I might have been cat's meat by now.'

Jowett, who knew his master, grinned, and said, 'But you ain't, m'lord, are you, so all's well. That ass, Tresidder, beggin' your pardon, m'lord, was so frightened out of his wits it took some time for him to tell us what was to-do. I see you've got things well in hand, as per usual. Send for the Runners to deal with him, shall I?'

'By no means. A mad doctor to treat him might be more useful. On the other hand, I think you can safely leave this matter to me to clear up. Let me think. Hmm, ah, yes, Mr Allinson discharged his pistol whilst inviting me to admire it. Why call the Runners in for that? Crime, not incompetence, is their game, eh, Allinson?'

'If you say so, m'lord,' came in a muffled wail through Devenish's ruined handkerchief.

'Oh, I do say so, and more beside when my belated saviours depart. You may go, Jowett. Oh, and take the pistol you will find on my desk with you. I don't think that Mr Allinson will be needing it again. It's quite safe. It's not loaded now.'

'I know, m'lord.' Jowett was cheerful. 'I heard the shot just before we came in. Knowing you, I couldn't believe that aught was amiss.'

'Your faith in me is touching—and one day may be unjustified—but not today. Silly boys are fair game for a man of sense.'

Allinson raised his head. His nose had stopped bleeding. He said mournfully, 'I suppose that you are right to mock me.'

'No suppose at all. Had you succeeded in killing me, you would have met a nasty end on Tyburn Tree. Had you made me give you back your IOUs, you would have ended up a pariah, gambling debts being debts of honour. Think yourself lucky that all you have to show for your folly is a bloody nose.

'And do stand up straight instead of cringing like a gaby. I've a mind to lecture you, and I want your full attention.'

'You have it, m'lord. I must have run mad to do what I did. But to lose everything—you understand—'

'Indeed, not. I am quite unable to understand that *I* should ever gamble away money which I didn't possess and a house which I did. As for compounding my folly by threatening to commit murder! No, no, I don't understand—and nor should you.'

Allinson hung his head. Whether coming to his senses had brought him repentance was hard to tell. He muttered, 'And after all, I am still ruined. I cannot expect you to show me any mercy now that I have threatened your life.'

Devenish sat down and motioned to Allinson to remain standing. 'Before you came in enacting a Cheltenham tragedy, or rather, melodrama, one of my more sentimental relatives was begging me to spare you. I was inclined to disoblige him, but on second thoughts it might disoblige him more if I did as he wished. He will not then be able to contrast my vindictive bloody-mindedness with his forgiving virtue!

'What I am prepared to do is to continue to hold your IOUs—'

Allinson gave a stifled moan. 'I might have known,' he muttered.

'You know nothing for you have not allowed me to finish. You would do well to curb your reckless impetuosity before you become gallows' meat. Hear me. What I am prepared to do is not to call them in so long as you refrain from gambling in future. Should you begin again I shall not hesitate to ruin you.'

This time Allinson groaned. 'The sword of Damocles,' he said at last. He was referring to the old legend in which a sword was held over Damocles' head, poised to fall, put there by the tyrant he had flattered in order to show him the limitations of life and power.

'Exactly. I'm charmed to discover that you learned something at Oxford—was it?'

'You know it was. You seem to know everything.'

'Enough.' Devenish rose. 'Do we have a bargain?'

'You know we have. You leave me no choice—'

'No indeed, again. Of course you have a choice—although I take your comment to mean a grudging acceptance of my generous offer.'

'Generous offer,' wailed Allinson. 'You mock me again. I am your prisoner.'

Devenish pounced on Allinson once more. He grabbed hold of him, gripping him by his over-elaborate cravat.

'Listen to me, you ungrateful young fool. You have, through my leniency, escaped the gallows because otherwise that is where your stupid escapade would have taken you. I offer you freedom and a chance to reform your dissolute life—and you jib at doing so.

'Answer me! Yes or no, unequivocally?'

'Yes—if you will stop strangling me,' Allinson croaked.

'Unequivocally, I said. Yes, or no?'

'Yes, yes, yes.'

'And remember what awaits you should you back-slide.'

'I'll not do that.' Inspiration struck Allinson. 'I'll…I'll buy a commission, turn soldier—that should keep me out of trouble.'

Devenish gave a short laugh and released him. 'God help the British Army, then! Now, go. I have letters to write and a speech to rehearse. Oh, and by the way, give Tresidder a guinea from your pocket to make up for the fright which you gave him.'

'I haven't got a guinea. My pockets are to let.'

'Then give him the pin from your cravat instead—and be gone.'

The relieved boy scuttled out of the room, pulling the pin from his cravat as he left. Devenish said aloud to the damaged portrait of his grandfather, 'God forgive me—although you wouldn't have done—for letting him off. I must be growing soft these days.'

And then he sat down to finish his letter.

He was late arriving at Lady Leominster's that night. He had written to Robert, naming a date for his arrival at Tresham—'and God help you if you have sent for me for nothing,' he had ended.

His speech in the Lords, asking for clemency and help for the starving Midlands framework knitters, who had recently rioted at Loughborough in Leicestershire, had created a great deal of excitement, if nothing else.

'What interest do you belong to?' one excited peer had shouted at him. 'You're Whig one week, and Tory the next.'

'None,' Devenish had shot back. 'I'm my own man and you'd better not forget it.'

'A loose cannon, careering round the deck then,' his neighbour, Lord Granville, had said languidly to him. 'Hit, miss and to the devil when anyone gets in your way.'

His reward for this shrewd comment was a crack of laughter from Devenish. 'By God, Granville,' he had offered, 'you'd be Prime Minister if you could make a speech half as incisive as your private judgements.'

'Not a remark anyone would make about you,' returned Granville, his perfect politeness of delivery robbing his words of their sting. 'You have no private judgements. Everything you say is for public consumption. So far as that goes, you're the most honest man in the two Houses.'

Remembering this interchange, Devenish smiled when he saw Granville and his wife across the

Leominsters' ballroom, talking to the Home Secretary, Lord Sidmouth. Some devil in him, which desired confrontation today, had him walking over to them.

Sidmouth's response to him was all that he had expected. 'Ah, here comes the noble advocate for the murdering Luddites I'm busy trying to control! What got into you, Devenish, to have you defending them?'

Devenish had a sudden vision of a mean street in a Northern town where a half-starved boy and his penniless and widowed mother had eked out a poor living.

He repressed it and said, 'I don't condone their violence, you know, but I do understand what causes it. Some relief, surely, could be given to those who wish to work, but who are unable to do so.'

'Not Jacobin tendencies then, eh, Devenish? No feeling for revolution?' Sidmouth said this quietly. He was a mild man. 'No, don't answer me, I know that on the whole you are more like friend Granville here and favour moderate and gradual change.'

He paused, 'Perhaps Lord and Lady Granville, you will forgive us both. Devenish is well met. I have need of a private and quiet word with him. You will both excuse us, I trust.'

The Granvilles assured him that they would. Sidmouth led Devenish into an ante-room and shut its double doors behind them. Without preamble he said, 'Do you intend to visit Tresham in the near future?'

Devenish said, 'I have thought of doing so, yes. It's years since I was there. My agent reproaches me every month for my absence, so I have arranged to go as soon as the House rises.'

'Yes, you take your duties seriously. As I take mine. I ask you because something odd has been happening there recently. The Lord Lieutenant of Surrey has brought to my notice that over the last few years two men, one a person of quality, have disappeared. The gentleman was later found murdered. Several women of the lower orders have also disappeared—one as recently as a month ago. No reason has been found for their disappearance, and apart from that of the gentleman, not one of their bodies has been recovered. He would like an enquiry made.

'Now, I have the hands of myself—and the few men I have at my disposal—overfull with this business of controlling radical revolution, to say nothing of Luddite discontent. I was speaking to an old friend of mine—Wellington, to be exact—and he told me that he has reason to believe that you are a sound man in a crisis involving danger. That being so I would ask you—discreetly, mind—to investigate this sorry business and report back to me should you find anything of moment.'

Devenish's first thought was of Robert's mysterious letter. He said nothing, however, other than, 'I think that the Duke overestimates my abilities, but I will do as you ask. As a stranger to the district it will not seem odd if I ask questions about it. I take it that that is all the information you have. Has no other landowner raised the matter?'

'Yes, Leander Harrington, the eccentric fellow who lives at Marsham Abbey, alerted the Lord Lieutenant about the second man who disappeared. It was his valet, and although he had no reason to believe that foul play was involved, he had given no warning of his imminent departure. On the other hand his clothes and possessions had gone, which seemed to indicate that he had left of his own free will.'

'As a matter of interest, have you any information about the murdered gentleman?'

'Yes, indeed. He was Jeremy Faulkner of Lyford, a young man of substance. He was found dead in a wood some miles from his home. His body had been brutally savaged by an animal, it was thought, although whether before or after death was not known. His widow, Mrs Drusilla Faulkner, the late Godfrey Stone of Stone Court's daughter, had reported him missing at the beginning of the previous week.'

'And Lyford House is less than a mile from my seat at Tresham. I see why you thought of me.'

'Coupled with what Wellington hinted, yes.'

Well, at least it would help to pass the time at Tresham—and perhaps serve to subdue his unwanted memories.

'I can't promise success,' Devenish said slowly, 'but I'll do my best.'

'Excellent, I shall be able to reassure the Lord Lieutenant that I am taking him seriously—although I shall not tell him who my emissary is. The fewer people who know, the better. This business might be more dangerous than it appears.'

Sidmouth paused. 'You're a good fellow,' he added warmly. 'I felt sure that you would oblige me.'

'Despite my reputation for never obliging anyone.' Devenish began to laugh. 'At least it will enliven a few dull weeks.'

Later he was to look back on that last remark and at the light-hearted fool who had made it, but at the time he walked back to the ballroom to congratulate Lord Orville on having won his beauty.

## Chapter Two

'Isn't it time, Drusilla, my love, that you left off wearing your widow's weeds? Jeremy has been gone for over two years now, and I don't believe that he would approve of your hiding yourself away from the world, either.'

Miss Cordelia Faulkner looked anxiously at her nephew's widow. She did not wish to distress her, but she thought that the time had come for something to be said.

'Dear aunt,' said Drusilla, looking up from her canvaswork, 'I am scarcely wearing widow's weeds. I have always chosen to dress modestly, and to live in like fashion, and I have certainly not hidden myself away from the world. I live a busy life locally, and only this week I have arranged with the parson of Tresham Magna that his annual fête to raise money for the poor children of the parish will be held in our gardens.'

'I expressed myself badly. I should have said the polite world. You ought to marry again, my love, not spend your life pining for my poor, dead nephew, and where better would you find a husband than in London?'

How to answer that? Drusilla looked away and caught a glimpse of herself in the long Venetian glass which hung on the other side of the room.

She saw a composed young woman in her very early twenties, dressed in a high-waisted gown of pale mauve, the colour allowed to a widow during her second year of mourning—a year which was now over. Her glossy curls were dressed on top of her head, one ringlet falling round a swan-like neck. Her eyes were the soft grey of clear water and her complexion was creamy, with only the faintest blush of pink.

Jeremy had always called her lips kissable—and he had often kissed them during the two years of her marriage. No, that was not correct, Drusilla reminded herself sadly, for eighteen months only. He had barely touched them, or her, during their last six months together.

It was the memory of those last sad months which helped to keep her in thrall to him. What had gone wrong with their marriage that he had absented himself from her not only bodily, but mentally? What had changed him from a carefree laughing boy to a brooding man? Was it something which she had unwittingly said or done?

Drusilla returned to the present with a start. Miss Faulkner was staring at her. She put her work down. 'I'm sorry, aunt, I was wool-gathering. But you already know that the polite world does not interest me, and I have no intention of marrying again.'

'So you say now,' remarked Miss Faulkner shrewdly. 'Later, you will surely change your mind.'

She sat down opposite Drusilla and said, her voice a trifle sad, 'I cannot recommend the single state, my dear. When I was young and foolish I turned down a man of solid worth because he was not romantic enough for me—my head was stuffed with cobwebs.

'By the time I realised that I was neither pretty enough—nor rich enough—to catch the handsome young fellow I thought I loved, and would have settled for solid worth, he had found another bride. And I, I never found anyone else who wished to make me his wife, and I led a lonely life until Jeremy kindly asked me to be your attendant when you married him. Do not reserve my sad state for yourself. You are younger, prettier and richer than I ever was. Find a good man and marry him.'

Picking up her canvaswork again, Drusilla told Jeremy's aunt what she had never thought to tell anyone. 'This time I would wish to marry for love. Oh, don't mistake me, my parents arranged our marriage and I was happy with Jeremy.'

Until the last six months, said her treacherous memory.

Repressing it, she continued, 'I'm not hoping for a grand passion, just a homely love. The kind of love my parents shared. What Jeremy and I had was friendship. I may be foolish, and I may have to settle for less again, but not yet, please.'

'Very well, my dear, so long as you don't wait too long—or settle for a fortune hunter.'

'Oh, I shall ask for your advice if one arrives. Would you forgive me if I settled for one who was young, handsome—and kind?'

Miss Faulkner smiled. 'Ah, you mean like Miss Rebecca Rowallan's Will Shafto, I suppose. There are not many of those on offer, I fear.'

Further conversation was stopped by an agitated rapping on the door, and the entry of Vobster, Drusilla's chief groom.

'Yes, what is it, Vobster?'

'It's Master Giles, ma'am. He's trying to persuade me and Green to allow him to ride Brandy instead of Dapple. I fear that, unless you have a word with him, he won't take no for an answer.'

Drusilla rose, shocked, her face paling. Behind her Miss Faulkner was making distressed noises. Giles was Drusilla's eighteen-year-old brother, who had a badly crippled leg as the result of a strange childhood illness which had kept him bedridden for months.

Dapple was a mild and well-behaved nag whom the doctor had reluctantly given him permission to ride, but Brandy was quite a different matter. He was the most high-spirited horse in the Faulkners' small stable.

'I'll come at once,' she said quickly. 'We can't have him trying to ride Brandy.'

'And so I said, but he wouldn't be told.'

'Well, he'll listen to me, I hope. I don't wish to ban him from riding at all, for I believe that it keeps him well and happy, but we can't have him risking his neck on fliers like Brandy.'

*   *   *

She arrived in the stable yard to find that Giles had finally persuaded Green to allow him to mount Brandy, by promising that he would not ride him, but would allow Green to hold him steady in the stable yard.

'I should so like to sit on a real horse for once,' he had said pathetically, 'instead of that rocking chair which is all Dru will allow me.'

'And rightly so, Master Giles, for you have not the strength to control Brandy. It was all Mr Jeremy could do to hold him.'

Giles knew that Drusilla did not wish to sell Brandy, although she could not ride him, because it would mean that her happiest memories of her husband would have disappeared with him.

He looked proudly down at his sister. 'See how well I sit on him, Dru,' he said. 'Pray allow me to ride him—if only for a few yards.'

Drusilla looked sadly at Giles. On horseback he appeared to be a handsome and well-built boy for his withered leg was hidden by his breeches and his spotless boots. She also saw a masculine version of her own face. Parson Williams had nicknamed them Sebastian and Viola, the beautiful brother and sister in Shakespeare's *Twelfth Night*, who were so alike that in boy's clothes they could be mistaken for one another.

'You know very well that you cannot do that. It is against the rules which the doctor insisted on for your own safety.'

'Oh, pooh to him! My arms are strong enough for me to control any horse. I refuse to be namby-pambied any more. At least allow Vobster and Green to walk me on him for a short distance. You may watch me and see how well I do.'

He looked down at her, his face on fire. Drusilla knew how much he resented not being like other boys, particularly since it was plain that if his leg had been normal he would have had the physique of an athlete.

'Very well,' she said, relenting, 'but you must promise to be good.'

His smile was dazzling. 'Oh, I am always good, Dru! You know that.'

'No such thing,' she told him ruefully, but gave Green and Vobster permission to lead him and Brandy out of the yard and on to the track which led out of Lyford House to join a byway which led to Tresham Magna. Vobster was shaking his head a little because she had, as usual, given way to headstrong Master Giles and nothing good would come of that.

He was right. For the first hundred yards Giles behaved himself, trotting along equably, with Brandy showing his annoyance at being curbed by tossing his head and snorting. One of the stable lads, Jackson, mounted on Drusilla's own horse Hereward, accompanied them. Drusilla herself, despite wearing only light kid sandals, brought up the rear.

The path was firm and dry and the July sun shone down on them. From a distance they would have made a suitably charming scene for the late animal painter, George Stubbs, to celebrate.

And then, as Drusilla afterwards mourned to Miss Faulkner, Giles had to spoil it. Without giving any warning of what he was about to do, he put spurs to

Brandy who, nothing loath, reared his haughty head, and set off as though he were about to charge into battle or win the Derby.

Green let go of his leading rein immediately. Vobster, more determined, hung on a little by one hand before prudence had him follow suit, lest he be injured. Jackson, urged on by the horrified Drusilla, tore after Giles in hot pursuit, for it was plain that the delighted Brandy, given his head, was going to be too much for his rider to control.

As though to demonstrate that he was in charge, Brandy immediately left the path, and charged across country towards Tresham Hall until he came to a tall hedge which he promptly jumped. Jackson followed suit, whilst Drusilla, Green and Vobster panted along behind them, delayed by having to push their way through a gap in the hedge.

Once through they saw that Hereward had unshipped his rider, but that Brandy had not, although Giles was slipping sideways in the saddle. Only his courage and his abnormally strong arms were preventing him from following Jackson's example as Brandy made for the next hedge.

But not for long. A final lurch to the right by wilful Brandy had him out of the saddle, too. Unencumbered by Giles's weight, Brandy tore madly on towards another horseman who had jumped the hedge from the other side and who only avoided being struck by the oncoming Brandy by swerving sharply.

He then had to swerve sharply again to prevent himself from trampling on the prostrate Giles—which manoeuvre almost had his own horse unshipping him! The happy Brandy, meanwhile, was bolting into the far distance.

Drusilla opened her eyes, which she had closed after Giles's fall and Brandy's near accident, to see that the new horseman had stopped, flung his reins to a drop-jawed Vobster, who had outpaced herself and Green, and was running towards Giles who was trying to sit up.

'No, don't,' said the stranger sharply, falling on to his knees beside the dazed boy and beginning to feel his arms and legs to check whether any bones were broken.

He had just discovered Giles's withered leg when Drusilla arrived—Green had gone to try to catch Hereward so that he might pursue Brandy, whilst Jackson was limping homewards.

'Is he badly hurt?' gasped Drusilla who had not run so far or so fast since she had been a hoydenish young girl.

The stranger looked up at her. 'Apparently not—and no thanks to the fools who let him ride a half-broken horse. You were lucky that he didn't kill himself.'

Drusilla could not help herself. She stared at him. He was the most handsome man she had ever seen. He resembled nothing so much as the statue of Apollo which Jeremy's father had brought from Greece. His hair, cut short in the latest fashion, was golden, and slightly curling. His eyes were as blue as the sunlit sea and his mouth was long and shapely: but for all his classic beauty there was nothing feminine about him.

On the contrary, he gave off an aura of cold strength and assured masculinity which was reflected in a voice so hard and measured that it shocked Drusilla into silence.

Not so Giles. He struggled upright and said indignantly, 'You go too fast, sir. And you're not to talk to my sister like that. My accident wasn't her fault, it was mine. I was stupidly disobedient and paid the price for it—and who the devil are *you,* anyway?'

The stranger laughed and rose. 'You might say the devil himself if you wished. But I would prefer you to call me Devenish. I apologise to your sister—and in the name of all that is holy, who are *you,* anyway?'

Brother and sister both stared at him. Giles croaked, 'Forgive me, m'lord, I had no notion that you were staying at Tresham, or I should not have been so short. I am Giles Stone, and this is my sister Drusilla Faulkner, the widow of the late owner of Lyford House.'

'Are you, indeed! If you were my young brother and responsible for riding a horse you couldn't control then I would think up a suitable punishment for you. I trust your sister will do the same.'

'But you ain't,' retorted Giles, struggling to his feet, to be helped by Devenish when he saw the lad's determination. 'And it's up to her to decide on my punishment, not you. Ain't it, Dru?'

'Ah, a youth of spirit,' drawled Devenish. 'How came you by that leg, anyway? Were you born with it?'

This matter-of-fact question, when most people they knew tip-toed apologetically round Giles's disability, pleased both brother and sister.

Drusilla suddenly found her voice. So this was Henry, Earl Devenish, nicknamed 'the Devil'. She could not allow the knowledge of his reputation to silence her. She answered him before Giles could.

'A childhood illness, m'lord. He contracted a long and lingering fever, which had him bedridden and his leg withering. But that was the least of it, most of the children around here who were so afflicted at the time lost more than that. They lost their lives.'

'Well, at least he kept his—and his impudence, too. Are you fit enough to walk to my horse, Master Giles, or would you prefer me to carry you? I can convey you to your home if your sister will lead the way.'

'Oh, Green will do that when he returns,' said Drusilla hastily. 'No need to put yourself out.'

'Oh, I never do that,' riposted Devenish. 'Very unwise. People would always be expecting it of me—most inconvenient. I needed amusement and entertainment this afternoon and you are providing it. I had not thought the countryside so full of incident.'

And that was that. There could be no gainsaying him. He helped Giles to hobble towards his horse, and with Vobster's assistance they hoisted him on to it, and set off for Lyford House.

Well, he had wanted entertainment and now he had it! What was better still, he could not have hoped for an easier entry to the late Jeremy Faulkner's home, together with an introduction to his widow. He had not known of the lively young cub's existence and could not be sure whether the lad's presence would make his task easier or harder.

As for Mrs Drusilla, she was a pretty young thing with, if he was not mistaken, a graceful figure beneath her Quakeress's gown. Was she still in mourning for the late Jeremy? Its colour would suggest so. After two long years? Did one then infer an undying love?

Probably, on the evidence of their encounter so far, the lad had all the spirit in the family—and all the character, too. Yes, undying love it must be, of the sentimental sort, ignoring all the flaws which the late Jeremy must have undoubtedly possessed.

Devenish's cynical musing was taking place whilst he talked nothings to the unworldly Miss Cordelia Faulkner. His hostess had insisted on seeing her brother to his room and sending for the doctor before she returned to take tea with them.

Drinking tea at an unfashionable hour held no attraction for him—he detested tea at any hour. Coffee was Devenish's drink, but he was prepared to sacrifice himself for once.

'Do you intend to stay long in this part of the world, m'lord?' Miss Faulkner was asking him.

'Oh, that depends,' he answered, 'on whether I find anything on which to fix an interest—or to entertain me. Now this afternoon I was provided with a great deal. To be nearly run down by a riderless horse, to avoid by inches trampling a lively youth to death, followed by meeting a charming widow—now that is a series of situations for a novel, do admit. Particularly since myself, horse, youth, and lady, are still alive and well.'

Miss Faulkner beamed at him. He was not in the least like his reputation. Such easy charm! Such grace! It was fortunate that mind-reading was not her game, for what Devenish was saying and what he was thinking bore no relationship to one another.

'I believe that your adventures this afternoon resembled those in the novels of Miss Jane Austen rather than the Gothic delights of Mrs Radcliffe. No murders, no haunted abbeys, mysterious monks or dangerous crypts,' she announced gaily.

Devenish forbore to point out to her that the former owner of Lyford House itself had been involved in one mysterious death. Tact must be used here, particularly since Mrs Faulkner, followed by the tea board, was now with them again.

He rose and bowed. Drusilla noted distractedly that his clothing was as perfect as his face and body. She had always assumed that a man nicknamed 'the Devil' must be dark and dour and dressed to match.

Nothing of the sort. The only thing about him which lived up to his name was his conversation, if the manner in which he had spoken to Giles was typical of it.

'I trust that Master Giles is beginning to recover from his accident,' he offered her.

'Master Giles,' returned Drusilla cheerfully, 'is behaving as he always does—as though he hasn't a care in the world. I am beginning to ask myself what would distress him.'

Devenish's smile was almost a grin. 'Better that way, surely, than a lad who always makes the worst of things.'

'Oh, indeed. He was distressed, I must admit, by my husband's death—but then he and Jeremy always dealt famously together. Not many men would have cheerfully given their wife's crippled young brother a home—and made a friend of him.'

'I had not,' Devenish lied smoothly, 'been informed of your husband's death. I regret that I was never kept up to the mark with local news. As you know, this is my first visit to Tresham in ten years. I trust that it was not a lingering illness.'

He saw her face change and added hastily, 'Pray ignore my question if it distresses you.'

'Not at all. It is two years since my poor Jeremy was found dead at some distance from his home. As to how and why he came to his end I suppose I shall never now know. You may imagine that at the time I was greatly distressed, but I have come to terms with it, if slowly.'

'A mystery, then.'

'Oh, indeed. The Lord Lieutenant came to see me, to assure me that everything in his power would be done to find the wretch—or wretches—who killed him. Alas, he wrote to me recently telling me that he regretted his failure to track them down.'

Drusilla was calm. Until very recently she would have found difficulty in speaking of Jeremy's dreadful end. She noted that Devenish's response to her was as coldly practical as his question about Giles's damaged leg had been.

'I commiserate with you, madam. You must miss him greatly.'

'Yes, we were childhood friends, and our life was happy, but pining for him will not bring him back.' The gaze she gave him was a frank one—which, like his, did not match her thoughts. She could never forget that last six months, never.

Devenish nodded his agreement. 'Yes, you are right there. Common-sense is always better than sentimentality. In the end, one has to come to terms with the discomforts of living.'

Drusilla nodded in her turn, and conversation died for a moment while Miss Faulkner, who had taken charge of the tea board, offered everyone more tea and muffins.

'Do you intend to settle in Surrey?' Drusilla asked him when tea had been poured and muffins refused, more to turn discussion away from Jeremy's death, she told herself, than to discover m'lord's intentions. In thinking this she lied to herself a little. Lord Devenish intrigued her. He was so unlike Jeremy, or, indeed, most of the men she knew.

It was not only his looks which fascinated her, but his barbed remarks, so carelessly tossed at his hearers. Even so, little about him appeared to justify his fearsome reputation.

She must have been staring mannerlessly at him, for he was smiling quizzically at her over the rim of his teacup.

Drusilla realised with a start that he had just replied to her question—and she had not heard him!

What was worse, he knew that she had not. She flushed.

He saw the flush and said gently, 'I collect that you did not quite grasp what I said. My intentions—like my recent answer—are vague. They depend on whether country living bores me—I have experienced so little of it, you understand, that I have no means of knowing whether it will please me or not. I am an urban creature, the town has always been my home, and I have yet to discover the delights of rural living so far as its scenery and its social life are concerned.'

He was talking to put her at ease again, something which surprised the cynical creature Devenish knew himself to be. She was a most unremarkable young woman, so why was he troubling himself with her? Normally he would have carelessly offered her a put down to punish her for her inattention—instead, of all things, he was trying to be kind by restoring her *amour-propre*!

To reward him for his consideration Drusilla offered eagerly, 'If you wish to see the countryside at its best, there are some picturesque views from the hills near Tresham Hall. And Miss Faulkner and I can offer you a splendid social occasion on Saturday.

'We are opening the grounds of Lyford House so that the incumbent of Tresham Magna church, Mr Williams, can organise his annual fête to raise money for the poor children of the parish. Your presence would add lustre to the occasion.'

Devenish rose and bowed. 'How could I refuse such a charming offer! Of course, I will attend. And you will, I am sure, inform Mr Williams that I shall be pleased to forward him a large donation. His cause is a worthy one.'

He was ironically sure that all his London associates—he told himself that he had no friends—would have been astonished to learn of his generosity since he usually mocked those who salved their consciences by giving large sums to charity. What they could not know was that she had named the one cause to which he always secretly gave: the relief of poor children.

Unaware of this, Drusilla murmured her thanks. He bowed again, saying 'Forgive me, ladies, if I leave you now. My agent will be in a rare taking if I do not return home soon. I told him that I would be gone for a short time—and now I have spent the whole afternoon away.

'He will be sending out search parties to find me for he is convinced that, though I may survive in dangerous London town, I shall be quite lost in the innocent countryside!'

The smile which he gave them at the end quite overset the pair of them. It transformed his face, turning it from a cold and stony beauty, like that of a statue, into something attractively human.

Seeing it, Drusilla experienced a totally new sensation. Her whole body thrilled so strongly that she became completely aware of every part of it. For the second time that afternoon she scarcely knew where she was.

Miss Faulkner's heart missed a beat. What a delight-ful man! She knew of his nickname and his reputation, but her immediate response was, *Oh, what a Banbury tale! Such a charmer as he is could not possibly be the man of whom I have heard.*

And so she told Drusilla when he had left them. 'You do know, my dear, that his nickname is Devilish, and that he is sometimes called Satan. He is supposed to be as hard as nails, and to have the tongue of a viper. As usual, I have to believe that, yet again, rumour lies.'

'Handsome is as handsome does,' remarked Drusilla as coolly as she could in an effort to reprove herself for her strong reaction to him.

She paused a moment before resuming. 'We know little of Lord Devenish other than that he is a charming and considerate person to entertain to tea and muffins. We can scarcely judge of him correctly on such a slight acquaintance.'

'Oh, you are always so commonsensical, my love. For once allow your feelings rather than your reason to command you.'

Drusilla could not retort that to give way to her feel-ings might be most unwise where Lord Devenish was concerned—it would be too dangerous—so she wisely said nothing.

'Forgive me, Rob, if I dashed away as soon as I arrived, but driving in a closed carriage, even for a short distance, always gives me the megrims. I needed to be out—and I was happy to be so. Particularly since I happened across a most charming local family, all bread-and-butter innocence—Mrs Drusilla Faulkner and her young brother, Giles. It was the lad's misfortune to fall from his horse. Assisting them made me late for my meeting with you'

'Now, you are not to sneer at them, Hal. They are all that you criticise them for being, and to know them would do your black heart good!'

'If my black heart were susceptible to tea, muffins and a spinster lady, as well as the brother and sister, then you might be right,' drawled Devenish, pulling a chair round and sitting astride its seat. 'Now, pray inform me what has been all a-bubble here that you send for me so peremptorily.'

He made nothing of being called Hal. It had been his childhood name and the only person in the world allowed to use it was square, solid and dependable Robert Stammers who was examining him so quizzically.

'Before I begin to do so I would wish you to allow one of your labourers, Caleb Hooby, to speak to you on a matter related to the misgivings which had me ordering you to do your duty here at last.'

'Reproaches, reproaches, Rob, they are all I ever hear from you, but, yes, send him in. I suppose that he has a story to tell?'

'That he has, and I would prefer him to tell it to you.'

'Very well, and I had best sit behind your desk, looking as solemn as befits the Lord of All visiting the peasantry both high and low.'

Caleb Hooby proved to be a middle-aged man, decently dressed and nervously turning an old-fashioned brown wide-brimmed hat in his hands.

'Most kind of you to allow me to speak to you, m'lord, most kind.'

Devenish waved his hand. 'No matter, pray begin.'

'It's this, m'lord. See, I have a daughter Kate, a pretty child, but naughty, just turned sixteen. A sennight since she disappeared late one afternoon. She told her mam that she was off to walk with a neighbour's girl, Ruth Baker, and would not be long. Not long, she said, m'lord, not long, but she never came back, and Ruth said as how she never met our Kate, nor had arranged to meet her.

'Not hide nor hair of her has ever been seen since. I feared that she had run away. She had been a wild thing this last few months, and would not be checked. I thrashed her the day before for not helping her mam with the little 'uns as she should, and mayhap that caused her to leave us. Her mam found that her few bits of clothes had gone, too. One of the labourers on Master Harrington's estate said that he had seen a lass like her waiting at the crossroads where the London coach picks up passengers.

'And then, this morning, her mam found her little box of treasures still in the cupboard in the room she shares with the little 'uns. And when she opened it, it was full of her little bits and pieces, as well as the few pence she saved to buy trinkets for herself and the little 'uns when the pedlar came round. But what worried us was, why did she leave the money behind if she were going to London? And where got she this, m'lord, as I shall now show you.'

Silent before the man's anguish, Devenish watched him fumble in his breeches pocket, before he added, 'And why should she leave such a valuable thing—and her savings—behind if she was off to London to make her fortune? For that was a jest of hers in happier days.'

So saying, he drew from his pocket something that shone and glittered in the bright afternoon sun, which filled the room, and laid it on the desk before Devenish.

Devenish picked it up. It was a necklace of thin fine gold, with a small pendant diamond in a delicately beautiful setting. He examined it carefully and handed it to Robert, who gave a low whistle, and said, 'Is this as valuable as I think it is?'

Devenish did not answer him, but said in a voice quite unlike his usual mocking one, 'Tell me the truth, Hooby. Have you ever seen this before?'

'Nay, m'lord. Never. What should a poor fellow like me have to do with such trinkets?'

'And you never saw your daughter wearing it?'

'Neither I nor my missis, m'lord. Who would give her such a thing? She was walking out with Geoffrey Larkin until a month or two ago, but she quarrelled with him. She said as how he was a rough fellow, and not for her.'

'And she had not walked out with anyone since?'

Hooby nodded agreement.

Without warning his face crumpled and tears stood in his eyes. 'What has she been adoin' of, m'lord? For Lily, her next sister, allows as how she has been leaving her bed at night and coming home she knows not when, bein' asleep herself. And now I learn this very day that more'n one maid round here has left her home and not been seen again. I am afeared for her, m'lord, and ask your help.'

'Which I shall give you, so far as it in me lies. You will leave the necklace with me, for it might help us to discover who gave it to your daughter and why.'

'Oh, m'lord, I fear I know why she was given it: as payment—which makes me fear the more for her.'

'Yes. I understand. But until we know more, we can neither fear the worst nor hope for the best. I have only been at Tresham for a few hours, but I shall make it my business to get to the bottom of this. Go home, comfort your wife and pray for good news.'

Robert saw him out and turned to Devenish, who was propping his chin with his hands and staring into space.

'That did you credit, Hal,' he said abruptly. 'Why cannot you always speak so?'

'What?' he exclaimed, staring at Robert as though he were returning from a long way away. 'Oh, you mean how I spoke to Hooby. Few people in this world deserve any compassion, Rob. When they do, I offer it to them. For the rest—' and he shrugged.

Robert was gloomy. 'So, your verdict is the same as mine. Some harm has come to her, I fear.'

'As does poor Hooby. And do you think this business of a disappearing wench is linked with that of the others—or with anything else? I have already learned that Jeremy Faulkner met a strange death.'

He thought it wiser not to admit—even to Robert—his knowledge of the other deaths and his conversation with Lord Sidmouth.

'As well as several servant girls, two men have disappeared over the last few years—one of them Jeremy Faulkner and the other Harrington's valet. Complete mystery surrounds the whole business. The numbers are slowly rising and no one seems to be able to discover the reason, and that is why I became uneasy, Hal, and sent for you.'

'And is Kate Hooby the first of my people to disappear?'

'As it chances, yes.'

Devenish rose and paced restlessly round the room. 'If we were living in a Gothic novel written by Mrs Radcliffe or Monk Lewis, we might suspect that a mysterious animal stalks the woods between Tresham and Marsham Abbey seeking and finding prey. But since this is southern England and the only mysterious animal around here is that huge mongrel which you still favour, then we must dismiss that supposition.'

He came to a stop by a map table on which lay a *gazetteer* of the district.

'Allow me to refresh my memory of my estates and those which march with them before I speak with you further. I fear that poor Hooby depends on a broken reed if he thinks that I may be able to help him. No matter. On Saturday, Rob, we shall both attend the fête given by Mrs Drusilla Faulkner in the grounds of

Lyford House in order to empty our pockets—and keep our ears open.'

He gave a short scornful laugh and said, 'But I am not hopeful, Rob, not hopeful at all, despite my brave words to that poor fellow.'

# Chapter Three

'How good of you, my dear Mrs Faulkner, to allow your beautiful grounds to be invaded by so many. Even for such a good cause as the poor children of the parish it is most magnanimous of you.'

Mr Williams, the incumbent at Tresham Magna, a portly middle-aged man, beamed kindly at Drusilla and wished that he were twenty years younger and unmarried that he might offer for such a treasure.

He turned to Devenish who had just strolled over to them, Robert walking at his rear, and said, 'I do not know, m'lord, whether you have had the honour to be presented to our hostess yet, but if not—'

Devenish cut him short. 'Oh, but we have met already, quite informally, so it is, unfortunately, too late for all the usual niceties, as I am sure Mrs Faulkner will agree.'

Drusilla had already been busily admiring m'lord's splendour. Beside him everyone looked provincial, or as though they were striving to appear as fine as he did—but had failed. Only Robert in his sensible countryman's clothing had not sought to compete with his friend and master.

Devenish was turned out so as to emphasise that even an event as small as this was worthy of his full attention. His bottle-green coat, his cream-coloured breeches, his perfect boots, his splendid cravat—a waterfall, no less—and his carefully dressed hair, gave him the air of just having sat either for a portrait by Sir Thomas Lawrence, or for a fashion plate designed to sell a Bond Street tailor's wares.

Now she smiled at him and the parson, saying in her quiet, pleasant voice, 'Since we have met, m'lord, allow me to present to you one of our guests—that is, if you have not already met him informally. I mean Mr Leander Harrington.'

She gestured at that gentleman who had just walked up to them.

'No, indeed,' said Devenish languidly, 'I have not yet had the honour.'

'No introductions needed,' interjected Mr Harrington before Drusilla could speak. 'I do not subscribe to the pantomimes of an outworn society, you understand, Devenish. And since we each know to whom we are speaking, that is enough. We are men together, no more and no less.'

'Well, we are certainly not women,' drawled Devenish, 'so I must agree with you in that, if nothing else. On the other hand, if Mrs Faulkner had not mentioned your name beforehand I would have been reduced to asking my good friend Stammers here who the devil you were!'

Several of the bystanders, previous victims of Mr Harrington's Radical views, sniggered behind their hands at this put down.

Nothing ever put Leander Harrington down, though. He smiled. 'Remiss of me, I suppose, not to mention that I am Harrington of Marsham Abbey—for what such titles are worth. I am but a citizen of the great world, and proud to take that name after Earl Stanhope's great example.'

'Ah,' said Devenish, and to Drusilla's fascination, his drawl was longer than ever, 'you are, I see, of the Jacobinical persuasion—as Citizen Stanhope was. Pray inform me, sir—as Stanhope, despite his desire to be at one with all men, threw away his title, but retained his estates and his wealth—I suppose that you have followed his example there as well and retained yours?'

Great men, like Devenish, could say what they pleased, Drusilla knew. What she also knew was that she had long considered Leander Harrington to be a fraud, and it was a pleasure to hear him called one so gravely and apparently politely.

Leander, though, was never bested in an argument. He ignored protocol and all the uses of polite society to clap Devenish on the back. 'Why, Devenish, until the great day comes when we are all equal in every way in the eyes of the law as well as God, I must sacrifice myself and husband what my ancestors have left me so that it may, at the last, be put into the pool for the common good.

'I bid you do the same, brother Devenish—and cleanse your soul.'

Behind Devenish, Robert made a choking noise. Those before him waited to see what riposte m'lord might make to that. His smile was enigmatic. 'Since I possess no soul to cleanse, that might be difficult, but I accept your suggestion in the spirit in which it was offered.'

Drusilla heard Miss Faulkner gasp behind her. She found that she had the most overwhelming desire to laugh, but dare not, for the bewildered parson was staring, mumchance, at the patron who had given him his living.

'You cannot mean that, m'lord,' he managed at last.

'At your pleasure, sir, and at both our leisures we must discuss my soul later,' said Devenish. 'Here and now is not the time. Mrs Faulkner, I would ask you to be my guide on this fine afternoon.' He bowed to Leander Harrington and said indifferently, 'Your servant, sir, and you will excuse us. Later you might care to visit the Hall and we can have a discussion on whatever subject you please.'

'Oh, very fine,' said Drusilla softly to Devenish. He had taken her arm and was walking her away. 'I compliment you, m'lord. Not many men could be as exquisitely rude and as exquisitely polite in two succeeding sentences as you have just been.'

Devenish looked down at her. Demure-looking she might be, but there was much more to her than that. He half thought that she was playing his own game with him by making cutting remarks in a pleasant but indifferent voice.

He briefly considered echoing her comment by saying, *Not many women have made half so observant a remark to me, and in such a manner that I am not sure that you actually meant to compliment me.*

Instead he merely offered, 'I trust that your brother has recovered from his fall.'

Drusilla looked up at him. For a moment she had wondered whether he would answer her in his most two-edged fashion. Since he had not, she was as coolly pleasant as he.

'Oh, very much so. I am fearful of what he might next wish to get up to—and what it might involve me in.'

'He is present this afternoon, then?'

'Oh, yes. I had thought that he might have tried to find you before now. He wishes to thank you for coming to his aid so promptly.'

'But I did very little for him.'

'Only because there was little to do. The thought was there, m'lord.'

Yes, there *was* more to her than he might have guessed.

Devenish looked around him at the house standing before them: a handsome, classically styled building in warm stone, a gentleman's residence, not too large and not too small. Over the front door was a stone shield with a falcon trailing its jesses on it: the Faulkners', or the Falconers', punning coat of arms. At the back of the house were three lawns, all at different levels on a slope running down to a wide stream.

Tents and tables had been erected on them. On the top lawn a target had been set up and a group of gaily dressed women were engaged in an archery competition. Their male escorts were standing about, keeping score, and urging them on before they took part themselves later.

'I must not monopolise you,' he said, abruptly for him, for his speech was usually measured. 'You have your duty to do to others.'

'Oh, m'lord,' Drusilla spoke softly, but firmly. 'My biggest duty is to see that you are introduced to most of your neighbours—if you will so allow.'

Oh, yes, he would allow. In the normal course of events he would not have permitted himself to be bored by making the acquaintance of a pack of nobodies, but he had given Sidmouth his word that he would try to discover what was going awry around his home, and he would do his best to be successful. Mrs Faulkner was going to save him the trouble of spending several weeks discovering who was who around Tresham Magna and Minor.

*Noblesse oblige* then—and perhaps it would do him good not to be selfish for once, and stifle his sharp tongue! As if to aid him in this decision Giles Faulkner hobbled up to him, full of a goodwill which it would be wrong to mock.

'Dru said that you might honour us with your presence, m'lord, and so you have. Now I may thank you properly for your consideration when I played the fool and received my proper payment by falling off my horse.'

He caught Devenish's sardonic eye and added ruefully, 'Oh, I see what you are about to say! That I didn't receive my proper payment for it because I didn't break my neck!'

'Well anticipated,' offered Devenish, 'except that I was only thinking it—not about to utter such a home truth aloud.'

This honesty pleased Giles immensely. He smiled and began to pull at Drusilla's sleeve.

'I say, Dru,' he exclaimed, 'you aren't going to tire my saviour out by dragging him round to introduce him to all the old bores of the district, are you? Much better if you went in for the archery competition, sir—if you can shoot, that is.'

'Giles, Giles,' reproved Drusilla, 'you mustn't run on so! Whatever will m'lord make of your manners? And do address him by his proper title. He will think you ignorant of the world's usages.' Giles thought this pomposity unworthy of his sister and was about to say so. Devenish forestalled him.

'Sir will do, my dear Mrs Faulkner. I am m'lorded quite enough as it is. I would be even happier if you were to address me as Devenish. You are my nearest neighbour, after all.'

He had no idea what made him come out with this unheard-of piece of condescension, but was left with no time to theorise as to the origin of it. Drusilla was surprised by it, but had little time to ponder on it because they were rapidly being approached by all those who wished to meet the great man who had avoided meeting them for ten long years.

Devenish knew Parson Williams because he had interviewed him in London when he had granted him his living, but he had never met Williams's junior fellow at Tresham Minor, George Lawson, having allowed Rob Stammers to make the appointment in his absence.

Lawson was the first to reach Drusilla and he made a low bow to his patron, murmuring, 'Too great an honour, m'lord, too great,' when Devenish, remembering his resolution to be pleasant to everyone, said he would be happy to entertain him to dinner in the near future.

He was a handsome young fellow in his mid-twenties, short rather than tall, dark in colouring, with an easy insinuating manner which Devenish instantly, and instinctively, disliked. He disliked most of all the expression on the fellow's face when he spoke to Drusilla, and the way in which he fawned on her, holding her hand a little too long after she had offered it to him.

He thought the dislike didn't show, but Drusilla registered it immediately. To her surprise, and much to her shock, she found that she was beginning to read Devenish's mind.

She smiled a little to herself, when, in swift succession, Devenish made further invitations to dinner to John Squires of Burnside, Peter Clifton of Clifton Manor, and a series of minor gentlemen. When Leander Harrington returned to ask m'lord to dine at the Abbey in the near future, he invited him as well.

'And you, too, Mrs Faulkner,' he added, 'and Master Giles. He is quite old enough at eighteen to join us and it is time he made his entry into the polite world.'

It was a pity, Drusilla thought, that she had always held Mr Harrington in dislike, for he was one of the few men who behaved to Giles as though he were a normally healthy person. For some reason which she could not explain, however, he made her flesh creep.

She would have been astonished to learn that Devenish was—to his surprise—registering her concealed dislike of the man. He thought that it showed her acumen as well as her good taste.

He had not expected to discover anything about the missing men and women on an occasion such as this. He moved about the grounds of Lyford House, being bowed to and responding with his most pleasant smile, his cutting tongue for once not in evidence. He was thinking, not for the first time, of the vast difference in life between the few fortunate men and women who surrounded him, and the vast mass of people at the bottom of the social heap.

Men—and women like the missing girls.

Here food was piled up in plenty on beautifully set tables. Elegantly dressed men and women talked and laughed in the orange light of the late afternoon's sun.

For the unlucky in their wretched homes a meagre ration was laid out on rough boards in conditions so vile that the workers on his estate would not have housed pigs in them. Their clothes were ragged, and the men and women who wore them were stunted and twisted.

Devenish shivered. He thought of Rob Stammers's surprise when he had ordered that the cottages on his estate should be rebuilt and the men's wages increased so that they might live above the near-starvation level which was common in the English countryside.

It was when he was in this dark mood which sometimes visited him at inconvenient times that John Squires approached him and asked diffidently, 'If I could have a serious word with you for a moment, m'lord, I should be most grateful.'

'As many serious words as you like,' he responded. 'But what troubles you, that you wish to be serious on a fête day?'

Squires coloured. He was a heavyset fellow in early middle age, ruddy of face, a country gentleman who was also a working farmer.

'It's this business of the missing wenches, m'lord, but if you prefer not to talk about it here, we could perhaps speak later—'

'No, speak to me now. I have had one conversation about a missing wench since I arrived in the district, and another will not bore me.'

'Very well, m'lord,' and he launched into a lengthy story of the miller's daughter in Burnside village who had disappeared six months ago.

'A good girl, her father said, until a few weeks before her disappearance, when she became cheeky and restless, and not hide nor hair of her seen since. Just walked out one evening—and never came home.'

His words echoed those of Hooby. Devenish decided to test him.

'And why should you—or I—trouble ourselves about missing girls?'

Squires stared at him as though he were an insect, lord though he might be.

'They are God's creatures, m'lord, and I have learned this afternoon that others are missing. It troubles me, particularly since one of them, Kate Hooby, was the miller's daughter's best friend.'

'Strange, very strange,' Devenish remarked, as though he were hearing that there was more than one lost girl for the first time. 'I share your worries about this. They cannot all have decided to run away to London to make their fortune on the streets.'

John Squires decided that he might have been mistaken in his first judgement of m'lord. 'Then you will cause an enquiry to be made, m'lord.'

'Indeed, I shall ask Mr Stammers to make a point of it.'

'My thanks then. The miller is a good man, and what troubles him must trouble me.'

Devenish watched him walk away, and decided that since the matter had been raised now by two others he might safely speak of it without any suspicions being aroused as to why he was doing so. He looked around for Drusilla and found her immediately. Despite the fact that she was carrying a fat baby boy, he decided to make a beginning.

'You are encumbered,' he drawled. 'Pray sit down, the child is too heavy for you, and sitting will be easier than walking.'

He waved her to one of the stone benches which stood about the lawns, and saw her settled before he sat down beside her.

'You know,' Drusilla observed quietly, watching him as she spoke, 'you are quite the last person, m'lord, whom I would have thought would wish to sit next to a woman holding a baby boy dribbling because he is teething. It only goes to show how mistaken one can be and should teach us all not to jump to over-hasty conclusions!'

'If you did not look as demure as a Quaker saint, I would think that you were bamming me, Mrs Faulkner.'

'Oh, dear, no, m'lord, just wondering what you have to say to me that is so urgent that you cannot wait until I shed my burden. And, by the by, do the Quakers have saints? I rather thought that they didn't.'

Robert, watching them from a little distance while he talked to Miss Faulkner, was surprised to hear Devenish's shout of laughter and wondered what Mrs Faulkner could have said to cause him to behave so informally.

'If they didn't, they ought to have,' Devenish finally riposted. 'I never thought that I should have to come into the wilds of the country in order to find a woman who would give me a taste of my own verbal medicine.

'Let me confess that I do have an ulterior motive in sitting by you. John Squires has just been telling me the surprising story that several of the local wenches have disappeared mysteriously. Have you mislaid any? Or is the Faulkner estate so considerately managed that no one from it has absconded to London to make their fortune?'

'Now, m'lord,' responded Drusilla seriously, wiping the little boy's dribbling mouth with her lace-edged linen handkerchief, 'this is not a matter for levity. The parents of the girls are most distressed, and no, none of my people has disappeared.'

'I stand corrected, or rather, I sit so. I see by your reply that I must take this matter seriously. Does that child have an endless supply of water in his mouth? Both you and he will be wet through if he continues to dribble at this rate.'

As though he knew that Devenish was referring to him, the little boy leaned forward, put out a wet and sticky hand, and ran it down the lapel of his beautiful coat before either he or Drusilla could stop him.

'Oh, dear!' Drusilla pulled him back with one hand and put the other over her mouth. 'I should never have consented to sit by you whilst I held Jackie. He is quite the liveliest child in the Milners' family, and I have been looking after him to give his poor mama a little rest.'

And then, without having meant to, quite the contrary, she began to laugh as Devenish fished out his beautiful handkerchief and started to repair the damage, his face an impassive mask—although his mouth twitched a little.

'I'm sorry,' she began. 'I shouldn't laugh, but, oh, dear—your face.'

'No, you shouldn't,' said Devenish agreeably. 'But then, as you have just rightly pointed out, I am responsible for my ruined coat by having first waylaid you and then allowed you both to sit by me. You do realise that he's about to be sick all down you at any moment?'

'No!' Drusilla leapt to her feet and, quite instinctively, thrust Jackie at Devenish so that she might begin to mop herself.

Devenish didn't need to mop himself because, having caught Jackie, he dextrously up-ended him and held him at arm's length so that he christened the grass instead of his already ruined jacket.

'Goodness me!' Drusilla exclaimed, scrubbing herself. 'I might have guessed that your invention would be as sharp as your tongue.'

The fascinated spectators to this unusual scene included a startled Robert and Miss Faulkner who stood aghast, her mouth open in shock, as that aloof Lord of Creation, Henry Alexander Devenish, Fourth Earl of Devenish and Innescourt, turned the squalling Jackie right side up and began to wipe him clean with his handkerchief.

Jackie, who had started to cry when subjected to this briskly sensible treatment, ceased his roaring immediately when Devenish told him sharply, 'Now, my man, stop that at once, or I shall be very cross.'

Drusilla said faintly, 'How in the world did you manage that? No one has ever been able to quieten him before once he has begun to cry. You really ought to offer yourself to the Milners to replace the nursemaid they have just lost. She was fit for Bedlam, she said, if she did not resign on the instant.'

Devenish, who had pulled his gold watch from his pocket with his right hand whilst he held Jackie in the crook of his left arm, and was circling it above his absorbed face, said abstractedly, 'I had a baby brother once.'

The Milners, who had just been informed of the brouhaha which their infant had caused, arrived on the scene to find their usually rampant offspring blowing bubbles of delight at Devenish as he tried to grasp the swinging watch.

'Oh, m'lord,' gasped Mrs. Milner. 'Oh, your beautiful coat, you shouldn't, you really shouldn't—'

'Not at all,' remarked Devenish coolly. 'Since I have been informed that this is the first time today that he has behaved himself, I think that I really should, don't you? For all our sakes.'

And since the Lord of All, as Drusilla privately called him, made such a statement, no one present dared to contradict him.

For some reason poor Miss Faulkner was the most disturbed by Devenish's behaviour. Later, her niece could only think that she had the absurd notion that it brought dishonour on the Faulkner name that he had arrived at such an unlikely pass.

She said sharply to Drusilla, 'My dear, I told you no good would come of your assisting the Milners' monstrous child. Look at you both! Your dress is ruined, and as for Lord Devenish's coat—'

'Very helpful of you,' remarked Devenish smoothly, 'to be so wise both before and after the event. You are quite right. Both Mrs Faulkner and I will be happy to be relieved of continuing to look after the incubus, and I'm sure that you will be delighted to care for him instead, seeing that his poor mama is already in the boughs over him—or so I am informed,' and he thrust Jackie into the astounded Miss Faulkner's arms.

'You may borrow my watch if he starts to cry again,' he offered helpfully. 'It seems to do the trick.'

'Oh, Devenish, you really are the outside of enough,' gasped Drusilla through laughing sobs. 'Give him to me, Cordelia, he cannot ruin my dress any further and I'll return him to his mama when she feels able to look after him.'

Mrs Milner had, indeed, sunk on to the stone bench where Drusilla and Devenish had been sitting, and was moaning gently while being comforted by her husband.

'She is increasing, you know,' Drusilla informed Devenish severely, in as low a voice as she could manage, 'and she needs a rest from him every now and then.'

'Really,' returned Devenish, quite unruffled by the commotion which he had created. 'I should have thought everyone needs a rest from him all the time. Pity we don't sacrifice to Moloch any more.'

'Devenish!' Drusilla and Robert exclaimed reproachfully together, whilst Cordelia Faulkner asked faintly, 'Why Moloch?'

And then, 'Oh, the God to whom they sacrificed children. Oh, Lord Devenish, you surely cannot mean that.'

'No, he doesn't,' said Drusilla and Robert together, and 'Yes, I do,' drawled Devenish, but he winked at Drusilla to show her that he was not serious.

She responded by kissing Jackie to show that she loved him if no one else did, and shaking her head at Devenish to reprove him for being flighty.

Giles, a fascinated spectator of the antics of his elders, said, 'I think babies are disgusting. If they ain't dribbling from one end, they're hard at it from the other. Can't think why anyone wants them.'

'Well, someone wanted you,' drawled Devenish. 'A bit of a mistake, d'you think?'

Drusilla said, 'I think it's time everyone behaved themselves. You know, Devenish, you're a really bad influence on us all. I quite agree with what you said earlier, you have no soul.'

But she was laughing when she said it. Giles looked after her as she removed Jackie from Devenish's corrupting presence by handing him to his now recovered mama and escorting them into the house where they might be private, and Drusilla might change her dress.

He said confidentially to Devenish and Robert— Miss Faulkner was panting in Drusilla's ear—'You know, sir, I don't think you're a bad influence on us at all. Why, since poor Jeremy died I haven't heard Dru laugh like that once!'

It was Robert who laughed at this artless remark and not Devenish, who said, as grave as any judge, 'Might you not consider that to make your sister laugh like that confirmed my bad influence on her rather than refuted it?'

'Not at all, sir.' Giles's response was as serious sounding as Devenish's. 'Why, when Jeremy was alive, she used to laugh all the time.'

He paused, a puzzled look crossing his open, handsome face. 'Except,' he said slowly, 'during the last few months before Jeremy was killed. She grew uncommon moody, as I recall. Jeremy told me that it was because she was unhappy at not providing him with an heir—although judging by the way that most babies behave, I can't understand why that should make her sad.'

'You will,' said Devenish, filing away Giles's strange piece of information in his retentive memory, 'until then, I shouldn't worry. You'll want your own heir one day.'

'I shall?' This seemed such an unlikely remark that Giles decided to ignore it. After all, Devenish didn't seem to be in any great hurry to provide an heir for himself, but he wisely decided not to say so.

Instead, he invited him to take part in the archery competition—'all the gentleman are expected to do so, and the prize is a silver medal which Dru will present at the end of the day.'

'I shall be delighted,' Devenish told him, which had Robert saying to him in the carriage on the way home, 'You were in an uncommon good mood today, Hal. I would have thought that it might be the kind of bread-and-butter occasion which would have brought out the acid in your speech.

'And, forgive me for asking, what was that about your having a baby brother? I always supposed you to be an only child. At least, your grandfather always spoke as though you were.'

'So he did, Rob, but then, seeing that he was invariably wrong in all his judgements, it's not surprising that he was wrong in that, too.'

He made no attempt to speak further on the matter, leaving Robert to expand instead on the charms of Mrs Drusilla Faulkner and the surprising fact that it had been Devenish to whom she had presented the silver medal for winning the archery competition.

'Another thing I didn't know about you—that you were a fine shot with a bow, except—' and he looked sideways at Devenish '—that you seem to excel at everything you do, however unlikely.'

'Don't flatter me, Rob, it doesn't become you,' Devenish returned shortly. 'Any success I may have is only because I choose never to do anything at which I don't excel.'

He seemed to be in an odder mood than usual so Robert remained silent for the rest of the short drive back to Tresham Hall. Something, he was sure, had occurred, or been said, that had set Devenish thinking, and thinking hard.

His face had taken on an expression which he had not seen since the days of their adventures on the Continent, and it was one which had only appeared in times of trial and danger.

Which was passing strange, because what times of trial and danger could there possibly be in sleepy Surrey?

## Chapter Four

The day's events had so excited Drusilla that she found it difficult to sleep that night—especially since the night was warm, even for summer.

For some reason she could not get out of her head the sight and sound of m'lord Devenish. One moment she was remembering his mocking voice, and the next she had a vivid picture of him holding little Jackie in the crook of his arm, displaying a strange tenderness of which she had not thought him capable.

Worse, he stirred her senses after a fashion which no one had ever done before—not even Jeremy. She was reluctantly beginning to understand that what she had felt for Jeremy was nearer to friendship than to passionate love.

And why was she thinking of Lord Devenish and passionate love in the same sentence? Could she passionately love such an apparently cold-blooded man? Especially since it was not his beautiful face which attracted her, but his beautiful voice saying shocking, unexpected things.

The kind of things which quiet, respectable Mrs Drusilla Faulkner had often thought but had never dared to say!

This insight into her deepest mind set her wriggling in the bed, her cheeks hot and her body strangely alive. She decided against calling for her personal maid, Mary, who had slept in a room near to hers ever since Jeremy's sudden death. Mary deserved her night's rest—and of what use could she really be? There was a pitcher of water and a glass by her bed, and she could surely pour a drink for herself without disturbing another's sleep.

A sound outside around eleven of the clock—a bird or a wild animal calling, perhaps—had her sitting up and deciding to open one of the windows to let in a little air.

Without using her tinder box to light a candle since it was the night of the full moon, she rose and threw back the curtains and opened the window just as the noise came again. It was neither a bird nor a wild animal, but stifled human voices, one of them laughing, the other murmuring 'Hush'.

Drusilla looked down. She saw, briefly in the moonlight, a man and a woman, fully dressed and holding hands, running across the back lawn, down the steps from it, and into the avenue below. She was unable to see their faces or identify them in any way.

Silence followed, broken only once by the cry of an owl. The man and the woman did not reappear. Who could they be? Servants, perhaps, but doing what—and going where? And who else would be in the grounds of Lyford House in the middle of the night. She would speak to Mrs Rollins, the housekeeper, in the morning.

This strange disturbance, added to her mind's refusal to let go of her memories of Lord Devenish, made sleep impossible for some time, but she heard nothing more.

A long time later she fell asleep for a few short hours before morning arrived all too soon. She ordered breakfast to be brought to her room and drank chocolate and ate buttered rolls in blessed silence.

Why did she think blessed silence? Because her mind was still in turmoil after yesterday's strange events. Cordelia Faulkner begged to be admitted, but Drusilla fobbed her off with a fib, saying that she had a megrim and would go to church only for the evening service.

One person whom she did admit was Mrs Rollins, the housekeeper. She was a tall, austere woman in early middle age, the terror of the under-servants. The Mrs was an honourary title for she had never married.

She had terrified Drusilla in the early days of her marriage, until she discovered that Mrs Rollins possessed a sense of loyalty to the Faulkners which was almost fanatical. That loyalty was now transferred to her.

Drusilla began without preamble, speaking of what she had seen the night before and asking if it were possible that she had witnessed a pair of servants who had left the house after nightfall without anyone's knowledge or permission.

Mrs Rollins heard her out before saying, 'It is quite impossible, ma'am, for any of the servants to leave the house at any time, particularly at night, without the knowledge of Britton or Letty Humphreys.'

Britton was the under-butler, a young man who had a room off the menservants' dormitory in the attic, which was locked by him at ten o'clock at night. The same arrangement held good for the maids who were similarly supervised by Letty, the chief parlour-maid, a stern elderly woman.

The senior servants had rooms of their own, but they were all of mature years and Drusilla was sure that the pair she had seen were young.

'Someone from one of the villages, ma'am,' Mrs Rollins suggested. 'Larking about the grounds at night.'

'But we are such a long way from either Tresham Magna or Tresham Minor,' Drusilla said, frowning. 'And why should they come here? It might be more sensible of them to lark in the grounds of Tresham Hall.'

'Harder to break into them,' suggested Mrs Rollins practically.

Drusilla had to let that be the last word, but for some reason the little incident had disturbed her—and why it should was mysterious. She told herself not to be troubled by such mental cobwebs, brought on, no doubt, by a poor night's sleep. She went downstairs where she found an anxious Miss Faulkner about to set off for morning service at Tresham Magna, Lyford Village possessing no church of its own.

'You look pale, my dear,' she told Drusilla agitatedly, 'It must be all the excitement yesterday. Lord Devenish may be a great man, but he is scarcely a restful person.'

Drusilla thought that Lord Devenish's sharp tongue must be catching for she found herself saying, 'One imagines that great men are rarely restful, Cordelia, but in any case I find his manner refreshing. We practise a deal of hypocrisy, you know.'

Consequently she said nothing of what she had seen the night before to Miss Faulkner for she did not wish to disturb her further.

She might have saved herself the trouble; when Miss Faulkner arrived back in the middle of the morning instead of at the end, her face was pale and she was trembling violently.

'Whatever can be the matter?' exclaimed Drusilla. 'What brings you back so early?' She poured out a glass of wine and handed it to her companion, 'Here, drink this, it may help you to compose yourself.'

'Nothing can do that,' gasped Miss Faulkner, 'nothing,' shivering as she drank the wine down in one unladylike gulp. 'I shudder to tell you, but I must. Of all dreadful things when Mr Williams arrived at the church this morning he found—oh, I cannot tell you, it is too dreadful.'

'My dear,' said Drusilla gently, 'I fear that you must.'

'Yes, I must, mustn't I? Oh, my love, of all things he found a dead sheep on the altar and the bishop must reconsecrate the church—Lord Devenish had been sent for, and I regret what I said of him earlier this morning. He was so kind. We are to use the chapel at Tresham Hall, he says, to save us having to go all the way to the church at Tresham Minor. So very gracious of him!'

Drusilla sat down, plainly shocked. 'Who could have done anything half so dreadful—and why?'

'No one knows. It seems that Farmer Ramsey had an argument with Parson Williams over the tithes—which he lost. But one cannot imagine such a jovial fellow as he is doing such a thing in revenge.'

'No, indeed,' said Drusilla faintly, thinking of the jolly red-faced man who had often given her sweet milk to drink, fresh from the cow, when she had been a little girl.

And so she told Devenish when he visited them that afternoon to reinforce his invitation to use his chapel.

'I thought that I ought to come to inform you that we shall make every effort to identify and punish the miscreants,' he told them.

Giles said eagerly, 'Vobster, our head groom, believes that it may have been Luddite sympathizers at work. Even down here, he says, there are those who talk and plan sedition.'

Devenish had surprised himself—and Rob Stammers—by finding that he needed to reassure the two ladies and young Giles that the authorities were not taking this matter lightly. He had ridden over to Lyford House as soon as he decently could, to be received with tea and muffins.

He said soberly, 'Oh, everyone has a different explanation, from Farmer Ramsey's annoyance over his tithes to a prank by unnamed villagers.'

'And which do you favour, sir?' asked Giles who had, much to Devenish's secret amusement, adopted him as a kind of honourary uncle of whom advice might be asked.

'I?' said Devenish coolly, accepting a cup of tea from Miss Faulkner, 'Why, I favour none of them until some kind of evidence emerges which might support any of the explanations offered. So far all we have is hot air and supposition.'

He looked across at Drusilla who was staring thoughtfully into space, 'You seem a little engrossed, Mrs Faulkner. Forgive me for questioning you, but is that because you have something of matter to import relating to what we are discussing?'

He was reading her mind again. Drusilla lifted her head and gave him a splendid view of a pair of candid grey eyes.

'I suppose,' she said slowly, 'that what I am about to say may be of the order of hot air and supposition. On any other day I might have dismissed what I saw late last night as mere innocent playfulness, but after this morning's events—who can tell?'

Devenish leaned forward. 'You intrigue me, madam. What exactly did you see last night?'

Without embroidery, Drusilla told him, as soberly as she could, of the two strangers in Lyford's grounds on the previous evening. She added, equally soberly, 'When I questioned her this morning, my housekeeper was firmly of the opinion that I had not seen two of my servants who had broken the staff rules by leaving their beds after lights out.'

Miss Faulkner exclaimed faintly, 'Oh, I wonder that you could have slept after *that*. I am sure that I couldn't have done.'

'Ah, but Mrs Faulkner is made of sterner stuff, are you not, Mrs Faulkner?'

Was there the usual faint tinge of mockery in his comment? Drusilla did not know. Perhaps not, because after he had leisurely demolished a muffin and the clock had ticked on in the silent room, Devenish said, 'Would I be considered to be grossly intrusive if I asked to be allowed to visit your room so that you might show me exactly what you saw—and where?'

'Or what I thought I saw,' said Drusilla challengingly. 'For I believe that you may be of the opinion that I might be indulging in hot air and supposition.'

'Oh, you don't think that, surely, sir?' exclaimed Giles. 'Why, Dru is the most sensible women I know—indeed, I would dare swear she is the *only* sensible woman I know.'

Devenish's beautiful mouth twitched. Miss Faulkner said aggrievedly, 'You want manners, Master Giles, and, as I have often said, if you are not to go to university, then a strict tutor ought to be employed to teach you the discipline you would otherwise have learned there.'

'You interest me, Miss Faulkner,' remarked Devenish. 'I would be happy to learn to which university you refer. None of those with which I am acquainted had much to do with teaching their under-graduates any form of discipline—quite the contrary.'

Giles threw him a grateful glance. Miss Faulkner, who was not sure whether she had been complimented or insulted, gave a hesitant, worried smile. Seeing her discomfort, Drusilla surveyed Devenish with a measuring, judgmental eye, and said coolly, 'Well, one thing is plain, m'lord, after that remark Giles would do well not to come to you to learn good manners—or perhaps Earls are exempt from them.'

'Oh, my dear,' gasped Miss Faulkner, 'I am sure that Lord Devenish did not mean anything wrong by what he said.'

'Oh, I am sure that he did,' retorted Drusilla. 'Did you not, m'lord?'

Her own daring in thus reproaching him for mocking poor Cordelia struck Drusilla when it was far too late to retract anything which she had said. She waited for the cutting riposte which was sure to follow.

It didn't. Instead Devenish rose from his chair, walked over to where she sat and lifted her hand to kiss it.

'You are right to rebuke me,' he said, his voice gentle. 'I have grown too accustomed to using my tongue to cut down those around me and who often feel unable to reply because of their lower rank. I must cease the habit.'

He turned to the astonished Miss Faulkner who stared at him, her mouth agape. 'Pray forgive me,' he asked, bowing to her, 'for I spoke ungallantly to you—and not for the first time. I promise not to do it again.'

'Oh, it was nothing, nothing at all, m'lord.'

'Ah, but it was. It was most wrong of me. And now, ladies, you will lead me to the room from which Mrs Faulkner saw—what she saw.'

The smile he gave then was his dazzling one. Drusilla, who was already overset because of the sensation which his kissing her hand had created, found that she was quivering with excitement. She told herself that this was partly relief because he had not taken offence at her rebuke, but she knew that she was lying.

Well behaved or ill behaved, he was having the most profound effect on her. Worse, however much she told herself to ignore it, she was unable to do so. All the way up to her room she lectured herself—in vain.

She watched him look around it. It was a lady's bedroom in splendid order and furnished in the most perfect taste. Devenish walked to the window, bidding her to stand beside him—Miss Faulkner was acting as their chaperon and hovered nervously behind them as Drusilla told her tale.

'And after they had crossed the lawn they went that way,' she ended, pointing to the steps down which the man and the woman had disappeared.

'Which leads towards—where? Remind me, we have turned so many times since I entered Lyford that I have lost my bearings.'

'Well, nowhere, really. I suppose that the nearest habitation in that direction is Marsham Abbey, Mr Harrington's place. There is a footpath across the fields which leads to it—but it is rarely used these days. It also runs in the opposite direction, but since Swain's

Hall was pulled down it goes nowhere, because the path to the highway beyond it has disappeared through lack of use.'

'I see.' After that Devenish fell silent. Drusilla had been right when she had said that what she had seen had been unremarkable, and would have been unremarked—save to her housekeeper—had it not been for the sheep on the altar.

'Does Harrington graze sheep on the Abbey's fields?'

'Oh, yes. But others around here graze them on their fields, including Farmer Ramsey—and you, of course.'

'Of course,' he echoed, and laughed. 'You are a shrewd lady, Mrs Drusilla.' He lowered his voice a little and asked, 'Did your husband find you so? And did your husband mind your sharp tongue?'

'Oh, I rarely had occasion to use it on him, m'lord.'

He laughed. 'Oh, so you reserve it for my deficiencies. I suppose that I do deserve it more. He was young, was he not?'

'Not quite twenty-five when he died.'

Devenish was grateful that the opportunity had been given him to ask these questions without seeming overcurious.

'And you had not long been married, I collect. I suppose, then, that you and he were rarely apart, so that his disappearance must have come as a great shock to you.'

'Oh, yes, but not so great a shock as his untimely and dreadful end.'

'And while he was alive, neither you nor he ever saw strangers in your grounds?'

'No,' Drusilla answered a little sharply, for she was not sure where this questioning was going—nor why Devenish was engaging in it.

But something, somehow, in the quizzical look which he then gave her jogged her memory.

'Except...' she began slowly, and then stopped. 'No, it could not be related to this.'

'Except,' Devenish mused, his bright blue eyes hard on her. 'I do dislike excepts—when they lead nowhere, I mean. They intrigue me, and for the rest of the day I am more bad-tempered as well as being ruder than ever, I fear. Pray finish and do not condemn me to that—you would not like it, and consequently I should feel the edge of your tongue!'

'Very well. He said one day, about nine months before he was found dead, that he was surprised that the path to the Abbey was being so heavily used, and that it must be at night, since he had never seen anyone on it during the day time.

'He told me that he would investigate the matter as it seemed rather odd. But nothing further came of it other than that he had spoken to Mr Harrington of it and he had assured him that he must be mistaken. Two of his gardeners used it. And that was that. The path had become worn, he said, and it did not need heavy use to cut it up.'

'Your husband never spoke of it again?'

'No, never. I am sure that it was simply one of Jeremy's whim whams—he was given to them. His father was the same, wasn't he, Cordelia?'

'Oh, yes. He had the oddest fancies which disappeared as soon as made, you know. Why, I remember old Mr Faulkner swearing that there were strange goings-on in the countryside around Lyford, but since his mind became very feeble before he died, no one thought anything of what he said.'

Another dead end. He could scarcely believe that the whim whams of the Faulkner men had any connection with dead servant girls and a sheep on an altar.

Except—and it was a good except, he thought wryly—that Jeremy Faulkner had died a strange and unexpected death. Like the sheep.

He dared pursue the matter no further even although it enabled him to stand next to Mrs Drusilla Faulkner and admire her pure and perfect profile. He dared swear that—like old Mr Faulkner—he was running mad to be so occupied by the charms of a country widow. Rob would be sure to twit him when he returned home.

All the way back to Tresham Hall what disturbed him the most was that it was not only her looks and figure which charmed him, but her ready, rebuking tongue. Who would have thought that such a gentle-seeming creature would be so morally fearless?

Rob met him in the stable-yard—and began to tease him immediately—and to warn him off.

'So, how was the pretty widow, Hal? Not so overset as that companion of hers, I dare swear.'

'No, not at all.'

'And did you find her in looks?'

'Why this inquisition, Rob? What point are you try-ing to make.'

'A serious one, and I advise you to take what I am about to say equally seriously. This is a good woman whom you are beginning to pursue, not one of the barques of frailty who haunt London, and may be re-garded as rightful prey. It would be wrong of you to treat her as a pretty toy to exploit in order to reduce the boredom of country living. You must not trifle with her affections. To do so would be most unworthy of you.'

'How many moral guardians must a man acquire in one short afternoon before he is allowed to make his own judgements?' Devenish murmured enigmatically. 'The world and his wife are determined to have me turn parson, I see. Yes, I found Mrs Faulkner in looks, but it is not her looks which intrigue me. I leave you to discover what does—you might as well have some-thing concrete to worry about rather than simply en-gaging in pious whim whams about my behaviour.

'And speaking of whim whams, tell me this. You have lived here these past ten years. Have you observed any whim whams in the behaviour of the Faulkner fa-ther and son?'

'Of the father, yes. He was light in the attic towards the end of his life. Of the son, no. He seemed a down-to-earth fellow to me, quite unlike his father.'

'And tell me another thing before we adjourn. Were there any persons recorded as missing during the life-

time of old Mr Faulkner—or is that simply a phenom-
enon of the past few years?'

If Rob thought that Hal was engaging in whim
whams himself he did not say so. He had too much
respect for his employer's intellect.

'Not that I know of.'

'And strange goings-on in the countryside, you have
heard nothing of that?'

Rob shook his head. 'Not until the servant girls began to disappear, and the two men of whom we spoke.
Why?'

'Nothing. Like my moral sense, my curiosity is light-
minded and frivolous—as you well know. Only people
are telling me different stories about the same thing.'

He did not elaborate, but left Rob looking after him,
wondering what Devenish was up to now. Rob sometimes thought that perhaps Devilish was not a bad nickname for his friend, even though he knew that it was
undeserved.

What was puzzling Devenish was why Drusilla and
Cordelia Faulkner—who both struck him as possessing
souls of simple truth—should believe that Jeremy
Faulkner engaged in whim whams like his father's,
whilst Rob, that man of sense, did not. There must be
a sensible answer to that, and one which he would en-
deavour to discover.

The advantage being that whilst he did so he could
further his acquaintance with Jeremy's widow.

## Chapter Five

'How very kind of Mr Harrington to invite me to accompany you on this visit to Marsham Abbey. The more particularly since this is the first time that he has ever asked anyone for more than a meagre supper. A whole week! It will be quite a holiday for us both.'

Miss Faulkner looked slyly across at Drusilla, and added, apparently absent-mindedly, 'I wonder if Lord Devenish will be one of the party.'

'Most unlikely if he weren't.' Drusilla was brisk. 'What's more, Mr Harrington has also asked Giles. Giles is over the moon for he thinks that this proves that he is no longer regarded as a child.'

'Oh, but will you agree to allow him to accompany us? He is given to saying the most remarkable things, you know.'

'Well, since Lord Devenish and Mr Harrington share the same failing, he will be in good company—and, being one of several, is less likely to be remarked upon himself.'

'Oh, my dear, you must surely agree that it is one thing for a great personage such as Lord Devenish to speak his mind, and quite another for young Giles. He wants discretion.'

'No, I don't agree, Cordelia. Lord Devenish should be more discreet and so should Giles. As for Mr Harrington, like Giles, he does not know the meaning of the word, but Lord Devenish most plainly does—which makes his conduct the worst of the three.'

'I thought that you liked him,' Miss Faulkner murmured plaintively.

'I do, but that does not mean that I am blind to his faults.'

It had become plain to Drusilla over the last week during which they had met Lord Devenish twice more that Miss Faulkner had no more sense than to begin matchmaking.

Her reasoning was as simple as she was and she was engaged in it whilst speaking to her late nephew's wife.

Drusilla ought to marry again. Lord Devenish needed a wife and an heir—what better than that they should marry? Their lands marched together; they were both young and handsome, which boded well for the future Viscount Innescourt when he arrived. In her daydreams Miss Faulkner was ensconced at Tresham Hall, the baby Viscount lay in his cradle and Drusilla and Devenish hovered over it, adoring him. Miss Faulkner herself was hovering somewhere in the middle distance.

She came to with a start. Drusilla was speaking. 'I need a new gown. Mary Swain must be sent for and shown the latest pattern books from London. I have some pretty pale green satin which would look well with the Faulkner pearls.'

'Mary Swain,' exclaimed Miss Faulkner aghast. 'Oh, no, you must go further afield and find someone who will make you as *comme il faut* as the London beauties who surround m'lord when he is in town.'

'Cordelia, I have not the slightest intention of competing with the London beauties. I am but a simple country girl and so m'lord must take me or leave me— if he thinks of me at all, which I beg leave to doubt.'

Saying which, Drusilla was aware that she was being deceitful. She might be but a simple country girl but she knew quite well that there was something particular in m'lord's manner when he spoke to her which told her a different tale.

He was, in fact, thinking of her that very afternoon. Leander Harrington had ridden over to present him with his invitation in person.

'If you accept it, Devenish, I intend to use this occasion to honour your arrival in Surrey and introduce you to as many notables as possible. Your late grandfather passed the majority of his life here and we should be charmed if you would do the same.'

'Would you, indeed?' replied Devenish drily. 'I'm not yet sure that I would be charmed to spend mine likewise. But I will accept your invitation in the same spirit in which it is offered.'

'And Mr Stammers? You will allow him to accept an invitation, too?'

'Oh, that is a matter for Mr Stammers to decide, not for me. May I say that I'm a little surprised that your Republican beliefs would allow you to approach me first.'

'But, then, Devenish, I was not yet aware that your attitude towards those who serve you was so very different from that of the late Earl. Every man in his place, knowing his place, was his motto.'

Oh, yes, that sounded like his late grandfather. Devenish smiled his most subtle smile.

'A useful motto for those whose place is secure, you will allow.'

'Oh, indeed, but in the new age of reason which will shortly dawn, all men will be judged by what they are and not by the bedroom they were born in.'

Devenish's smile grew more subtle still. 'That age not having arrived yet, sir, we must continue to endure our present fortunate condition. And that being so, I shall enjoy your hospitality at Marsham Abbey, as will I expect, my good friend Rob Stammers. Until then, I bid you adieu.'

It was Leander Harrington's *congé* and he knew it. He gave his sweet smile and left. One of the delights of the new age of reason, he thought, would be a guillotine set up in Trafalgar Square where the liberated masses would cheer as each aristocratic head rolled in the dust—most particularly when m'lord Devenish's landed there.

Nothing of this showed, however, when Devenish arrived at Marsham Abbey in the middle of a fine early

August afternoon. Both men smiled at one another as though they had been bosom companions since boyhood. There was already a goodly sprinkling of guests on the lawn before the Abbey, that noble relic of the days of Catholic glory.

A long-gone Harrington had built his house using the Abbey's north wall as his southern one, and retaining, Rob had told Devenish, the staircase down to the huge crypt. Over the centuries Marsham's abbots had been laid to rest there, and there was still a chapel at one end of it, with a ruined altar.

This afternoon, though, no one was eager to visit dim underground rooms, least of all Devenish, who wished to mix with his neighbours as much, and as soon, as possible. His host led him on to the lawns where trestle tables had been erected and set out with food and drink and where burly footmen stood around ready to help those too helpless to help themselves.

Many of those already present were known to him and greeted him with the deference suitable to the honour of a peer. Devenish was just growing weary of being bowed and scraped to when he saw Drusilla Faulkner standing alone before a bed of roses, a glass of lemonade in her hand.

She looked divinely cool in white muslin and a wide-brimmed straw hat worn in such a fashion that it did not hide her charming face. The old trot, as Devenish unkindly thought of Miss Faulkner, was for once not with her.

With a muttered 'Excuse me,' he rescued himself from a tedious discussion about the respective excellencies of different breeds of sheep and walked over to her, picking up a glass of lemonade for himself on the way.

'Alone for once,' he offered, 'no Gorgon of a duenna dancing attendance on you, no high-spirited younger brother ready to insist on your full attention. I am in luck.'

Surprised, for she had not seen him coming, Drusilla still had the presence of mind to riposte, 'Now, is not that exactly what I should expect of you? That you would always wish the undivided attention of those whom you are with!'

'Is not that what we all wish?' he parried.

'Oh, indeed. But few of us are lucky enough to get it.'

'And you least of all,' he told her. 'For whenever we have previously met you have been surrounded by demanding others. Not so, now. And, if I see them coming, I shall whip you away down the nearest alley, claiming that I wish to admire the scenery with you, when all I wish to admire is you.'

This was plain speaking with a vengeance which surprised even the man who was uttering it. He had not intended to be so plain, so soon, but the sight of her had wrenched it from him.

Drusilla coloured; delightfully, Devenish thought. 'You cannot mean that,' she said at length, not quite sure how she ought to respond.

'Oh, but I do. And in token of my truthfulness I shall ask you to stroll down that very alley, and I shall admire you—but respectfully and from a discreet distance. Come.'

He held his arm out for her to take, and after a little hesitation, Drusilla took it.

That she had not been admired greatly before was very plain, Devenish thought. He wondered what the young husband had been truly like. Nevertheless she comported herself admirably, not tittering, or murmuring, 'Oh, my dear lord, you honour me too greatly,' or the rest of the female piff-paff which had so often been served up to him in the past.

She possessed the blessed gift of quiet, and so they walked along in the golden afternoon sun leaving the noisy lawn behind until they came to an open spot which looked out on the green and wooded countryside before them.

A sundial stood in yet another bed of roses. 'I tell only the sunny hours' it proclaimed, but strangely there was a skull and cross bones on one side of the pillar which supported it, and the face of a demon on the other. Someone had tried to erase them, but had failed.

For some reason the sight set Drusilla shivering, warm though the afternoon was. Such a chill sensation ran through her that her face turned white and her lips blue.

'You are cold,' Devenish exclaimed. He looked about him, and discovered a low stone wall. He began to strip off his fine deep-blue jacket. 'Sit down a moment,' he ordered her, 'and let me put this round your shoulders.'

Still shivering, Drusilla did as he bid her. He sat down beside her and took her hand—to find, to his astonishment, that it was as cold as ice.

Devenish chafed it, saying, 'Are you subject to these fits, madam?' for he could find no rational explanation for her changed state.

Drusilla looked at him, trying to stop her teeth chattering.

'No, indeed,' she whispered. 'This is very odd and you may think me odder still if I tell you that I suddenly had a feeling of the most profound evil, something cold and monstrous—like that thing there,' and she pointed to the defaced head of the demon. 'If you took your coat back, I should like to go away from this place. I think that I might feel better.'

Reluctantly Devenish lifted his coat from her shoulders and resumed it. 'You are sure you feel well enough to return?'

'Quite sure. It is only staying here which is distressing me.'

'And all I wished to do was admire you,' he said, trying to be light as they walked away. 'And instead I took you to what Dante called "the place of horror". Though why that should be, I cannot think. You are beginning to look better already. The next time I wish to be alone with you I shall make sure that we visit somewhere which I know must be free of such frightful associations.'

'You will think me stupid, I fear.'

Devenish stopped and turned her to face him just before they walked into the sight of the other guests.

Her colour had already returned and the shivering had stopped.

'Not at all,' he said, and was quietly serious after a fashion which he had never shown her before. 'I have reason to know that the black devils may appear without warning and that their power is strong. I felt nothing there, but you did, and I know you to be a woman of sense. In another place I might be affected—and you not. Do you feel ready to return to the normal prattling world again?'

Drusilla smiled at him. 'You are very kind, and the answer is yes.'

'Good.' He bent down and kissed her very gently on the cheek, a brotherly kiss, nothing like the passionate one which he wished to give her. 'Do not go there again, I beg of you, with or without me.'

Drusilla had to bite back the words which she wished to say. *I would go anywhere with you, m'lord, for I now know that you would always be ready to protect me.* Instead she smiled and said nothing.

If a few curious eyes watched them as they returned so quickly from their solitary walk, neither she nor Devenish remarked on it. He walked her to one of the tables and handed her a glass of strong red wine and a sweet biscuit. Taking a glass for himself, he raised it in a toast to her, and had the pleasure of seeing her eyes sparkle again and the colour fully restored to her cheeks.

'And now I must leave you for the time being,' he told her, 'lest I cause you to be gossiped about unduly.'

He bowed his *adieux* and she gave him her hand—which he held only a trifle too long.

Long enough for a man's voice to say in her ear, 'I had no notion that the next time I saw you, dear Drusilla, you would be widowed and in the company of a man as dangerous as the devil.'

Drusilla swung round exclaiming, 'Toby, Toby Claridge, I thought you were in France.'

Sir Toby Claridge, a handsome man of her own age, gave her the wide smile which she remembered from the days when they had played together as boy and girl. She had not seen him since the summer before Jeremy's death. At first after she had accepted Jeremy, having already refused Toby, Toby had been jealously at outs with Jeremy—another childhood friend—for quite a long time. It was only during that last year before he had left for France that they had suddenly become like brothers again.

'No, indeed. I am here, and as an old childhood companion I think that I have a duty to warn you to have as little to do with Devenish as possible. You owe it to Jeremy's memory to stay away from someone of whom he would never have approved.'

These were strong words indeed. Drusilla thought of the tender kindness with which Devenish had so recently treated her.

'What should make you speak so of him, Toby? He has a cutting tongue—but otherwise—'

He would not let her finish. 'No otherwise, Dru. He is a devil with women, my dear, and more than a devil with men. Women he merely ruins—men, he kills.

Why, he killed his best friend in a duel—over a woman, they say. And he is a devil with the cards as well. No, steer clear of him.'

'Gossip,' said Drusilla bravely. 'Besides, I don't believe he wishes to ruin me.'

Toby raised ironic eyebrows. 'No? That foolish duenna of yours tells me that he is being most particular with you and you with him. She is silly enough to think that he will marry you. I warn you for your own good, you know.'

And perhaps for yours, thought Drusilla a little dazedly. For with Jeremy gone these two years, Toby was free to propose to her again. But he would always be her friend. For all his easy charm she could not imagine him as her lover, but she had never been cruel enough to tell him so.

Devenish, now...

Could what Toby had just said possibly be true? She supposed dismally that it was. A roué and a murderer. No, she could believe many things of him, but not the last. Most men of his station were roués, often after marriage as well as before.

But murder—that was quite a different thing. She was suddenly aware that she was so *distraite* that she had not been listening to Toby, nor had she answered him. She said, a trifle hastily, 'Oh, I assure you that neither of us is contemplating marriage—nor the other thing—and as yet one might scarcely call us friends.'

'The looks he is giving you are not those of a man who thinks of a woman as a friend,' responded Toby drily.

Drusilla stared at him. This was not the sort of remark which Toby would have made before he had gone to live in France—but she could scarcely tell him so.

Instead she murmured, 'I assure you that you are mistaken—and even if you are right you must also know that at the moment I am not at all inclined towards marriage with anyone—least of all Lord Devenish.'

'Oh, I don't believe for a moment that he is thinking of marrying you—which is why I am offering you this warning. Purely as your friend, you understand.'

Now why did she doubt this? Drusilla asked herself. What she did not doubt was that this line of conversation ought to be brought to a rapid end. So she offered Toby nothing more than banality, saying, 'You must be hungry, and I see that Mr Harrington has provided us with an excellent array of food. We ought to do him the honour of thanking him by sampling it.'

She followed this by walking towards one of the laden tables, with Toby gallantly following, murmuring in her ear, 'You do believe that I am your friend, Dru, don't you? As we were years ago.'

Hardly that, was Drusilla's inward and amused response. Then friendship consisted of climbing trees and hiding from a governess or tutor—not at all the sort of thing which they might consider doing now!

On the other hand she was sure that what Toby was contemplating doing with her was quite another thing: taking his dead friend's place now that a suitable time had elapsed!

Nevertheless, talking pleasantly to him, she betrayed nothing of her true thoughts, but, for once, was quite relieved when George Lawson, the parson from Tresham Minor, came over to them and told Toby that Mr Harrington was asking after him.

'He wishes to speak to you about your travels in France, Sir Toby. I believe he would like to know whether the spirit of revolution is still abroad in that benighted country.'

As usual, there was something unpleasantly mocking in Mr Lawson's speech, although Toby seemed to notice nothing amiss. His manner, when he turned to speak to Drusilla after Toby had left them, became unctuous in the extreme.

'Allow me to tell you how charming you look today, madam. You always seemed to be accompanied by the spirit of summer—today, even more so!'

What could she say to this other than, 'I fear you flatter me, Mr Lawson,' something which provoked him to even further excesses.

'No, no,' he exclaimed, bowing towards her and putting his hand out to touch her arm, 'not at all.'

The effect he had on Drusilla was quite otherwise from that which he had expected. At the moment that his fingertips touched her wrist, Drusilla suffered a recurrence of the odd black horror which had struck her earlier in the garden.

For a brief second she feared that she was about to faint. Her colour disappeared and, to Mr Lawson's alarm, her eyes closed and she began to fall against him.

He put out his hand to support her, but she swayed away from him, fearful lest his touch distress her again, saying as calmly as she could, 'No, no, a passing megrim. I had one earlier. It is a thing from which I normally suffer. It is perhaps the heat. I will repair indoors immediately.'

She turned to leave, but Mr Lawson, all gallantry, exclaimed, 'Pray allow me to assist you. I fear that you may take harm if no one accompanies you.'

For some strange reason this kind offer distressed Drusilla further. She wanted him away from her but could not say so—nor think how to deter him from his well-meaning kindness.

Help came from an unexpected quarter. As Mr Lawson put out his arm to support her again, a cold voice said, 'Forgive me, sir, but as an old friend of Mrs Faulkner's I think that she might be more comfortable if I were allowed to assist her indoors. Besides, you have your duty to Mr Harrington's other guests, and as your patron I must direct you to assist them.'

It was Lord Devenish, and a less likely Good Samaritan Drusilla could not imagine. She allowed him to supply the kindness which she had rejected from the unfortunate Mr Lawson who dare not refuse to obey his patron's orders. He bowed and reluctantly moved away while Devenish led her through the open French windows into the Abbey.

Once inside he said, 'Would you like me to fetch Miss Faulkner to assist you to your room?'

'No, indeed,' replied Drusilla, recovering some of her normal briskness. 'She would fuss me to death and that is the last thing I need. Pray be as severe with me as you please—and, by the by before I forget, when did you and I become old friends? It is little more than a week since we first met!'

'Oh, I thought a little judicious fibbing was in order when I saw that you were resisting that oily fellow's attempt to manhandle you. It may be officious of me but, by your looks, I thought that you were suffering from another attack of what distressed you in the garden.'

'And so I was. You will think me but a poor thing, I fear. And I fibbed, too, when I informed Mr Lawson that I was subject to such fits, for I have never suffered from them before.'

'No?' Devenish was looking around him. 'I wonder where we could be private. The library, perhaps. One of the flunkies pointed it out to me earlier. I think that it's this way. We are sure to be undisturbed there. None of our fellow guests appear to me to be great readers— quite the contrary—ABC looks beyond most of them.'

Drusilla could not help herself. She began to laugh. He had the habit of saying all those dreadful things which she often thought—but could never publicly utter.

'There,' he said encouragingly, patting her hand. 'You are feeling better already. A good laugh cures many ills. May I ask what brought that one on?'

'Oh, it was because you come out with such outrageous remarks. Do you say such things to everyone— or am I especially favoured?'

They were in the library now, a large room full of books, most of which looked as though they had never been disturbed for years. There was a massive table in the middle with a pair of chairs before it. Devenish led her to one of them.

'This is more comfortable than I had expected,' he told her approvingly. 'And, yes, I have noticed that my naughtier *bon mots* meet with your approval—particularly when we are alone. I have observed that when I perpetrate them in company, in your desire to be seen as an innocent young widow you always suppress your natural instincts to laugh.'

He must have been watching her carefully during the short time in which he had known her to be so aware of what she was doing and thinking. Drusilla did not wish him to know what she had just learned of him although the temptation for her to confront him with her new knowledge was great.

Instead she said, roasting him a little for that was all he deserved, 'It is not every man, m'lord, who, seeing a woman in distress, would regard a library as a suitable place to take her to recover herself.'

'But you are not every woman, either, or I would not have brought you here!'

Whether he knew it or not his cavalier manner with her was assisting her to recover, Drusilla thought. She was sure that he did know. For once his usually impassive face was full of an amusement which transformed him quite. She suddenly saw a different man from the one he usually showed the world.

The question was—which was the true man?

Thinking this, Drusilla ignored his compliment—if such it were—and allowed the quiet coolness of the room to envelop her. Devenish said nothing further, but walked to the far wall to examine the books ranged there. This enabled her to watch *him*.

He pulled a book from the shelves and examined it carefully. He was truly the most contained, controlled person whom she had ever met. He made everyone around him appear callow and unformed—even older persons like Leander Harrington and Parson Williams. As for Toby Claridge and George Lawson, they seemed like children beside him.

He was speaking to her again, amusement still written on his face, 'You may,' he told her, 'return from whatever distant country you have just visited in order to inform me whether I am correct in finding it odd that Mr Harrington has so many abstruse theological works in his library. Tom Paine I would have expected, and Rousseau, for they are the Gods whom Jacobins like Harrington worship, but not this well-thumbed motley collection,' and he waved his hand at the shelves before him.

'Perhaps,' ventured Drusilla, 'he inherited them from his father.'

'Maybe,' said Devenish. 'But many of them are of recent origin.'

He frowned, 'I dislike mysteries.' He shut the book he was holding, replaced it and walked to another wall to examine what was shelved there.

'Poetry,' he announced, 'and old novels, all as pristine as when they left the bookshop.' He pulled a volume from the shelf, and opened it, saying, 'Lord Byron as I live and breathe, how very apt.'

Silence fell as he turned the pages for a moment, before he lifted his head and began to recite, his eyes hard on her. His voice was as beautiful as his face, and the words flowed slowly from his mouth like thick cream poured from a jug.

> She walks in beauty, like the night
> Of cloudless climes and starry skies;
> And all that's best of dark and bright
> Meets in her aspect and her eyes.

Drusilla was entranced—as he doubtless meant her to be.

Devenish put the book back on the shelf, walked over to where she sat, bent down and took her face in his hands. He kissed her lightly, not on her mouth but on her eyelids, for her eyes had closed at the moment that he had touched her.

He said, or rather breathed, 'You have no notion how much I wish to make love to you, here, in the library.'

He released her even as he spoke.

Drusilla opened her eyes and said as softly as he, 'Make love—or make lust, m'lord? Which?'

His answer was a short laugh. 'Pray, madam, what's the difference?'

Her response was as steady as her grave grey eyes. 'Oh, you know better than that, m'lord, both you and Lord Byron, for all your cynicism. When we love our aim is to give pleasure to our partner, but in lust we consider only our own.'

Devenish's expression had become unreadable. He nodded his head, and assumed her gravity. 'Rightly rebuked, but I was not being frivolous, you understand, I meant what I said. And...' he paused for a moment '...I suppose that young Claridge was warning you that I might behave exactly as I have just done. Am I right?'

'Indeed, you are. And did you speak so in order to disarm me or to prove him correct in his assumption that you wish to seduce me—and live up to your nickname by doing so?'

This time his answer was to bow low to her, 'Ah, madam, if I had known that I was going to meet such as you in the country I would have visited it long ago.'

'Then your visit would have been wasted, for I would either have been too young to attract you, or too recently married to a man I loved to listen to your blandishments.'

She rose. 'We have been together overlong, and tongues will be wagging. I will leave you now, I think. I am quite recovered.'

'Unkissed?'

And whether he was mocking her, Drusilla could not tell.

'Better so,' she told him, before turning to open the door.

'Do not fear for your reputation,' he said coolly, 'for I shall now take Paley's sublime work on moral philosophy with me into the garden, beard Mr Harrington and ask for his opinion on it as though I have just been reading it for the first time. He is not to know that I read it long ago and will therefore believe that I have spent my time indulging in the higher thought instead of in the lower!'

Such shamelessness! Drusilla had difficulty in suppressing her desire to laugh. She decided to reprimand him instead.

'I see, m'lord,' she said, 'that you are well practised in those low deceits which are designed to throw the curious off the scent. I shall expect you to provide me later with the details of your dialogue with our host. Preferably in public this evening after supper—unless you have earlier drunk too well of Mr Harrington's good wine. Until then, *adieu*.'

She was gone, having had the last word, as usual. Devenish threw his head back and laughed, before tucking Paley under his arm and going to find his host—who was delighted to discover that m'lord was more serious-minded than he had supposed, so he rewarded him by treating him to a lecture on the mistakes which the Reverend Mr Paley had committed in his erudite text—displaying his own superior learning while he did so.

It was also to be supposed that Lord Devenish appreciated his condescension since, his head on one side, and an expression of intense concentration and admiration on his face, he endured Mr Harrington's sermon to its long-delayed end, uttering 'Quite so' at regular intervals.

What he was actually considering was Mrs Drusilla Faulkner's terse and telling definition of the difference between lust and love and wondering by what miracle this quiet and chaste country girl could have achieved such wisdom.

And what was Mrs Drusilla Faulkner considering? Why, Lord Devenish, of course!

What mainly concerned her was how to hold him off. His assault on her virtue was so subtly organised, so delicate that she was in danger of succumbing to it. For every step he took forward, he seemed to take two steps back.

He had kissed her lightly—and then withdrawn. She was in danger of finding herself beneath him without knowing how she had got there!

She could not help contrasting him with the husband of her distant cousin, a country squire, whom she had met for the first time almost a year after Jeremy's death on a visit to their home. She had thought him kind, for he had made sure that her visit was a happy one.

Alas, one evening, half-cut after dinner, he had cornered her in a corridor and pressed her against the wall, his breath hot on her neck.

'Come,' he had muttered, 'let us engage in flapdoodle, my dear. 'Tis a year since you were widowed—you must be ready for it.'

She had staved him off easily enough for he was not a man to assault an unwilling woman. She was dismally aware that he might have misunderstood her friendly overtures to him, taking them for more than they were worth. It had made her wary of all men. She had found an excuse to go home soon afterwards, knowing that a long friendship with her cousin was at an end.

Flapdoodle! She had laughed at the word later when she was safe home again, and now she contrasted his boorish approach with that of Devenish's—and knew that the latter's subtlety was the more dangerous. It did not assist her composure to know that Toby's reading of him appeared to be correct.

Or was it? She remembered most vividly the strange expression on Devenish's face when she had refused him and had offered him her distinction between love and lust.

Had he, after all, been pleased that she had not fallen into his arms? Was it possible that he, in his devious way, had been testing her? And if she had allowed herself to be seduced, would he have found her wanting—been disappointed, even, not triumphant?

It was a strange thought—but then he was a strange man. For there was not only the puzzle of what he truly felt for her to occupy her mind but something quite different which had nothing to do with her at all. It concerned Leander Harrington.

The problem was that her memory failed her when she tried to recall what it was that he had done or said which had led her to believe that his interest in Leander Harrington and in Marsham Abbey was that of more than simple curiosity.

But then, there was nothing simple about him, was there?

## Chapter Six

'What in the world was all that piff-paff you were engaged in with our esteemed host, Hal, about the Reverend Paley and the evidences of Christianity? I never knew that you were interested in such stuff.'

'Nor am I, but our host is. He has the oddest mixture of books in his library.'

'Oh, so that was where you absconded to with the pretty Mrs Faulkner. I suppose it *was* quite useless of me to try to persuade you not to seduce her.'

'Not at all—I have not the slightest intention of doing so. As for the lady—well, pretty she may be, but strong-minded she is, and reprimands me severely every time I seem to make a move in that direction!'

Rob Stammers and Devenish were chatting together in Devenish's suite of rooms before supper. His friend's last reply set Rob laughing.

'Sits the wind in that quarter, then? I would have thought a provincial nobody would have been easy prey. That she isn't must be a new experience for you.'

Devenish cuffed playfully at Rob's head as though they were still lads together. 'You know me better than that, Rob. First of all, I don't regard women as prey, and secondly, anyone I have made my mistress has come to me willingly and without coercion. Indeed, like Lord Byron I may safely claim that with some of them I have been the seduced, not the seducer.'

'So you say. But your determination to talk philosophy with our host still baffles me.'

'Does it? Tell me, how does he strike you?'

Rob thought for a moment before replying. 'As a rather silly man with his maunderings about the Rights of Man which sits ill with his air of being the local magnate and determined that everyone shall know it. You have put his nose a little out of joint, you understand, by choosing to visit your estates here.'

'Would it surprise you that I don't agree with you about his silliness?'

Rob laughed. 'Not at all. You are usually contrary. But what makes you think that?'

'Nothing that I can offer you as evidence. Just an odd feeling.'

'An odd feeling.' Rob stared at Hal. Hal had experienced odd feelings before, and the fact that they were now alive, well, expensively dressed and waiting for dinner in a great house in the country was due solely to them.

'No evidence at all?'

Devenish hesitated a moment before he replied.

'None you would like. Only—Mrs Faulkner's two attacks of the megrims in which she experienced a feeling of panic, fear and intense cold.'

Rob laughed again. 'Oh, is that all! Put on to intrigue you, I suppose.'

'Oh, I might have thought that, too, except that she experienced the second one when I was not with her. It appears that Mr George Lawson's touch was enough to set her off.'

'George Lawson? You mean the parson? I can scarcely believe that. She must be bamming you. And why do you connect Leander Harrington with it? She was never with him, I collect.' He paused and then added slowly, 'But you said that you have had an odd feeling, too. Is it at all like hers?'

Devenish studied his perfect reflection in the long mirror set in the wall opposite the windows before dismissing it.

'No, indeed. Merely what you know I have experienced before. An intense unease. A feeling that the universe is out of kilter. That there is something hidden which should not be hidden—and which will shortly affect me. Stupid, isn't it? I had rather have been a gypsy scryer whom they say sees the future in a crystal ball. A vague feeling of something wrong is not the most useful tool in the world.

'As for connecting Leander Harrington with Mrs Faulkner's distress, it is *his* territory on which these events are occurring. His gardens, his home—and his guests.'

Rob stopped being sceptical and became practical. 'And your unease also has to do with Mrs Faulkner, Leander Harrington, George Lawson and Marsham Abbey?'

'Indeed—but in no particular order. Will you be my eyes and ears, Rob? Tell me if you see, or hear, anything untoward.'

Rob sighed. 'As before, and despite all my reservations about this mystic nonsense of yours, I will do as you ask. But I see no sense in any of this, you know. None at all. I think that, for once, you have been undone by a woman's megrims.'

Devenish simply said, 'Humour me, Rob. That is all I ask—and all I can tell you.'

This last he knew only too well was not quite true. He was deliberately not telling Rob of the mission on which Sidmouth had sent him for he believed that the fewer people who knew of why he was really visiting Surrey, the better. To preserve his secret he was willing to endure Rob's critical banter.

He pulled his gold hunter from his watch-pocket and studied it. 'Time for supper,' he announced. 'We must not be late, or, at least, I must not be, since as the senior person present no one may enter the supper room until I arrive.'

The smile he gave Rob was a rueful one. 'You have no notion of how odd that circumstance seems to me—I don't think that I shall ever get used to it.'

It was not the first time that he had made such a remark to Rob, and Rob, as always, pondered on its meaning, coming as it did from a man so supremely in command of himself, his surroundings and his staff. But he said nothing, and followed his friend downstairs.

The first person Devenish saw in the drawing room was Mrs Drusilla Faulkner. She appeared to be quite recovered from her afternoon's distresses.

She looked particularly enchanting in a pale green silk evening gown, with a cream silk sash around a high waist. She was carrying a small cream fan with crocuses painted on the parchment which carried its ivory sticks. Her jewellery was simple: a string of small pearls circled her elegant neck, pearl ear-drops, and a silver pearl studded bracelet on her left wrist completed her *ensemble*.

Perhaps he saw her first because, for him, she was the person of most importance in the room. Unhappily he was unable to enquire whether or no she was re-covered, for Mr Harrington approached him to intro-duce him to the Dowager Lady Cheyne who had ar-rived but a few hours earlier. He was delegated to escort her into the supper room as the only lady of a rank to equal his own.

To say that the lady was pleased to be introduced to him was an understatement. She was, Devenish dis-covered, not so very much older than himself, touching forty, he thought, but her manner and dress were that of a very young girl and did her no favours at all.

She shook her gold curls at him, and pouted pretty painted lips. 'Oh, how delightful. I had heard of you from my cousin Orville, but I never thought to meet you here in the wilderness.'

She spoke as though Surrey was a jungle filled with ferocious animals, and Devenish was tempted to an-swer her in kind, by advising her not to stray too far in the Abbey gardens lest she fall prey to a passing lioness.

Instead he gave her his most charming smile, and remarked that fortunately Surrey, although far from town, had nothing more dangerous to offer than a few foxes which rarely appeared in the day.

'Too amusing—' she twinkled at him '—you destroy all the romance in life. Next you will be telling me that Marsham Abbey is nothing like those in Mrs Radcliffe's romances. I am not to expect banditti, nor horrid happenings in the Abbey crypt! There is a crypt, I am sure.'

'Indeed there is,' returned Devenish gravely, amused by her inconsequence. 'I understand that few Abbeys are without them.'

'Oh, famous.' Her voice rose an octave and she placed a pretty hand on his arm. 'Then you will help me to persuade Mr Harrington to allow us to visit it. I have never visited a crypt and would wish to know whether they are as horrid as report paints them.'

As the lady prattled merrily along, not pausing to allow him to reply, Devenish was able to watch Drusilla without seeming to. She had been paired off to go into supper with George Lawson and he wondered, a little anxiously, whether his company would distress her.

On the contrary, apparently, for she immediately began an animated conversation with him. But he also noticed that she was careful to hold herself away from Lawson a little to avoid any chance of him touching her, or her him.

The supper room was a large one which had been used as a refectory in the days before the Abbey was dissolved and partly destroyed in the reign of Henry VIII. It was cold and draughty even though the evening was warm and a huge fire had been built in its hearth. Its high ceiling and thick stone walls seemed to have retained the frosts of winter.

Drusilla, with George Lawson on one side of her, Rob Stammers on the other, and Devenish and Lady Cheyne opposite to her, was not the only woman who began to shiver.

Leander Harrington, who was himself warmly dressed, apologised for the cold, and suggested that one of the footmen be sent to inform the ladies' maids that their mistresses would need warm shawls.

'I had thought that the fire and the heat of the day would warm the room sufficiently, but it seems not,' he offered. 'These old buildings are difficult to heat and one would hardly wish to install one of Count Rumford's grates: it would quite spoil the room's beauty. Think how the poor monks must have suffered in winter, eh, Devenish?'

Devenish, thus appealed to, found himself saying, quite why he did not know, 'Very odd, don't you think, Harrington, that the houses of the religious were always so cold when we are reliably informed that the Devil was the master of the cold? One might have supposed that their prayers would have kept him away.'

He was astonished at the reception of what he had meant as an idle witticism. Lady Cheyne gave a hysterical titter and hit at him with her fan. Giles Stone, seated at a little distance from his sister, exclaimed merrily, 'You must have been reading Monk Lewis's masterpiece, Devenish!'

Leander Harrington, however, frowned, and George Lawson who had just lifted his glass of wine in order to toast Drusilla, gasped, and dropped it. The red liquid ran along the white damask of the cloth like blood gushing from an artery.

'Pray forgive me,' he almost stuttered. 'But you startled me, m'lord, by speaking of the Devil so lightly.'

Devenish raised the quizzing glass which he always wore but rarely used, and stared at him through it.

'Why, sir,' he drawled, 'as a man of the cloth I would have expected you to startle the Devil, not the opposite.'

This witticism, at least, found its mark. Toby Claridge laughed uproariously and exclaimed, 'Caught you there, Lawson. Get out your bell, book and candle, eh.'

'Hardly a remark in good taste,' retorted Lawson. Devenish was fascinated to see that his face had turned paper-white, nay, almost green, and wondered why his and Claridge's idle remarks should have disturbed him so.

The sense of unease which had plagued Devenish since he had set foot in the Abbey grew stronger still. He had named the Devil, and by doing so seemed almost to have conjured him up. He had become used to jokes on his own nickname, and the reaction of some of his hearers surprised him.

Leander Harrington said, 'Which supernatural being controls the cold is of no import, since unfortunately, the responsibility for the warmth of this room rests with me, and I have failed you by not controlling it.

'Ah, here come the maids with the shawls and the soup is ready to serve. Between these two phenomena we will, I trust, soon be warm again.'

His little speech ended the awkward silence which had fallen on the company and conversation became general again. Drusilla, mechanically taking her shawl from her maid, was careful to avoid Cordelia Faulkner's troubled eye, as well as George Lawson's.

For a brief second when Devenish had mentioned the Devil she had been fearful that she might feel again the dreadful cold which had twice overcome her that day, but fortunately, no such thing had occurred, and equally fortunately the rest of supper passed without further incident.

Later, in the drawing room, Devenish, with Lady Cheyne still firmly attached to him, was apologised to by Leander Harrington for the lack of warmth in the supper room. Before he could reply, Lady Cheyne carolled at her host, 'Why, Mr Harrington, you come apropos, Lord Devenish and I have decided that we wish to visit the Abbey crypt in order to discover whether it is as horrid as Mrs Radcliffe says they are!'

'No, not horrid at all, ma'am,' replied Mr Harrington hastily. 'Boring, in fact—and dark. No one has set foot in it for years. You would not like it at all.'

'Oh, I'm sure I should, shouldn't I, Lord Devenish? One expects a crypt to be dark, but you would be able to provide us with lights, would you not? What else are footmen for?'

For whatever reason, it was plain to Devenish that Mr Harrington had no wish for anyone to visit the crypt.

'It's damp,' he muttered, 'there would be rats—and smells, perhaps.'

'Rats and smells, eh! Do you hear that, Lord Devenish? I thought you said that there were no ferocious animals in Surrey! I am more than ever determined to see this horrid place. A few pistol shots would suffice to dispose of the rats before we go down. I am not a woman to allow such small drawbacks to stop me from such an adventure.'

The look on Mr Harrington's face was an agonised one. So agonised that the strange something which took Devenish over occasionally had him vigorously seconding Lady Cheyne's tactless efforts to make Mr Harrington do something which he most palpably didn't want to do. Why in the world did he not want anyone to visit his damned crypt? It was only a cellar, after all.

'Oh, come, Harrington,' he drawled. 'If the lady asserts that she is prepared to brave the worst which you can suggest to her, it is surely the part of a gentleman to allow her to indulge herself.

'Besides, I have a sudden burning desire to see the crypt myself. Most odd. I have never been interested in them before.'

Beleaguered, Mr Harrington reluctantly gave way. 'Oh, very well, but you will both have to wait a little. I must send some men down to make sure that all is safe there.'

'Oh, capital,' exclaimed Giles, who had been an eager listener—with several others—to this discussion. 'I have often wanted to visit a crypt—ever since I read Monk Lewis's book, in fact. Thank you for the opportunity, sir.'

'Now, Giles,' said Drusilla anxiously, 'are you sure that you will be able to manage the stairs in the semi-dark?'

His face fell so much that Devenish drawled, 'Have no fear, Mrs Faulkner, I myself will lend an arm to see he makes the descent safely.'

Lady Cheyne was not best pleased by this offer, saying ungraciously, 'I was depending on your arm to assist me, Lord Devenish.'

'Never fear,' said Devenish smoothly. 'Mr Stammers will be only too happy to assist you, I'm sure.'

Drusilla's cough to conceal her amusement at the sight of Rob Stammer's stunned face as Devenish made this handsome, but unwanted, offer on his behalf, was the only response other than that of Miss Faulkner's.

She said, her voice as disapproving as she could make it, 'I'm sure that when Mr Lewis wrote *The Monk* he could not have known what a brouhaha it would cause, inconveniencing Mr Harrington and giving us all nightmares. I wonder at you allowing Giles to read it, Drusilla.'

'Oh, she didn't, aunt,' responded Giles cheerfully. 'I borrowed it from a friend and read it in the Folly. I never brought it into the house at all.'

'Very enterprising of you, Giles,' drawled Devenish, 'There's nothing for it, Harrington. You'll have to escort all these enthusiasts into the crypt as soon as possible.'

'I'm sure I shan't go,' Miss Faulkner muttered at Drusilla. 'I recommend you not to, either. There might be horrid things lying about.'

'Not after three hundred years,' returned Drusilla, who had been amusedly watching Devenish's devious efforts to rid himself of the leech-like Lady Cheyne. She hoped that he would soon be free of her for she wished to twit him about his sudden desperate desire to visit the crypt.

Had he seconded Lady Cheyne in order to inconvenience Mr Harrington, or was it for some other reason? She doubted that he was an enthusiast either for Mrs Radcliffe or Monk Lewis. She had no desire to visit the crypt herself for she was fearful that it might set off another strange attack. She would ask Devenish about it when he returned.

This thought amused her. Since when had she become so familiar with him that her first thought these days was always of him and his doings?

Fortunately both Devenish and Rob Stammers were relieved of Lady Cheyne's company by their host who, fearing that he might have offended her by his reluctance over the crypt, felt that it was his duty to give her a guided tour of the ground floor of the Abbey.

This enabled Rob to hiss at Devenish, 'What the devil were you up to, Hal, saddling me with that painted gossip?'

'Oh, I didn't think that I deserved to be the only sufferer,' retorted Devenish. 'I thought that you would be pleased to learn that she was one woman whom I didn't want to seduce!'

Only the nearby presence of Drusilla and Giles prevented Rob from doing his friend and patron some violence. To steady himself he turned to Drusilla and said, a trifle savagely, 'I would imagine, Mrs Faulkner, that you were a little surprised to learn that Devenish here was such an enthusiast for the Tales of Terror that he could not wait to visit a crypt.'

Drusilla's smile was poisonously sweet. 'Oh, nothing Lord Devenish did would ever surprise me, Mr Stammers, and ought not to surprise you, seeing that you have known him since you were boys together, I understand.'

Devenish's laugh was a genuine one. 'Bravely said. You see, Rob, others know us better than we know ourselves.'

Rob gave Drusilla an ungrudging smile. 'You rebuked us both equally, and I think that we both deserved it. You know, Mrs Faulkner, I think that it would do Lord Devenish a power of good if he had someone like yourself to bring him down to earth occasionally.'

'Occasionally?' Devenish's beautiful eyebrows rose and he bowed at Drusilla. 'Nonsense, she never stops. Her conversation with me is one long reprimand—

charmingly delivered. Yes, I was wrong to foist Lady Cheyne on Rob, but he deserves a little punishment for constantly misreading all my better motives.'

'Which are?' asked Drusilla, raising her own eyebrows.

'You may ask, but I shall not answer. I do have them, you know.'

Giles, puzzled a little by the turn which the conversation had taken, said in his forthright manner, 'Take no notice of Dru, Devenish. She means well—I think,' he ended dubiously and set the company laughing.

After that there was nothing for it but to persuade Mr Harrington when he returned that there was no necessity for him to clean the crypt—most of the company were determined to visit it as soon as possible on the morrow and would brook no delay.

To which demand he had no option but to agree—with reluctance.

'I see, m'lord, that you are suitably dressed for this excursion. I might have guessed that you would not go down into the bowels of the earth in dandy fashion.'

Devenish bowed in acknowledgement of Drusilla's mild teasing of him—he was growing used to it. He and the rest of Leander Harrington's guests were standing in the ruins of the Abbey church near to the trapdoor in the stone pavement which led down to the crypt. They were passing the time while waiting for their host's arrival by gossiping mildly.

Lady Cheyne had Rob firmly in her toils and was regaling him with the convoluted plot of *The*

*Necromancer of the Black Forest.* Beside her stood George Lawson, a long-suffering expression on his face.

'Indeed, Mrs Faulkner,' Devenish replied as he straightened up from his bow, 'as you see, I have come prepared. I expect to find cobwebs, dusts and spiders, and perhaps a few pools of water awaiting us. Boots and gaiters and a dark frock-coat seemed to be the order of the day, not my usual finery.'

'You should have warned Lady Cheyne, Devenish. Her turnout seems to be more suitable for a garden party,' was Giles's immediate and irrepressible remark.

'Hush, Giles,' ordered Drusilla. 'She will hear you.'

'All the better for her, then,' he riposted. 'It might serve to persuade her that her pink silk frock and white kid slippers ought to be exchanged for something more practical.'

Devenish came to Drusilla's rescue. 'Come, Master Giles,' he said in his most honeyed voice, 'has no one ever informed you that no true gentleman ever makes personal remarks about those around him?'

Very little could silence Giles. 'But you make them all the time, Devenish,' he protested.

Drusilla rolled her eyes heavenward. Devenish adjusted his minimal cravat—no waterfalls or Napoleons for him this morning—and drawled, 'But I am not a gentleman, Master Giles, I am a nobleman and may do as I please—short of murder, that is. Ah, here comes our host, and the footmen with flambeaux to light our way.'

'You will be careful, Giles,' begged Drusilla. 'Do not allow yourself to become over-excited.'

'Really, Dru, you are nearly as much of an old fuss-pot as Aunt Faulkner these days,' said Giles crossly. 'I *am* eighteen you know.'

'Quite an elderly gentleman,' said Devenish reprovingly. 'Take my arm and try to behave like one. We shall shortly set off on our expedition. The trapdoor is open, the footmen have gone down, and all that we have to do is negotiate the stone stairway. You are sure that you will not come with us, Mrs Faulkner? I am quite capable of looking after both you and Giles.'

'I dare not risk making a fool of myself for two days in succession,' was her reply. 'You may tell me of it when you return.'

'If we return,' he said with something uncommonly like a grin. 'Who knows what may be waiting for us down there?'

Lady Cheyne heard him and shrilled, 'Oh, something horrid, I do hope. I shall scream, I know I shall. You must be sure to catch me if I faint, Mr Stammers. I should not like to dash my head on the stone floor.'

No, but Rob might, was Devenish's inward and unkind comment, but he said nothing, concentrating on assisting Giles to descend safely underground.

The steps were uneven and Drusilla's misgivings proved to be reasonable. Giles, for all his determination to live as though he were not crippled, made heavy weather of them—as did Lady Cheyne who was immediately ahead of them.

They found themselves in a large chamber with a surprisingly high roof. At the east end of it the remains of a stone altar stood upon a low dais. Each side of the long room was filled with ledges on which stone coffins—now empty—stood. Their stone lids had been thrown down, broken, and heaped around the door by which they had entered.

The footmen's flambeaux threw flickering and grotesque shadows on the walls, floor and the faces of the company. The corners of the crypt were hidden in pools of darkness. A musty smell, the smell of long ages gone by, filled the air.

Even Lady Cheyne was silenced. She said no more after breathing the one word 'Horrid.'

It was left to Devenish to break the silence. 'They must have conducted services down here,' he remarked. He had helped Giles to sit and rest upon one of the larger pieces of stone, and now strolled towards the altar.

'Yes,' said Mr Harrington. 'The Abbots were brought down here after death. The coffins were opened, their bodies were removed and thrown into the lake at the back of the Abbey at the time of the dissolution of the monasteries. The valuables in the coffins and the church were looted by the locals, I understand, before King Henry VIII's Commissioners arrived to deal with the property.'

'Like France in 1789,' commented Devenish, who alone of the party appeared not to be affected by his dark and gruesome surroundings. 'The crypt is not used now, I suppose.'

'No, indeed. I really should have impressed on you how very little there is to see,' frowned Mr Harrington. 'I hope that you are not disappointed. I think that we ought to return now.'

Lady Cheyne found her voice again. 'Oh, I am not disappointed, Mr Harrington, not at all. This exceeds all my expectations. So romantic, so horrid. And the smell...' She sniffed the air like a pointer. 'I do believe that I can still smell the incense which they used so long ago.'

Giles's sniff was one of disbelief. Rob Stammers, always practical, murmured, 'How safe is it down here? Our ancestors' grasp of architectural principles was not as strong as ours.'

'Oh, quite safe,' said Mr Harrington, moving towards the door. 'I think that we may leave now. You have seen all that there is to see.'

Devenish, listening to him, caught a note of desperation in his host's voice. He seemed resolutely determined that the party's stay in the crypt should be as short as possible. Now, why should that be? As he had expected, the crypt had turned out to be merely a glorified cellar. Like Lady Cheyne he was intrigued by the smell. He, too, could have sworn he smelled incense.

Which was nonsense, of course. The party was now filing back upstairs and he was the furthest away from the door. His duty to Giles meant that he ought to prevent him from trying to essay the stairs on his own. He turned towards the exit just as the footman nearest to him moved away and left him in the dark.

Unlike Lady Cheyne he found nothing romantic in this. He walked forward—and caught his foot against a broken piece of stone left behind when the remains of the coffin lids had been moved. He stumbled and, to prevent himself from falling, caught at the stone altar, but even then, landed on one knee.

He began to rise, kicking away the piece of stone as he did so. His eyes had adjusted rapidly to the dark once the light had gone, and he saw that moving the stone had revealed something on the ground which had been trapped and hidden between the stone and altar.

He bent to pick it up. It was a gold signet ring.

He stared at it, and some instinct—the same instinct which had often warned and protected him—had him slipping it into his breeches pocket without examining it further, or saying anything of it.

The footman with the flambeau, hearing him stumble, turned towards him, stammering, 'Forgive me, m'lord. I thought that you were with me, or I would not have left you in the dark. You are not hurt, I trust.'

'Not at all. My own fault for dallying,' said Devenish. The small incident had caused Mr Harrington to walk agitatedly towards him. He had been standing at the bottom of the stairs, helping his guests on their way. He had Giles by his side.

'It is as I feared, Devenish. I thought this adventure ill-advised and now you have proved it so. As a consequence of that silly fellow's negligence, you might have been injured.'

'Not his negligence, mine,' said Devenish quickly. 'As you see, I am A1 at Lloyds, quite ready to help Master Giles up the stairs.'

'Oh, I think I could manage walking upstairs without help,' returned Giles. 'But Mr Harrington insisted that I wait for you. He said that he wanted to be the last person out.'

'And so he will be,' smiled Devenish. 'Except for the footman, of course. You will not wish to be left in the dark.'

Mr Harrington was offhand. 'Oh, the dark does not trouble me,' he murmured. 'I have good night vision.'

Devenish became conversational as Giles took his arm. 'One wonders why our ancestors were so fond of dungeons, crypts and oubliettes, seeing what difficulties they must have had in lighting them.'

This served to set Mr Harrington off on a long disquisition about the habits and customs of the Middle Ages which, as Giles later told Drusilla rather irreverently, seemed to be a bad habit of his.

'He thinks that we are all as interested in his dry-as-dust hobbies as he is, although I must admit that Devenish was the soul of politeness, asking him questions as though he really wished to know the answers.'

'Perhaps he did. We are not all ignorant heathens like you, Giles.'

'He nearly fell, though. In the crypt.'

'You mean Lord Devenish fell? Was he hurt?' She had not meant to sound as agitated as she did. After all, what was it to her that Devenish might have injured himself?

'Oh, no. It wasn't a real fall. The footman was stupid and left him in the dark, but Devenish didn't want Mr Harrington to blame him. He was unhurt, he said, and only went to his room to change his clothes. He said that he didn't want to spend the day dressed as a game-keeper!'

'How exactly like him,' exclaimed Drusilla. 'I never met a man so determined to be exactly right for every occasion in which he finds himself. He is the exact opposite of you, Giles.'

Giles nodded mournfully. 'I'd love to be like him, you know, but it would be the most fearful hard work.'

Neither Giles nor Drusilla was to know that Devenish had not been quite truthful with him. His real reason for returning immediately to his room was that he wanted to examine the ring which he had found—and his right hand.

He did not immediately send for his valet. He walked to the window in order to examine his hand. Down the side of it and inside his finger nails were smears and traces of black candle grease, the result of his grasping at the altar to save himself from falling.

Now that was odd. For had not Mr Harrington quite explicitly told him that the crypt was never used? But the grease was soft, not hardened with age, and when he sniffed at it he could smell the slight remains of its burning. He thought for a moment before shaking his head.

Something tugged at the edge of his mind—but what? He did not waste time trying to recall the wisp of memory—it would come if he left it alone. Beside there was the mystery of the ring. He pulled it out of his breeches pocket and examined it carefully, to discover that engraved on it was a falcon with its jesses trailing, exactly like the one on the shield over the door at Lyford House. The falcon which was both the arms and emblem of the Faulkners of Lyford.

Devenish turned it in his hand. Presumably it had at one time belonged to the owner of Lyford Hall. But which owner? And how in the world had it come to be in a crypt which was rarely visited, if Mr Harrington were to be believed?

He walked to his portable writing desk, an object which no one but himself was allowed to touch, and unlocked the small drawer beneath its lid and placed the ring inside it before re-locking it. Finally, he rang for his valet and only when he was *à point* ordered him to find Mr Stammers and ask him to come to m'lord's room at once.

How to raise the matter? It would not do to blurt out apparently pointless questions about a ring which he had found in a supposedly unused crypt. And how stolid Rob would stare at him if he babbled about fresh candle grease!

Devenish sat down. He picked up a book and began to read—to little avail—because pecking away on the edge of his mind like a bird worrying at a meaty egg, determined to open it, was the suspicion that the ring had something to do with Drusilla's late husband.

And, if as he was beginning to suppose, Jeremy Faulkner's death was linked to the mystery of the missing girls, then he must try to fulfil his promise to Sidmouth by pursuing the matter.

He was still in a quandary when Rob entered. 'I understand that you wish to see me.'

'True. I'm bored. Unbore me, Rob.'

Now this was cavalier, even from Devenish. 'That sort of demand,' Rob declared, 'is enough to drive any notion of how to entertain you out of my head. Will the weather do?'

'I think not. Perhaps we could discuss this morning's damp squib. What a nothing of a thing the visit to the crypt was. Although I suppose that your *belle amie* found it exciting.'

Rob swore at him. 'If by my *belle amie* you mean Lady Cheyne, she finds everything exciting. And I will forgive you for sending for me to talk nonsense because it enabled me to get away from her. Failing you, she seems to think that I would make her a useful second husband.'

'Why not?' drawled Devenish. 'Think of her lovely money.'

'You know, Hal, there are times when I find you intolerable. I heard that you had a slight fall after we had gone. Harrington was troubled that you were concealing an injury.'

'Oh, I conceal many things, but injuries are not usually among them. Let me be truthful. I was thinking about Mrs Faulkner—which led me to think of her husband. You knew him, you said. Have you no notion why anyone should wish to murder him?'

Rob thought that when Hal said 'Let me be truthful', he usually meant the opposite! On the other hand, he seemed to have Mrs Faulkner on his mind.

'The only explanation was robbery. That he was set upon by a thief or thieves and his money and belongings were taken. They were all missing—and some of his clothing.'

'Hmm. I doubt that he would be carrying much money. Was he the sort of man who wore flashy jewellery?'

'Not at all. A fob watch and a signet ring were his only ornaments. They were not on his body when he was found. Why?'

'Why what?' Devenish was languid.

'Why are you interested?'

'I was thinking how disappointed the murderer must have been to have committed such a grave crime for nothing.'

Rob shrugged. 'The only real mystery was how Faulkner came to be so far from home when all his horses and his carriages were in the stables and coach house at Lyford Hall.'

An even bigger mystery, thought Devenish, as he accompanied Rob downstairs to take lunch, was, how did Jeremy Faulkner's signet ring arrive in the crypt at Marsham Abbey if he was killed miles away from both Marsham and his home?

## Chapter Seven

'I wonder,' said Leander Harrington to Devenish after cornering him in the drawing room before supper was announced, 'whether your careless words about the Devil last night provoked him into putting you in some danger in the crypt this morning. I trust you are recovered.'

'I am not recovered since I was never damaged. Besides, although I am well aware that the Devil is wicked, I had never thought him to be petty! His revenge on me would surely have been more dramatic and certain. Something like a mysterious bolt of hellfire which would have left me dead and smoking before the altar would have been his way, not a minor stumble!'

'You are pleased to jest, but such frivolity might be dangerous, you know.'

Devenish fished out his quizzing glass and stared at him. 'I had understood you to be a man of sense, the essence of reason, the late Jean-Jacques Rousseau's disciple in person. A belief in the Devil hardly sits well with his version of theology!'

'I believe in God,' enunciated Mr Harrington gravely, 'which means that I must also consider the existence of the Devil. How else can we explain the inexplicable acts of the wicked?'

'How else, indeed?' drawled Devenish. 'It is enough to put one off the splendid supper which you have ordered for us.'

'There, I was sure you would agree with me,' smiled Mr Harrington a trifle triumphantly. 'Forgive me for saying so, but a man who is nicknamed the Devil is scarcely in a position to deny him.'

Now, what the deuce is he getting at? wondered Devenish. He thought that there was a double meaning in his host's words and the look which he was offering his guest was a meaningful one.

But what sort of meaning? It was like reading a book in a strange language, or hearing someone speak it as though you were expected to understand what was said.

'I didn't give myself that nickname,' he said at last, for Mr Harrington was plainly expecting some sort of reply. 'Others did. I make no claim to his attributes, or to his name. On the contrary, *Vade retro Sathanas.*' He wondered what sort of answer this plain speaking would provoke.

He was not to know for even as Mr Harrington translated his Latin into 'Ah, yes, "Get thee behind me, Satan",' Lady Cheyne, who had just entered, interrupted him and the moment was lost.

She was all charming vacuity. 'So pleased,' she trilled, 'to have been allowed to visit your holy of holies. I mean the crypt. I could quite persuade myself I was back in Henry the VIII's time and imagine the pageantry which has, alas, disappeared from our prosaic age.'

Her intervention had one benefit. It allowed Devenish to make his escape—but he was not allowed to escape very far. Toby Claridge buttonholed him and, like Mr Harrington, began to twit him about having raised the Devil who had then pursued him into the crypt. His small accident, thought Devenish morosely, seemed to be the sole topic of conversation of a house party which was desperate to have something to talk about.

He evaded Toby by offering him the same explanation which he had given Leander Harrington: that he had never thought the Devil petty. Giles came up to him as he finished and opened his mouth, doubtless to make some similar remark.

'Master Giles,' he said, 'as you love me, do not mention the word Devil, nor ask me how I fare.'

'How strange, that was what Dru said. She told me not to mention this morning's mishap or link it with the Devil, for you would be sure to be displeased.'

'Did she, indeed? She has the most damnable habit of being right—but we must not tell her so.'

'Rather not. Females get above themselves so easily if you praise them. Or so Parson Williams says.'

He stared, puzzled, when Devenish broke into uncontrollable laughter after he had come out with this profound statement.

'I was not funning, sir, I assure you,' he said earnestly.

'I know, that was the joke, Giles. When you are older I will explain it to you.'

'Why not now? I say, Dru, you were right, Devenish does not like to be twitted about the Devil.'

Drusilla, who had been watching Giles talk to Devenish and was sadly aware that he was probably displaying his usual lack of tact, said gently, 'That being so, why do you dwell on it?'

'I didn't mean to, Dru. Somehow it slipped out—but for the life of me I cannot see why he should mind.'

To Drusilla's relief Devenish laughed again, and patted Giles on the head. 'Honest boy, go and amuse yourself by baiting someone besides me with the truth.'

Drusilla said quickly, 'I am sorry if he has been troubling you—he speaks without thinking.'

'Not at all. I needed Giles to show me the folly of my own vanity. Twit away at me, do. Why should all the world stick darts in me—but not you?'

Drusilla could not resist his charm. 'Perhaps it is because I have already stuck so many in you.'

'And you wonder why Giles is honest? He catches it from his sister—but he has not yet learned to refine his delivery. He is too blunt—but time will change that. You are very much alike, you know, and not only in looks.'

Rob Stammers listened to this conversation with some amazement. He had never known his acid-tongued friend to be so easy with anyone.

He said, 'It is only natural that your slight mishap should arouse such interest.'

'Granted, Rob, but tell me this, and if you cannot offer me an answer, then perhaps Mrs Faulkner might. Why is everyone so hipped on the Devil that, since I mentioned him last night, everyone is including him in their conversation?'

'Perhaps,' said Drusilla slowly, 'it is because we are in a spot which was once devoutly religious, and when one speaks or thinks of God, his adversary, the Devil, may not be far away.'

The looks both men gave her were respectful. 'Well said, Mrs Faulkner,' was Devenish's offering, whilst Rob nodded his head slowly. George Lawson, who had come up to them while they were speaking, said a trifle disagreeably, 'I had hoped that we might have another subject for discussion tonight, but I see that Lord Devenish is determined that we shall not.'

'I?' said Devenish, his tone haughty. 'It is not I who am obsessed with him—he may rest unmentioned for all I care. Let us talk of idle matters, the piff-paff of the daily life of society, whether it be in the country or the town.'

This rebuke from the great man silenced Mr Lawson—to Drusilla's secret amusement. She was beginning to discover why Devenish found her and Giles so entertaining—it was their lack of cringing respect for him.

Devenish, however, had his wish granted. The Devil disappeared from the supper-table conversation. Unfortunately he was replaced by something equally repulsive. Someone had informed Lady Cheyne of the disappearing girls—but not of Jeremy Faulkner's murder.

She began a loud and tactless speech on the subject. 'Here I was,' she declaimed, 'contrasting the quiet life of Surrey with the lurid events of which Mrs Radcliffe and her sister authoresses wrote, without knowing how mistaken I was to do so. I am given to understand that there have been several mysterious disappearances of young girls of the peasant sort, as well as murders involving the better part of society. Has no effort been made to trace the miscreants? We are, after all, not living in the wilds of central Europe!'

Leander Harrington looked up. From his expression, the discussion of disappearing girls was as distasteful as talk of the Devil.

'Oh, I understand that there is no mystery connected with their disappearance. It is to be supposed that, as a consequence of rural poverty, they have run off to London to seek their fortune.'

The lady nodded her over-curled head. 'Ah, yes. A reasonable supposition. But the murders, what of them?'

Mr Harrington avoided looking at Drusilla's white face. 'Thieves, ma'am, thieves. I have spoken to the Lord Lieutenant on both matters, and he is quite satisfied with this explanation.'

Not quite, thought Devenish, remembering his conversation with Sidmouth, but perhaps he had told Harrington a different tale. The difference between his version of events and Sidmouth's troubled him.

The unease he suddenly felt rendered the food he was eating distasteful. He put down his spoon, leaving most of his soup untouched. With one part of his mind he was listening to Lady Cheyne, with the other he was trying to identify the source of the unease.

His answers to the lady were mechanical. He suddenly became aware that Drusilla Faulkner's thoughtful eye was on him, and he knew immediately that his unease was visible to her if no one else.

Devenish pushed this disturbing thought away. He had never wanted such an intimate tie with another, but it was becoming increasingly apparent to him that, from the very first moment that he had met Drusilla Faulkner, a rapport had sprung up between them which was increasing every time that they met.

So strong was it and so upsetting that once supper had ended and he and the rest of the men rejoined the ladies who had left them to their port, he went over to her, sat himself opposite to her and murmured so softly that no one could overhear them, 'You are not to do that to me, Mrs Faulkner—particularly at the supper table.'

Drusilla, who had indeed registered his strange disturbance and wondered what had caused it, said, as innocently as she could, 'Do what, m'lord?'

'Do not pretend that you do not know what I mean, madam, it does not become you. It is the outside of enough that I should have someone walking about my head, trying to read my inmost thoughts.'

Her head swam. How could he know that she had read him? She had kept her face as impassive as she could whilst watching him and feeling his unease. What had given her away? Was *he* inside her head?

It was his turn to read her. 'Now you know of what I speak. You cannot easily deceive me, as it seems that I cannot deceive you. If I asked you to take a turn outside on the terrace with me, would you answer a strange question which I wish to ask you?'

Drusilla felt as though the mesmerist whom she had once seen on her solitary visit to London was exercising his powers over her. Devenish's blue eyes were holding hers after a fashion which left her helpless to refuse him anything.

'If you wish,' she said and as he stood up and put out his hand to assist her to rise, it was as though it was not her will which brought her to her feet, but her emotions.

They left by the glass doors which led to the terrace and he walked her along it until they reached the end where they could see the ground falling away before them, down to the stream which had been the Marsham monks' supply of water long ago.

The full moon shone its silver light on them. Devenish released her hand, saying gently, 'I would never coerce you, madam. You may return to the drawing room as soon as you wish. Now, if it pleases you.'

He had suddenly become ashamed of using his iron will to bend her to do as he wished. He might have known that he had deceived himself—as she had—for Drusilla, released, suddenly realised that he had not, after all, compelled her to do his bidding. She had come of her own free will, but had needed to persuade herself that she had not!

But that was not it, either. Rather from the moment that he had taken her hand they had become mentally one and as she had surrendered her separate self to him, so he had done the same to her in return. Freeing her hand had made them two again.

'No,' she told him, 'you did not coerce me. Ask me your question. I will answer you freely.'

'I don't want to distress you by raising the matter, but it is important for me to know. You mentioned to me not long ago that your late husband had spoken to Mr Harrington about the use of the road at the back of Lyford House and which leads to the Abbey. Tell me, how friendly were you and your husband with Mr Harrington?'

It was an odd question and she could not read him and know why he had asked it, for their rapport did not extend to that. It was an exchange of feelings, of emotions, not of words and facts.

She said slowly, 'We met as neighbours do in a small village. We dined together. I had the impression that in the last six months of his life Jeremy and Mr Harrington became much closer together than they had been before. After he spoke to him about the use of the road, I believe.'

Drusilla stopped. Something else struck her of which she did not speak to Devenish. It was after that meeting that Jeremy had changed so much. His last unhappy months of life had coincided with his growing friendship with Mr Harrington.

Devenish did not know exactly what she was thinking—he was only aware that she was greatly disturbed.

'You have remembered something else?' he ventured.

To tell him, or not to tell him? She had told no one else. Why should she trust him? Because they shared something strange? Was that enough?

She said, slowly again, 'No one but myself knows how much my husband grew away from me—and his other friends—in the last months before he died. The change in him began about the time he sought out Mr Harrington. I thought at first that it was because he was beginning to share his radical views—but it soon became plain that he did not.'

She stopped and smiled tentatively at Devenish. His face was stern in the moonlight. 'This sounds very weak and woolly, namby pamby almost. You had best ignore it.'

Devenish shook his head. 'No, I would not dare to judge you so harshly. You knew your husband well, I am sure, and I know your judgement to be sound, surprisingly so for one so young, cut off from the world of consequence and power.'

He fell silent again and they stood for a moment, looking across the obscured view.

'And that is all?' Drusilla said, at last. 'You have no further questions for me? May I ask why you wish to know about such an odd and unimportant matter?'

Devenish took her hand in his again, turned it over and kissed its palm. 'Perhaps because I might not consider it unimportant? Perhaps because I wish to know of the relationships which exist between the people among whom I have come to live. Or, perhaps, mere idle curiosity.'

'Oh, no!' It was Drusilla's turn to shake her head. 'Do not deceive me, m'lord. Curious you may be, idle never!' She spoke quickly to try to deny the effect that his kiss had had on her.

How strange that even the lightest touch from him caused her body to vibrate and shiver. She had been married to a man whom she thought she had loved and who had said that he loved her, and his touch had never moved her as Devenish's did.

If he knew of his effect on her, he did not betray it. Only, as once before, he bent his head to kiss her, not on the eyelids this time, but on her mouth. It was a tender kiss, with nothing demanding about it.

But, involuntarily, as he broke away from her, Drusilla gave a little moan. It was as she thought—he was seducing her, slowly and painlessly, gaining an inch every time they met, and leaving her feeling desolate, as though a light in her life, briefly lit, had been immediately extinguished.

'Come,' he said. 'We have been alone again, and long enough for the gossips to begin to weave their webs. When we return I shall retire immediately, pleading that country air wearies me more than town air does. Better that you leave when others do. Fortunately our rooms are in different wings, and I gather that Miss Faulkner sleeps in an anteroom to yours. That should serve to silence gossip.'

Drusilla, as usual, could not resist the urge to tease him, 'Is it my reputation—or yours—m'lord, of which you are so careful?'

He stopped dead and caught her around the waist. 'Hussy,' he growled into her ear, 'you know that I have no reputation to save. Do not tempt me, or you will be in the same case.'

It was her turn to break away from him. 'So, m'lord, let us return at once, as you bade me. As it is, dear Cordelia Faulkner will reproach me.'

Which, of course, she did. Drusilla bore her admonitions patiently, saying gently that her stroll with Devenish had been perfectly innocent, that only fools would engage in violent love-making on a terrace outside a busy drawing room and she and Devenish were not fools.

She said nothing of Devenish's question about Jeremy, although later she spent a few moments wondering what could have provoked it.

Devenish shared with the great Italian thinker Machiavelli the belief that our life is governed by equal mixtures of planning and chance, and that what is sometimes better—and sometimes worse—is that chance can alter all our careful plans.

Chance had led him to the signet ring under the altar and chance was to do him yet another favour. Afterwards he was to wonder what might have happened if he had not been plagued with sleeplessness after he had retired. He had dozed fitfully for a little time before waking some time after midnight. Sleep eluded him so completely that even picking up a book and beginning to read—his favourite stratagem to defy insomnia—did not help him.

Finally he rose, and dressed himself country-style in the clothes he had worn to visit the crypt. He would tire himself by taking a walk in the Abbey grounds. He put on his lightest shoes in order not to disturb his fellow guests.

Thus equipped he made his way down the backstairs. Much to Rob Stammer's amusement, he always learned the geography of any house he visited—a hangover, he told his friend, from the days in wartime Spain when such knowledge might save his life. Tonight he used it to avoid meeting anyone.

He let himself out of the Abbey by opening a window in the small porch at the back entrance and climbing through it.

Outside the air was balmy. A light breeze was blowing. He walked away from the house, turning once to see that no lights were visible in any of the windows. When he reached the lake he sat down on one of the rustic benches by it and gazed thoughtfully at the starry heavens, identifying the constellations and trying to imagine the immense distances of space.

Sleep began to claim him, but it would not do to be found in the morning, lying across a rustic bench in the open. He gave a little snorting laugh, remembering a time when the bench would have been more comfortable than—

He stopped that line of thought. He refused to remember those days. They were long gone. He began to walk back towards the Abbey.

Devenish never knew why he changed his mind at the last minute and decided to visit the Abbey church before he returned to his room. He had been in the open as he rested by the lake. Here, all was darkness. Trees clustered in and around the ruined building, so that he was forced to pick his way carefully so as not to trip over truncated pillars and fallen masonry.

For a time he looked about him, trying, as Lady Cheyne had suggested, to visualise what the church must have looked like before the Reformation had destroyed it.

Curiosity satisfied, tiredness claiming him, he turned to go. Then, as he reached the remains of the far wall over which he had to step to take the path to the back door, he heard a noise behind him.

He turned, to see that the noise was the creaking of the trapdoor to the crypt as it was lifted to allow three men to climb out into the open. His hair stood up on the back of his neck. Some primitive instinct held him silent and still, lost in the shadow cast by the trees and the house wall.

The trapdoor replaced, the three men stood together. One, by his height, was Leander Harrington. The other two were harder to distinguish, standing as they were, half in shadow, until one of them moved away from the others. It was George Lawson.

Harrington spoke to him, and in the clear night air his voice, though low, was audible to Devenish's keen ears.

'As I expected, nothing untoward for him to see. An expedition for nothing.'

'Not for nothing. Besides, how can we be sure he knows nothing? How came he to speak so of the Devil—and in such a knowing fashion?'

An owl, perched on the house roof, gave a sudden cry and swooped downwards. George Lawson started back and echoed the bird's call in his fright.

Harrington said reprovingly, 'Tut, tut, you are too fearful. There's naught to be worried about. He suspects nothing. I spoke to him later. The fellow is a shallow fool for all his title. It was unfortunate that he should light on that one word when that stupid bitch started to prattle about visiting the crypt.'

The third man spoke at last, and his voice was agitated—all its usual cheerfulness missing. 'We should be careful—in case he is not so innocent as he looks. No more meetings until he has left the county.'

It was Toby Claridge speaking—and of what? Why was the crypt so important?

Harrington said brusquely, 'Nonsense. You start at flies. And it's time we left. Fortunately we have no wives to miss us.'

He said something else in an even lower voice which set them all laughing and they moved away, not to the back of the house, but to the side, leaving Devenish alone in the shadows considering what he had overheard.

Wherein lay its significance? The three men plainly disliked his speaking publicly of the Devil, were fearful that he had seen something that he shouldn't have done in the crypt, and were accustomed to meeting frequently there.

There were three problems connected with finding an explanation which might make sense of all this. For the life of him he could not imagine why they should be disturbed by his speaking of the Devil. As for what he might have seen in the crypt, what could it possibly be? It could not be Jeremy Faulkner's signet ring, for they had not mentioned it, and judging by the place in which he had found it, he doubted whether they knew it had been there.

And finally, why should they stop meeting because of what he might have thought he knew about them and, as a rider to that, why were these meetings secret and held in the crypt?

But if they *were* holding meetings there it would explain the fresh candle grease on the altar for they would need light to see by when they met.

One explanation might be that they were members of a drinking club, using the crypt because it amused them—but in that case, why Lawson's heavily expressed fear and why the secrecy?

Devenish gave a great sigh as he silently negotiated the backstairs which he had reached in his musings. And his final thought, before at last he climbed into bed again, was, had all this odd behaviour anything to do with the missing girls and young Faulkner's mysterious death? And if so, what?

His major difficulty in solving these mysteries lay in the fact that he dare not show his own interest in them overmuch for fear of alerting those responsible who might—or might not—have some connection with Leander Harrington and his two friends. He was working in the dark in more ways than one, and not for the first time.

Sleep was long in coming, and when it arrived, proved a traitor, since it brought him no real rest. For the first time in several years he had a recurrence of one of the nightmares which had plagued him since his early adolescence.

He was an eleven-year-old child again, running down the back street of a northern town to escape his pursuers. He clutched a stolen penny loaf to his ragged chest. It would serve to prevent his mother and his little brother, Ben, from starving. He managed to feed himself by picking up stale and unwanted food, left over from the daily market in the little town's centre.

The three of them were quite alone in the world. Six months earlier his father had been accidentally killed in a tavern brawl. The boy whom Hal had been remembered his father as a big jolly man whom he had adored. In his waking life he knew only too well that Augustus Devenish had, in reality, been a feckless and careless fool and spendthrift who had embraced ruin like a mistress—and taken his family down with him.

But now, Devenish was in the lost past. He was small, always hungry, Hal again, who knew nothing of who and what his father had been and how he had come to end his wasted life in a dirty alehouse, leaving his young son to turn into a thief in order to survive. Hal had been driven to steal small sums of money, and scraps of food to stave off his family's final destination—the workhouse.

Until she had grown too ill to work, his mother had been employed as a sempstress, making delicate baby clothes for the wives of the wool merchants whom the long wars of the late eighteenth and early nineteenth century had made rich.

Breathless, and relieved that he had evaded capture and prison once again, Hal arrived at the tenement where the Devenishes rented two rooms in the garret. He ran swiftly up the stairs, dodging the landlady who shot out of her kitchen, demanding to know when she might expect the rent to be paid.

'It's two weeks overdue,' she howled after him.

He ignored her, reached the garret and pushed open the bedroom door, panting, 'I'm back, Mama, I'm back.'

He received no answer. His mother was sitting up in bed, holding small Ben in her arms. He had been born after his father's death. She looked at him with lacklustre eyes, the marks of recent tears on her face.

'What is it?' He ran over to the bed.

His mother, white-lipped, muttered, 'He's gone, Hal. Ben's gone.'

He did not at first know what she meant. 'Gone?' he echoed, 'how can he be gone? He's here. I can see him.' He loved his little brother dearly, played with him, held him, washed and changed him when his mother had become virtually bedridden.

She took his hand to hold it against the small cold face. 'He died, Hal, shortly after you left. It's my fault. I had so little milk, and he was never strong. God has taken him. Better so, perhaps.'

'Then damn God,' he cried, the loaf falling unheeded to the bare wooden floor.

'No, Hal, you are not to take on. It is God's will, and we must obey it.'

'I won't, I won't.' He took the little body in his arms and said fiercely, 'He's not dead. He's only cold, I'll warm him. He'll be better soon.'

But he knew that it was useless. His mother held her arms out to them both and said, 'I'm going, too, Hal, before long. I shall have to disobey your father. I cannot leave you all alone in the world, to be sent to the workhouse.'

He had no notion, then, what she meant by saying that she would disobey his father: he was to learn that later.

He only knew that the worst had happened—or, perhaps, not the very worst: that, too, was to come later. It was at this point that he always woke, sitting up, the tears running down his face, for he was still back in the past, mourning the lost little brother who would never walk and run with him.

'I'll teach him his letters when he grows a little,' he had promised his mother, for until his father's money had run out they had lived in a better part of town and he had attended an academy for young gentlemen.

Sometimes he saw them on the way to school, laughing and talking, rosy and well fed, carrying their books. When he did so he always ran down a side street, or shrank into a doorway so that they might not see the ragamuffin which he had become.

Devenish recovered himself. He reminded himself that small Hal was long gone, that he had become a man of power and consequence, and whether it was a good thing or a bad thing that he would always remember his harsh past was difficult to judge.

Apart from his growing friendship—if that was the right word—with Drusilla Faulkner, the rest of Leander Harrington's house party was something of an anticlimax for him. Nothing occurred which might suggest secret or strange goings-on of any kind. Indeed, so bland was the conduct of all the party that Devenish might have supposed them to have been a convocation of Methodist ministers on holiday.

True, Lady Cheyne was as eccentric as ever, and George Lawson had developed a habit of sidling away if he found himself in Devenish's vicinity. Toby Claridge, on the other hand, sought him out rather than otherwise, although when he was alone with Drusilla he continued to warn her of Devenish's possible perfidy.

He only did this once in Giles Stone's hearing, for Giles immediately squared up to him, bristling at all points, the picture of youthful aggression. 'I wonder at you, Sir Toby, slandering Devenish behind his back. It is not the action of a gentleman. I dare say you would not care to repeat it to his face. Too dangerous.'

Toby's laughter at such impertinence held a hint of fear. It was only too likely that blunt and tactless Giles might repeat his words to Devenish. And then, what? Pistols at dawn, perhaps, bearing in mind m'lord's reputation. Toby was not sure that he agreed with Leander Harrington's dismissal of Devenish as a shallow fool. He made certain he did not risk himself again by being frank in front of Giles.

It was left to Drusilla to reprimand her brother for his plain speaking. 'After all,' she ended, 'Toby only seeks to protect me.'

'From Devenish?' Giles began to laugh. 'Not by the way he looks at you, Dru. He respects you.'

It was Drusilla's turn to laugh. 'You offer me that from your great experience of life and love, Giles?'

Giles hung his head a little and muttered beneath his breath, 'More than you know, Dru.'

Aloud, he said, 'I do know this. Devenish would never hurt you, but I am not sure of Sir Toby.' Even Giles was not quite certain where this last remark came from. He only knew that he liked Devenish and did not like Sir Toby. He hoped that Dru was not thinking of marrying *him*.

Much better that she married Devenish, but he had enough sense not to tell her so.

Drusilla might have defended Toby to Giles except she was beginning to find his constant denigration of Devenish tedious. It implied that her own judgement was faulty if it needed to be made. She tried to examine both men impartially and came to the not-very-helpful conclusion that Toby was a lightweight and Devenish was a mystery!

She told him so before dinner on their last day at Marsham Abbey. The dinner was a formal one and was to set the seal on what Mr Harrington rightly proclaimed had been a happy week.

Not that she referred to Toby, only to Devenish's own consummate air of total control—based upon what?

'Tell me your secret,' she said, 'for I have the feeling that I should like to be as much in charge of my world as you are of yours.'

'It's an illusion,' he told her gravely. 'In reality I am driven by time and chance like all humanity.'

'An illusion?' queried Drusilla. 'How so? The magician pulls strings, as it were, to produce his. What is your secret?'

Devenish looked down at her laughing face and slowly smiled. He took his handkerchief from his sleeve, showed it to her, crumpled it up in his hand so that it disappeared from view, and then opened his hand—which was empty.

'No secret,' he told her, watching her surprised face carefully, 'a trick, that's all.'

'But where has it gone?' she asked, bewildered.

'Here,' he said, and apparently plucked the handkerchief from her sash before handing it to her.

He had never performed such an illusion before an audience in his adult life, although it was a trick which he had learned at the age of twelve from a travelling magician, and one, among others, which he occasionally practised in private. His reward was Drusilla's amusement when she returned the handkerchief to him.

'It was a parable you were offering to me, was it not?'

'Indeed,' Devenish said, not surprised at all by the speed of her understanding.

'To prove that things are often not what they seem.'

'Exactly.'

Giles, who had been watching, his jaw dropped, said, 'Will you teach me how to do that, Devenish?'

Devenish shook his head. 'A magician, however lowly, never gives away his tricks.'

Giles had not been the only spectator. Leander Harrington, standing by, had watched the little scene with interested eyes. For the first time he wondered whether he had been correct to dismiss Devenish as a shallow fool.

## Chapter Eight

Drusilla, like Giles, found being home again a trifle dull. She missed sparring daily with Devenish, as Giles missed the society of other than his immediate family. Miss Faulkner, on the other hand, was relieved.

She had been persuaded to think that, contrary to her early beliefs, Lord Devenish was a bad influence on both Giles and Drusilla. Mr Harrington, who for his own devious reasons, had no wish to see a marriage between the owner of Lyford House and the owner of Tresham Hall had, quite subtly, suggested to her that m'lord Devenish was not a suitable person for Mrs Faulkner to marry.

'It is not, I think,' he had said in his most magisterial tones, 'that I consider Lord Devenish to be an evil, or a wicked man, but neither is he the sort of person whom I consider dear Mrs Faulkner ought to marry.'

He then retailed to her all the lying gossip about Devenish—and some embroideries of his own—which he could remember, and in the doing convinced poor Cordelia that she had been very wrong to try to push for a match between them.

She was careful, however, not to criticise him over-much to either Drusilla or her brother because she was well aware how much they valued his friendship. On the other hand she no longer echoed Giles's admiration and said nothing if Drusilla appeared to second it.

Giles was particularly restless when he returned home and Miss Faulkner privately thought that it was Devenish's fault. He either mooned about the house or spent long hours away from it, doing goodness knows what.

She bearded him late one afternoon when he had reappeared after several hours' absence from the house.

'And where have you been, young sir?' she asked him. 'You have been gone so long we were growing worried.'

'Nowhere,' he said defensively, 'just to the little copse beyond the park with my book,' and he held it up. 'It's too hot to frowst indoors.'

'Now you know that your sister does not like you to disappear on your own. With that poorly leg of yours, it's not safe.'

'Oh!' and charming Giles was, for once, a trifle nasty. 'Well, I'll have you know that I can walk further on my one good leg and one poorly one than you can on your two well ones.'

Since this was unfortunately true, Miss Faulkner was left with nothing else to say to him—although she complained to Drusilla later.

Drusilla heard her out patiently, saying, 'We can't mollycoddle him too much, you know. It is merely asking for trouble.'

To Miss Faulkner's further complaint that it was all due to Lord Devenish's bad example and his spoiling of him, Drusilla felt constrained to reply, 'I was not aware that Lord Devenish was urging him to take long walks.'

'He is encouraging him to be rebellious, which comes to the same thing.'

Drusilla sighed. What with Giles's adoration of m'lord, Miss Faulkner's new-found dislike of him, and her own repressed feelings of desire which he had aroused, his arrival among them had caused a rare commotion.

'He's growing up, Cordelia. He'll soon be a man, and we must let him learn to make his own mistakes.'

But even Drusilla became worried one fine afternoon when Giles did not turn up for nuncheon—something very out of character for a young man who loved his food.

Miss Faulkner was in a fine old taking, bustling about agitatedly and visiting the stables—something which she rarely did—to discover whether any of the outdoor servants had seen him since early morning.

She found Drusilla in the dining room, looking out of the window, nuncheon untouched on the table. She turned as Miss Faulkner entered, saying, 'I have questioned the housekeeper and most of the indoor servants. He has not been seen since shortly after breakfast. He took his book with him and told Jenkins here—' and she waved a hand at the tall footman by the door '—that he was going to the copse to read in the shade, the day being so hot. I have sent one of the other footmen to fetch him in. He may have forgotten the time.'

'Forgotten the time, indeed!' snorted Miss Faulkner, disbelievingly, secretly a little pleased that her forebodings were proving true. 'I doubt that greatly for I have never known Giles miss a meal before. He has always been a great one for favouring his stomach.'

'Well, I refuse to be too worried until the footman returns—Giles with him, I hope. I don't believe that he can have gone far.'

But when the footman returned it was without Giles, and Drusilla was compelled to admit that Miss Faulkner had been right to be worried about him. A search of the grounds, and the land beyond the grounds, was immediately set in train.

Although, thought Drusilla, we shall all feel very foolish if he shortly wanders in saying that he did not mean to frighten us by falling asleep because his book was so boring.

The afternoon wore on, however, with no sign of him. One of the grooms rode over to Tresham Hall to see if he might have decided to visit Lord Devenish on foot. M'lord was out for the day, visiting the Lord Lieutenant, Rob Stammers said, and they had not seen Giles since the end of the Marsham house party.

When late afternoon found him still missing Drusilla was almost frantic, and Miss Faulkner had turned from being a tower of strength into a watering pot.

'I fear I may have somehow brought this about by worrying overmuch about him!'

A sentiment which Drusilla roundly told her was fit only for a sensational novel. She refused to lose heart, but even her stoic calm was beginning to falter when time continued to pass and there was still no sign of him.

By dusk her spirits had reached their lowest ebb. She was standing on the terrace, wearing her oldest boots, after walking over to Tresham Minor to ask whether he had visited Mr Lawson, when she saw Vobster and Green coming across the park carrying Giles between them, his arms around their shoulders.

She ran down the steps, Miss Faulkner faltering behind her, to discover that Giles was semi-conscious, that his head was bloody, and that he had lost his boots, jacket and watch. They had found his book thrown down on the path nearby.

He roused himself enough to give Drusilla a rueful half-smile. 'Sorry, Dru,' he mumbled.

'Exactly like the master,' Vobster told her when Giles had been carried to bed and the doctor sent for. He had been dragged into the undergrowth—as Jeremy had been—and it was only because they had remembered how his body had been concealed, that Vobster and Green had searched it thoroughly instead of walking by it. Giles had been groping around, dazed, trying to stand up, when they had found him.

'Not far from the stream by Halsey's Bottom,' Vobster ended.

'By the stream near Halsey's Bottom,' echoed Drusilla. 'Whatever was he doing there?'

Halsey's Bottom was a field next to Halsey village which consisted of a dozen labourers' cottages and was part of Devenish's estate.

'Who knows, madam?' said Vobster. 'He might have been carried there, of course.'

'But why?' exclaimed the distracted Drusilla. 'Who would want to hurt Giles?'

'For his possessions, madam. Like the late master. He told us when we found him that he had no notion of what had happened to him. He thought that he was having a nightmare and was trying to get out of bed.'

Giles confirmed this to her later, after the doctor had been, his head had been bound up and he had been given laudanum to relieve his pain.

'I can't remember anything much after I left the copse to go for a walk,' he mumbled, when Drusilla asked him if he had any notion of how he came to be attacked, or why he was so far afield. 'Only that the weather was fine and I was tired of reading. I remember thinking that a little exercise might do me good— and after that, nothing.' He gave her a small, wan smile.

Vobster and the doctor had both warned her that this might be the case. Vobster had been in the Army as a boy and said that soldiers wounded in battle, particularly in the head, often lost their memories of recent events when they recovered.

'Some lose them altogether,' he told her glumly.

Fortunately this was not the case with Giles. But since he was unable to tell her anything, and the laudanum was beginning to take effect, she left him to sleep. Sleep, the doctor had said before he left, was a great healer.

I wish it would heal me, thought Drusilla sadly, later that night. The attack on Giles had revived all the dreadful memories associated with Jeremy's disappearance and death and, like Devenish a few nights earlier, she found sleep a long time in coming and her dreams unhappy when it finally came.

Devenish did not learn of the attack on Giles until he was eating breakfast in his room. He had arrived back late on the previous night from his visit to the Lord Lieutenant and Rob had already retired.

'Something you ought to know of, Hal,' Rob said, after he had discussed the business of the day. 'Giles Stone disappeared yesterday afternoon, and was found much later by a pair of grooms from Lyford House. He had been attacked and left unconscious by the stream at Halsey's Bottom. I gather that they had the doctor to him immediately; although he is not in danger, he has taken a nasty blow.'

Devenish stopped eating to stare at Rob. 'Do I gather that this is a similar attack to the one on his brother-in-law?'

'Indeed, very similar. He was found far from home and had been robbed. The thief, or thieves, took his watch, his jacket and his boots and shoved him into the undergrowth. Vobster remembered how his late master had been hidden and had ordered the search to be very thorough.'

Devenish immediately thought of poor Drusilla. First her husband—and now this.

He flung his napkin down and rose. 'I shall visit Mrs Faulkner immediately. She will need to be comforted. Whilst I change into riding clothes I beg you to order my best horse to be saddled and ready for me. And, for once, I shall take a groom with me. After all that has passed I don't think it safe to ride, or walk, un-accompanied. Do you do the same, Rob.'

Rob's eyebrows rose. This was most unlike Hal, who usually took little note of possible danger. He shrugged his shoulders. Well, even the steadiest of us have their whim whams, was his internal comment as he went to do Devenish's bidding.

Drusilla seemed her normal serene self when Devenish arrived at Lyford House. If her face was a little pale and there were mauve shadows beneath her eyes, well, that was to be expected. But her voice and manner were composed when she greeted him.

'It is very good of you, m'lord,' she said, after Devenish had enquired as to Giles's condition, 'to come over so promptly. He will be pleased to learn of your concern.'

Devenish had kissed her hand on his arrival, and was now seated opposite to her. Above her head was a portrait of the late Jeremy Faulkner, a handsome enough man, but his face was not a strong one, Devenish thought.

He spoke kindly to her, asking her for full details about Giles's disappearance and his discovery by Green and Vobster.

Drusilla was only too glad to have a sympathetic ear. She poured out her story of the previous unhappy afternoon, adding, 'I suppose that I didn't worry about his absence soon enough, but since he has taken to disappearing for long periods since we got back from Marsham Abbey, I assumed that he was walking and reading in the grounds near home. By the time we realised that something was amiss a great deal of time had passed. It was fortunate that Vobster and Green found him when they did.'

Fortunate, indeed, thought Devenish, and being a man who took nothing on trust, he also thought, Exactly what has Master Giles been up to lately? There is more amiss here, perhaps, than his sister realises.

Aloud, he said, 'If he is fit enough to receive me, I should like to visit him. But the decision is yours, madam.'

Drusilla hesitated for a moment, and then said with a sudden smile, 'I can think of nothing better. His delight at your kindness must surely outweigh any possible strain entertaining a visitor might cause. I shall take you to him at once—and afterwards you will stay for nuncheon, perhaps. I am alone, Miss Faulkner is spending the day with an old friend.'

Devenish bowed and followed her up the stairs. By agreement she left him on the landing while she entered Giles's bedroom, and he heard her ask, 'Giles, my dear, are you strong enough to receive a visitor?'

'Depends on the visitor,' he replied, 'I don't think that I could wear Miss Faulkner. She will be sure to put the blame on me for being attacked!'

'No, it's not Miss Faulkner. I rather think that it's someone you might wish to see,' and she beckoned Devenish in.

'Good Lord, Dru, why didn't you tell me it was Devenish you were babbling about! I'm always ready to see *him*.'

Giles was sitting up in bed, his face white, and his head bandaged, but evidently still his old irrepressible self.

'Sit down, do,' he exclaimed as Drusilla tactfully left them alone together. 'And, before you go, try to persuade Dru that I really do need more than gruel to keep me in trim. It's not my stomach that's been damaged, it's my head.'

'Happy to see you as lively as ever,' drawled Devenish. 'I had thought to find you on a bed of pain.'

'Well, I was last night,' declared Giles, leaning back on his pillows, for he was not feeling quite as well as he was claiming to be. 'But I'm much better this morning—or I would be if this confounded headache would go away.'

'It will,' Devenish told him, 'but you must co-operate with your sister and the doctor. Drusilla has quite enough to worry her without you playing the goat. And, by the by, without taking poor Miss Faulkner's part, what *were* you doing, larking around Halsey's Bottom?'

Giles closed his eyes and leaned back in an invalidish manner, before saying feebly, 'Do you know, I don't remember. Everything after I left the copse at the back of the house to go for a walk has quite gone from my mind.'

'Everything? You've no notion of where you were going, or of who might have struck you?'

'No, indeed.'

'Or how you came to be at Halsey's Bottom, so far from home?'

Giles blinked and sank even further back into his pillows, trying to look weak and wan.

'Why do you keep asking me that, Devenish? I have already told you, no.'

Devenish leaned back himself. 'So you said. Now, why do I believe that you are not telling me the truth? Oh, I accept that you have no memory of the attack, or even of a short time before it. What I don't believe is that you were carried any distance to Halsey's Bottom by those who attacked you. In the middle of the night, perhaps, but in the day, no. I think that you know very well why you went there.'

Giles muttered something unintelligible. Devenish leaned forwards, cupping his ear in a parody of a deaf old man. 'Eh, what's that, then? Your sister tells me that you've been disappearing for long periods of time lately. Where to, and why? And don't you want the villain who did this to you caught? He'll not be if you don't tell the truth about your doings.'

'I'm ill. I don't like to be badgered and questioned,' whined the goaded Giles pathetically.

'No? Then why not end the questioning by biting the bullet and telling me the truth?'

Stricken, Giles looked away. 'I don't want you to go peaching to Dru if I tell you—'

'Listen to me, young Giles. I promise to keep your secret if you tell me now. If I find out later, I shall certainly tell her as a punishment for your lying to me and delaying my attempt to find your assailant. Your choice, my lad, your choice.'

This was a new Devenish. A hard man whom Giles scarcely knew. But a man to respect. He swallowed, and gulped out, 'Oh, very well. It's like this, everyone treats me as though I'm made of china, a rare old mollycoddle, not a man at all. Other fellows have fun, I don't—' He stopped.

'Oh, spit it out,' said Devenish inelegantly. 'You'll feel much better when you do. If you've been dallying with one of the village girls, say so and have done.'

Giles was so surprised that he sat up sharply, then fell back groaning as his head protested at this cavalier treatment.

'How did you know?' he gasped.

'I've been eighteen myself. Besides, you live in a house full of women, protected from life. What more likely than that, at your age, you'll kick over the traces. Which one?'

Giles gaped at him. He had expected reproaches, a sermon, perhaps, not this cool acceptance.

'Betty,' he said. 'Betty James. She lives at Halsey.'

'Ah,' said Devenish. 'The village Venus. Not that the villagers know her as that. I hope you don't think that you were her only patron.'

Giles hung his head. 'No, I know I wasn't.' He paused. 'She was kind. She didn't laugh at me.'

'And you were on your way to see her.'

'Yes, and I truly don't remember anything much after I met her. She said, or I think she said, "Oh, Giles, I've something to tell you—" and then, nothing. Truly. If I did remember anything I'd tell you, Devenish. Truly.'

He was becoming agitated. Devenish said gently, 'Lie down, Giles, and try to rest. I'm sorry that I had to be so harsh with you when you were feeling ill, but it is important for me to know exactly what happened if we are to find those who hurt you.'

Giles bit his lip, and hung his head.

Devenish said, 'Don't worry, Giles. I understand why you felt as you did and why you went with Betty. You aren't the first lad to sneak off to enjoy himself, and you won't be the last. You've been unlucky, that's all. On the other hand, when you're feeling better, we'll have a little talk before you start—adventuring—again. And I shan't tell Dru.'

Giles closed his eyes and sank even further back into the bed again. 'First you make me think that you're a beast, and then you're kind. What was it that you said about illusions at Marsham Abbey?'

Devenish rose and looked down at him. He pulled the covers over the sleepy boy, and thought, If he had lived, Ben would have been older than Giles, and possibly no wiser. The question is, Has Giles made me wiser by telling me the truth? And what was Betty James going to tell him? Had it anything to do with the assault on him, or was it merely one of her rustic lovers attacking the young gentleman out of jealousy?

Well, one way to find out would be to go and question Betty. After he had taken nuncheon with Drusilla Faulkner, that was.

'How did you find him?' Drusilla asked him anxiously. She was not sure that she had done the right thing in allowing Devenish to see Giles when he was still so poorly, but Devenish's cheerful air seemed to suggest that he was not too distressed.

'Battered,' he said, 'but surviving. He has no memory of being attacked. I dare say that in a few days he will be over the shock of it. If I might be so bold as to advise you, I would not mollycoddle him overmuch. Are there no other lads in the neighbourhood with whom he could mix? He lacks the companionship of his equals.'

Devenish had kept his promise to Giles by an act of omission, saying nothing of his visit to Halsey's Bottom and his affair with Betty James. He was pleased to hear that Drusilla was also worried about Giles's isolation.

'I was about to ask for it,' she said, 'as to whether Giles should attend one of the two Universities. What worries me, of course, is his damaged leg.'

'Well,' Devenish replied, seating himself in the chair which Drusilla offered him, 'if Lord Byron could successfully go to Cambridge with *his* damaged leg, and play cricket there, then I see no reason why Master Giles should not do the same. Sooner or later you will have to let him fly the nest. You have several excellent servants, any one of whom could accompany him.'

Drusilla felt that a great weight had been lifted from her shoulders. She might have known that she would get a sensible answer from him. She was beginning to think that a true heart was hidden behind Devenish's tart tongue.

She looked across at him to meet his burning gaze and looked hastily away again. Did he know the effect that he had on her? Only the entrance of the servants with nuncheon, which they laid out on the sideboard, prevented her from making an absolute fool of herself by stammering something meaningless at him.

By the time that they had been dismissed she was in command of herself and she was able to thank him for his kindness. The only problem was, that for all her outward calm, the sight of food was making her feel ill. This attack on Giles, resembling as it did that which had caused Jeremy's death, was distressing her more than she liked to confess.

The whole world was beginning to seem unsafe. She tried to calm herself by picking up her plate and selecting a variety of meats, a small chicken pasty and some bread and butter and taking it to the table which the servants had earlier set.

Devenish followed suit, pouring them both a glass of red wine and coming to sit beside her. Her unease was a palpable thing, and the psychic bond which existed between them had never been so strong.

He watched her struggle to eat what lay before her—and fail. Finally she pushed her plate away and said unsteadily, 'You will think me a fool, I know, but I have never felt so overset. The assault on Giles, coming on top of Jeremy's death, has reduced me to near hysterics—something to which I have never normally been prone. It also seems to have revived the dreadful feeling of cold which I experienced at Marsham Abbey. You must forgive me if I cannot eat.'

Her beautiful eyes were full of unshed tears. They affected Devenish profoundly.

He put down his knife and fork and picked up her untouched glass of wine, saying in his usual composed fashion, 'Not at all. Most women would be reduced to the vapours or would have taken to their beds long ago. The more I see of you, the more I admire your stoic calm. The only thing I would ask of you is that you drink your wine,' and he handed her the glass.

Whether it was his blue eyes which held her in thrall so that she did as she was bid, or her own wish to please him, Drusilla never knew. Obediently she took the glass and tipped the crimson liquid down her throat. The taste and feel of it set her whole body aflame, coming as it did after many hours of fasting.

Her cheeks flushed scarlet, her eyes shone, belying the fear which had fuelled her distress since Giles had been found to be missing. And then, oddly enough, reaction set in. The unshed tears reasserted themselves and ran down her face like twin pearls.

Devenish leaned forward. After putting a fingertip on first one teardrop and then the other, he pressed it to his lips. Drusilla gave a little cry. In response he leaned forward again and kissed her on each cheek at the point which his fingertip had touched.

He whispered, 'You are not to worry. Giles is recovering, and as for your husband, what is past, is past. I shall do my best to protect you.'

As he spoke he slipped from the chair to his knees and put his arms around her. She leaned forward to rest her head on his shoulder. He turned his head a little in order to kiss her on the lips this time.

He met with no resistance, only co-operation. She was shuddering against him, whether from passion or fear, he could not tell, and it was Devenish who broke off the kiss, not Drusilla.

'Come,' he said and, rising, scooped her into his arms to carry her over to a *bergère*, where he held her close to him, doing nothing while she hid her face in his chest, blindly seeking his protection. He was cradling her as though she were a baby, and when passion began to stir in him, he ignored it. There was a time and a place for everything and this was neither the time nor the place to indulge his desires.

'I feel safe now,' came from her in a thready whisper, 'but I cannot expect you to spend your life comforting me in this position.'

'Had I but world enough and time,' he said, revising the words of a long-dead poet, 'we could spend eternity comforting one another, but since we have not, this must have a stop—but not yet.'

'I am comforting you?' Her voice was stronger this time.

'Yes, and you must understand that for the bad man that I am, to come to you in your innocence and not violate it comforts me, for I had forgotten that I might be able to behave so.'

Drusilla did not need to be told that this was a rare confession on his part. 'You have never been bad with me,' she breathed, and kissed him on his cheek where it was soft, just above the point where he had shaved his beard away, and where his skin was nearly as tender as hers.

'That is because you are as good as any faulty human being can be,' he told her, still sternly repressing his wish to have her in his arms, consenting to whatever he might wish to do. 'Goodness can beget goodness as evil can beget evil. And do not trust me too much, for I sometimes make vows which I cannot keep.'

'Do not we all?' she said drowsily, for if the wine had begun by rousing her senses it was ending by making her want to sleep.

'But I am worse than most of all,' he told her, but he was smiling when she opened her eyes and looked at him again, 'as doubtless Miss Faulkner and Toby Claridge have both told you.'

'Oh, I take no note of them. It is your actions which I judge you by, and so far you have been kindness itself.'

'But I shall not be kind much longer,' he said, sliding her out of his embrace and seating her beside him, 'for you are temptation itself, and when I am tempted I have to say as I did at Marsham—'

Drusilla finished his sentence for him, '*Vade retro Sathanas*. You know, it's an odd thing. I remember Jeremy, who was no Latin scholar, being annoyed when I quoted that to him not long before he died. When I explained what it meant he said that I was not to say it again, for one might call up the Devil merely by uttering his name and I would not like that. I told him not to be superstitious and he told me that there was more to superstition than we liked to think.'

She paused and said slowly, 'He became very angry with me when I said that no one believed in the Devil any more, and shouted that I might be surprised to learn that there were some who still did.'

Devenish became very still. 'Did he, indeed?' He thought it surprising that so many who lived around Tresham Magna disliked to hear the Devil spoken of disrespectfully. All desire had suddenly fled from him—which could not be the Devil's fault since surely he would have preferred him to seduce Drusilla, not behave chivalrously towards her.

He had learned something about himself since he had arrived at Lyford House: that he had fallen in love with the pure woman beside him and would do nothing to hurt her or those whom she loved. How far this love would take him he did not know. He had always vowed that he would never marry, but that vow had been made before he had met Drusilla Faulkner.

'Let me ring for your maid,' he said. 'I am sure that you did not sleep well last night, and a little rest would restore you. No, do not say that you will not give in to a passing weakness. Even the strongest of us must pause now and then, and let kind Nature take its course.'

'Very well. It's true, I couldn't sleep last night, but now that you have seen Giles and he was able to talk to you I feel much better.'

Devenish waited until she was safely on her way upstairs before he returned to the stables where he had left his horse and his groom. He needed to visit Halsey in order to find Betty James immediately—what he did not need was any witnesses to his visit to her.

Consequently when he reached the stables he ordered the groom to return without him. 'I have a mind to take a short ride on my own, and do not need company. Tell Mr Stammers I shall not be long returning.'

If the groom wondered why his master had changed his mind he did not say so. Devenish waited until he was safely on his way back to Tresham Hall before setting off alone to question Giles's village inamorata in the hope that she might be able to offer him some valuable information.

Halsey might be small, but it was not poor. One of his first acts on inheriting the title had been to have the wretched hovels in which his tenants existed, rather than lived, improved.

He rode through Halsey's Bottom before he entered Halsey village, and, as he had expected, found nothing there which might help him to discover who had attacked Giles. The undergrowth was trampled where

Vobster and Green had searched it, and he dismounted to look around for any evidence which they might have missed. But, of course, he found none.

It was a different matter when he rode down the muddy lane which served as Halsey's main street. Heads turned, men doffed their hats and women curtsied. He knew where the James family lived and rapped on the door with his riding crop.

It was opened by old man James himself—Betty had been the youngest and wildest of his eleven children. A look of profound relief swept over his face at the sight of Devenish.

'Oh, m'lord, 'tis pleased I am to see you. I was about to visit the Hall to see if any there knows aught of what has happened to our Betty. She went out yesterday well before noon and has not been seen since.'

His anxiety was plain, as was that of his worn-down wife who peered anxiously around him.

'Come in, m'lord, dunnot stand in the street. Gertrude, put out a chair for m'lord, and a cup of the tea you've just made.'

Devenish had no wish for either chair or tea, but pleased his humble host by accepting both. After he had drunk a little of the tea he asked as gently as he could, without appearing to criticise Betty's father in any way, 'Did she often stay out all night?'

Mr. James was uncomfortable. He looked away. 'Aye—oh, you know what she is, m'lord, everyone does. There's no ruling her. But she has always returned before breakfast before.'

No point in beating about the bush or in pretending the girl was other than she was. 'And have you no notion of who she was with this time?'

'No, m'lord. I dunno who she met yesterday. It could have been Tom Orton, or the lame boy from Lyford House—or it might have been anyone else she fancied. Who's to know? I asked young Tom if he'd been with her, yesterday, and he said no. I thought I'd ask at Lyford on the way to see you.'

Devenish knew, without being told, that what Betty earned from pleasing her various admirers, either in money or in kind, was a useful addition to her family's budget.

It was time that he informed them why he was there. 'No one has told you, then, that young Giles Stone was attacked and left injured in Halsey's Bottom yesterday?'

Mrs James gave a gasp and threw her apron over her head. Her husband said, 'No, we knew naught of that. The Bottom's a mile away, and you're the only visitor we've had in the last week.' His face paled. 'Did Master Giles say whether he had been with her?'

'Master Giles has no memory of the attack. Indeed, his last memory is of deciding to go for a walk. He knows nothing after that.' He had decided that the less people knew that Giles's last memory was of being with Betty, and that she was about to tell him something which she thought important, the better.

'Aye, so then there's none knows who she met, or where she can be.'

Where, indeed?

Mrs James flung her apron down again, and cried out, 'Niver say that she's gone like them other poor girls, niver to be seen again.'

This was, indeed, what Devenish feared. She had been with Giles when he was struck down, must have seen his assailant, and was now added to the list of the missing.

'Oh, m'lord, say as how you'll try to find her for us.'

Devenish stared helplessly at his tea, conscious of how difficult that was going to be. 'Yes, indeed, but you must tell me this. Was she friendly with any of the missing girls?'

'Nay,' began Mr. James, 'not her,' only for his wife to contradict him.

'Oh, but she was, our Will. She was right friendly with the last to leave, Kate Hooby. D'you think she's run off to London, too?'

Devenish doubted it very much. He was growing more and more certain that there was a link between what had happened to Faulkner, young Giles, and the disappearance of the girls, although what it might be baffled him completely.

All that remained for him was to comfort Betty's family, even though, in honesty, he did not think that he could offer them any real hope.

'Rest assured that Mr Stammers and I will do all we can to find her,' he told them. 'In the meantime, you must ask her friends whether she was going with anyone new or strange in the district.'

He rose. Mr James clutched at his hand, and began to thank him profusely. Mrs James on the other hand, stood there, her mouth dropped open, her eyes distant, as though she were trying to think of something.

He was halfway back to his horse, which he had left tethered to a tree, when she ran after him.

'M'lord, m'lord, I've just remembered. Our Betty's not been quite herself since Kate disappeared. And as to having truck wi' a stranger, she must have been meeting someone wi' money, for she'd been given a pretty necklace wi' a nice white stone in it which she allus wore beneath her dress. I saw it by accident and she swore it were a trumpery thing some lad she'd met at Tresham Fair had given her. But it looked better'n that to me.'

Devenish thanked her and rode slowly away. At last, a link between two of the missing girls: both of them had been given a valuable necklace of a similar design. But, like the other mysteries in this sad tale of death and loss, he could, for the moment, make nothing of it.

More than that, the sense of growing danger surrounding him was not lessened by his conviction on the ride home that unseen hostile eyes were watching him. He had experienced this odd sensation on more than one occasion before, and it had always proved to be correct.

In the end, his musings invariably took him back to the strange business over the crypt at Marsham Abbey, but again, what that had to do with anything was a mystery.

He remembered a toy he had been given not long before his father died. It had consisted of several odd pieces of wood with colours painted on them, and when the pieces were fitted together correctly a picture appeared.

The bad thing was that, so far as the puzzle he was faced with at Tresham was concerned, he was rapidly becoming aware that he did not possess all of the pieces necessary to complete the picture. The good thing was that today he had acquired one more.

And even that was not an unmitigated good for he was certain that it had taken Betty James's death to provide him with it.

# Chapter Nine

'I understand that Lord Devenish visited you today and that you ate nuncheon with him—*alone*.'

Cordelia Faulkner invested her last word with a doom-laden quality which suggested that Devenish and the Devil were as synonymous as rumour had it.

Drusilla's reply was a quiet, 'Yes, he did. He was kind enough to visit Giles—a visit which I understand did him a power of good. Afterwards we ate together, and he encouraged me to rest a little—which I did. Nothing occurred which need trouble you in the least.'

'But I am troubled, my dear. I don't think that Lord Devenish has marriage in mind—far from it—and if you do wish to marry, would it not be wiser to consider someone sound of your own age? Sir Toby Claridge, for instance. He was a great friend of dear Jeremy's and would make you a most suitable husband.'

Drusilla's patience with Jeremy's meddling aunt snapped at last. She rose, and said in as level a voice as she could manage, 'Dear Miss Faulkner, may I remind you that you are not my guardian, and furthermore, that you are here as my guest to be a companion for myself and Giles. I welcome your advice, but I have made it plain to you that so far as Lord Devenish is concerned I must allow my own judgement of him to be my guide. That being so, I must ask you not to raise the matter again.'

Had a mouse bitten her Miss Faulkner could not have been more surprised. In her two years at Lyford House Drusilla had allowed her to air her prejudices without contradiction. Like most female bullies, when crossed she took refuge in tears.

Out came her handkerchief. She hid her face in it for a few moments, surfacing only to say in a reproach-ful voice, 'I am sure that I only speak with the best intentions in mind.'

'No doubt,' said Drusilla, sorry to have been driven at last to speak her own mind, 'but I do not wish to hear either your best or worst intentions concerning Lord Devenish. As for Sir Toby Claridge it is I who will have to live with him as his wife, so you must leave me to make up my own mind about him also.'

She did not tell Miss Faulkner that, beside Devenish, Sir Toby seemed even more callow than he was. She thought that she had said sufficient to silence Miss Faulkner, at least for the time being.

'I shall go up to poor Giles to see how he fares,' Miss Faulkner declared self-righteously, privately con-vinced that Devenish's visit could have done him noth-ing but harm.

'Oh, I wish that you will not. His nurse says that he is sleeping peacefully after managing to eat a little, and it would not do to wake him.'

Trembling a little, Miss Faulkner picked up her canvas work and announced that she would retire to her room. All the way upstairs she silently lamented Drusilla's stiff-necked attitude over her attempts to warn her off Devenish. She also decided that she would privately urge Sir Toby to press his suit with her lest others be there before him.

Once she had gone Drusilla sighed unhappily. If Miss Faulkner thought that she was attracted to Devenish she was correct, but that did not give her the right to act like a mother-hen with one chick. She remembered that Giles had said after Devenish's arrival at Tresham that it would set all the biddy hens from ten miles around clucking and gossiping as nothing else had done for the past ten years.

'And every mama with a marriageable daughter will set her cap at him,' he had added.

Well, that was true enough. What neither of them had bargained for was that Giles would come to regard Devenish as either his lost father or the older brother he had never had, and that Drusilla would fall head over heels in love with him.

'There's a letter waiting for you, Hal. The Lord Lieutenant sent it by special messenger. He said that it was urgent. I put it on the desk in your study.'

Devenish tossed his riding gloves on to the boule table in the back hall. 'That's prompt of him, if it's what I think it is.'

'Did you find out anything useful about young Stone's attack?' Rob enquired casually.

'Only that it was most probably robbers at work since he was foolish enough to stray too far afield,' replied Devenish equally casually. He was not about to tell anyone, not even Rob, of his suspicions: better so. He would pass on the news of Betty's disappearance later as though it had nothing to do with Giles. He had a strong suspicion that Giles, having lost his memory, would be safer if his attack and Betty James's disappearance were not connected.

Rob did not say *I told you so* to the news about the robbers. He did not need to, his face said it for him. Well, that suited Devenish down to the ground, and he grinned a little ruefully at his own ability to deceive even his best friend.

He opened the Lord Lieutenant's letter immediately. It was as he had thought. He had asked, earlier that morning, for a list of the dates on which first Jeremy Faulkner had disappeared, and then the girls. The letter told him that the Lord Lieutenant's secretary had been sufficiently interested to keep a log of everything to do with the matter, and had immediately compiled a list for m'lord's use which he had enclosed.

Devenish ran his eye down it quickly. One thing he found there interested him mightily. The first girl's disappearance had been reported a week before Jeremy Faulkner's. The others had been reported at several-month intervals—the next, indeed, occurred six months after Faulkner's death.

He put the paper down and walked to the window to stare across the Park. Was he running mad to think

that there was something significant in the two disappearances being so close together in time?

Not that it told him anything directly useful. He had
battered his brains long enough on the subject, and decided to let it rest for the time being.

He pulled out his fob watch to check the hour. He
was giving a small dinner party for some of the local
gentry and their wives and the two Parsons, Williams
and Lawson. As Lawson had no wife he had been reluctantly compelled to invite Lady Cheyne to join
them.

To be honest, he would have preferred to ask
Drusilla but he did not wish to encourage gossip by
publicly seeming to be over-partial to her. He knew
that Miss Faulkner was not the only local busybody
who disapproved of her friendship with him. If they
thought that it was love—or seduction—their tongues
would never stop clacking—and he did not want her
to be hurt.

That he was wise in so thinking was confirmed when
he met Rob on the way upstairs.

'I never asked you how you found young Stone,' he
said, 'I was more concerned with informing you about
the letter. It's a pity that it was he who was attacked
so brutally, since it means that you will be compelled
to visit Lyford House frequently to check on his condition, thus giving ground for further gossip about you
and Mrs. Faulkner.'

Devenish's fine eyebrows rose. 'Further gossip? I
was not aware that there had been any. No, do not tell

me of it. I have no wish to know who cannot be trusted to mind their own business and not mine.'

Rob coloured. 'I thought it something which you ought to know,' he began defensively, and somewhat incoherently. 'I have only your best interests at heart.'

'Whenever anyone says that to me,' returned Devenish, 'my one instinct is to disbelieve them absolutely. What they are really saying, is that they are much better able to use their judgement than I am! Allow me to be the best judge in my own cause, and, as you love me, do not mention Mrs Faulkner to me again, other than impersonally. This evening I have to endure Lady Cheyne and that is quite enough—if not too much.'

Like Miss Faulkner Rob sighed and shook his head as Hal bounded upstairs as though he were running a race against time. Why was it that wilful people would never believe that you really did have their best interests at heart?

Dinner was as tiresome as might have been expected. Much idle discussion of the attack on Giles told Devenish nothing that he did not already know. No one seemed to connect the attack on Giles with that on his brother-in-law. Labouring men, thrown out of work by a local and unpopular landowner, were blamed.

'We have no Luddites to contend with down here,' was the general verdict offered by Mr Williams, with the added gloss, 'but we do have troubles of our own. It behoves us all to be careful where we walk and not to do so without a companion.'

He added ruefully, 'We have suffered another strange occurrence at the church. Someone stole the two large white candles which stood on either side of the altar and replaced them with black ones.'

Lady Cheyne shivered, 'Strange indeed. It reminds me of something I read once. I cannot think what!'

This unhelpful offering would have amused Devenish at any other time, but after the news about Giles and young Betty the lady's inconsequence only served to irritate him. Particularly since something had tugged at his memory while Mr Williams had been speaking and the lady's idle comment had driven it away.

The evening's so-called entertainment over, and all the guests safely on their way home, Devenish turned to Rob, who privately thought that Hal was not quite his usual sardonic self and had seemed preoccupied during dinner.

He said, 'One moment before you retire. I did not speak to you of it earlier but it will be current gossip soon enough and I did not wish it to be hashed over during dinner.

'When I visited Halsey this afternoon to try to find out if anyone there had seen Giles yesterday, the Jameses told me that Betty had disappeared yesterday. She had left home around noon—and never returned. It seems that the James family were not worried until she had failed to come down to breakfast this morning. They were apparently resigned to the fact that she was given to staying away overnight.'

Rob nodded, and said wryly, 'A pity, that. The trail will be cold.'

'True.' Devenish waited for him to make the inevitable connection with Giles having been struck down on the same day. He did not have long to wait.

'Strange that it should have occurred at the same time that Giles was attacked.'

'Perhaps the same man,' offered Devenish. 'Who's to know? Most likely it's a coincidence.'

Rob looked doubtful, but did not pursue the matter—nor did Devenish tell him about Giles's rendezvous with Betty.

Later, alone in his room, his head buzzing, Devenish sat down and began to make a list of the odd events of the last two years to see if there were any pattern to them.

It was while he was writing down a brief account of his accidental finding of Jeremy Faulkner's ring in the crypt at Marsham Abbey that the memory which had been teasing him during dinner came back.

He remembered his surprise when, after falling beside the altar in the crypt and catching his hand against it to steady himself, he had found black candle grease under his fingernails.

So, someone had been burning black candles in the crypt. Had that same someone placed them in the church and, if so, why? There was no doubt in his mind that the sheep had been placed on the altar to desecrate the church—was that also the reason for black candles being substituted for white ones?

And what had Lady Cheyne not remembered? Or had she been chattering away mindlessly as was her wont?

There were other connections but they demanded leaps in logic to make them. So be it. He had done such a thing before and had often been proved right later.

For example, two of the missing girls were wearing similar expensive necklaces which no village lad could have given them. That must mean that they were involved with a man of means, a gentleman most likely.

And then Giles was attacked when Betty was about to tell him something. Now what could that be? Something, perhaps, which might incriminate others, since it seemed increasingly likely that Giles had been hidden and left to die—like his brother-in-law—in case Betty had had time to tell him anything incriminating.

The necklaces must have been given to the girls for services rendered—and if so, what were they? It must have been for more than simple sexual favours from various gentlemen, married and unmarried. No one would commit murder to hide such a commonplace activity as that. No, the girls must have known of something discreditable for such extreme measures to have been taken.

And if Betty and Kate had been killed in order to silence them, then could it be that the other missing girls had been disposed of for the same reason? He was beginning to find it difficult to believe that any of them had gone to London, as was commonly supposed.

Had Jeremy Faulkner been killed because he was involved in something wrong and was about to inform the authorities of it? Was that the explanation of his changed behaviour during the last six months of his life?

But what could it be? Nothing so far gave him any clue as to what could be happening of so grave a nature that, rather than have it revealed, those responsible for it were prepared to organise an orgy of murder.

Which brought him back again to the strange conversation which he had overheard at Marsham Abbey. To make sense of that he needed to discover what secret Harrington and his friends were hiding which had them meeting at dead of night.

This odd incident reinforced his growing belief that more than one person lay behind the deaths, assaults and disappearances. Yet another link with Marsham Abbey was that one of the deaths, or disappearances, was that of Leander Harrington's valet.

The trouble was he could scarcely, without any real evidence—other than his intuition—go about questioning apparently respectable gentlemen and suggesting that they were engaged in a programme of murder and deadly assault. Babbling about black candles and necklaces would not serve at all. Or rather it would serve to make him look and sound like a ridiculous masculine version of Lady Cheyne.

No, he would wait until he had something firm to act on, and then—then what? Why, chance might tell him, or Lady Luck, those twin deities whose hands might not be forced, but who dispensed their favours on mortal man most often when they were least expected.

Dog-tired, Devenish lay back in his chair, trying to summon the energy to undress and put himself to bed—he had dismissed his protesting valet for the night long ago. What kept him from doing so was another vague tugging at his memory, a tugging which told him that he had seen or heard something of moment and had not understood its importance at the time—and which he had immediately forgotten.

He leaned forward and propped his chin on his hands. Yes, he was tired, but sometimes the tired mind gives up its secrets when it ceases to concentrate.

He closed his eyes and tried to think of nothing. He saw nothing and was nothing, floating away on a tide of non-being.

And then, as from a great distance, he heard Leander Harrington speaking. He was back in the supper room at Marsham Abbey and Lady Cheyne was demanding to know whether the crypt was as horrid as Mrs Radcliffe had suggested.

'No, not horrid at all, ma'am,' Mr Harrington was saying hastily. 'Boring, in fact—and dark. No one has set foot in it for years...'

Devenish was back in his body again. He opened his eyes. How could he have forgotten that ringing statement from Leander Harrington which was easily disproved not only by his discovery of Jeremy Faulkner's ring there, and the presence of candle grease from candles recently used, but everything which he had overheard Harrington and the others saying at dead of night?

Harrington had lied.

The crypt had been used, but he did not want anyone to know that it had been.

Why?

Which meant—what? The memory was significant but it still left him with nothing firm to act on. Until he had, he must not attract suspicion from those whom he now thought had not hesitated to kill to preserve their secret, which was connected with the crypt.

And of the three men whom he now thought were involved the one with whom he must be most careful was Harrington. The weak links were the Parson and Sir Toby Claridge.

He was inclined to think that Claridge might be the weakest. He had left the neighbourhood shortly after Jeremy Faulkner's death, had only recently returned and Devenish's opinion of his intellect was not high. The Parson had sounded fearful in the dead of night, but he was an opinionated man and in the daylight might be less inclined to panic.

No, Claridge it must be. But how to set about suborning him? Not now, he told himself, yawning, I'm only fit for bed. God send me no nightmares.

But God was not kind and sent him one of his worst, which he realised, even as he suffered from it, had been caused by his musing on the puzzle into the early hours.

\* \* \*

A week later, during which time Devenish was distracted by a letter from Lord Sidmouth asking him if he had made any progress and did he require the assistance of a Bow Street Runner, as well as by an unwanted, if brief, visit from the distant relative who was his heir, Drusilla was seated in her front drawing room, writing a letter to an old schoolfriend, when Leander Harrington was announced.

She had been hoping that her visitor might be Devenish whom she had not seen since the day after Giles's attack, but she allowed herself to betray no sign of her disappointment in her welcome to Mr Harrington. He had come, he said, to commiserate with her over the attack on Giles.

'How is the young fellow?' he asked jovially, after accepting a glass of Madeira and some ratafia biscuits.

'Restless,' said Drusilla, smiling. 'He is feeling so much better that he wishes to get up but the doctor says that he must wait a little longer. Head injuries are not to be trifled with, he says.'

'No, indeed. The brain is a delicate instrument, easily damaged. His mind is not affected, I trust.'

'Not at all. If anything he seems livelier than usual.'

This polite chit-chat was interrupted by the maid who announced that Lord Devenish had arrived and wished to know if Mrs Faulkner would receive him.

'By all means.' Drusilla was always ready to receive m'lord Devenish. She and Mr Harrington rose when Devenish came in, and the maid was sent for Madeira and biscuits for m'lord also.

Devenish was absolutely *à point*. He had ridden over wearing his most snowy breeches and a black jacket, both of which fitted him to the degree that they showed off his muscular figure to perfection. His boots were perfection too, as well as his hair. He had remarked to his valet before he set out that if he was fit for nothing else he was a splendid advertisement for his tailor, his hairdresser and his bootmaker.

'You are pleased to jest, m'lord,' returned his valet stiffly. His master was always a credit to him as he often boasted in the servants' hall, but he did so wish that m'lord took the whole business of dress more seriously. He made far too many jokes about it for his liking.

Devenish was surprised to find how much it annoyed him to discover Leander Harrington already ensconced in Lyford House's drawing room. He had hoped to speak to Drusilla alone.

Like Mr Harrington he asked all the right questions about Giles, and received similar answers, Mr Harrington nodding an unnecessary agreement with each word Drusilla spoke.

That over, Mr Harrington leaned forward and addressed them both in confidential tones. 'I suppose, Devenish, that the Jameses being your tenants, you are already aware that young Miss Betty has disappeared. Has the news reached you yet, Mrs Faulkner?'

Drusilla said as calmly as she could, 'Oh, no. It's possible that since Giles's accident no one has cared to touch upon it lest it distress me further.'

Devenish said quietly, for he could see that Drusilla was disturbed, 'I did not wish to trouble you with it. I heard the news after I had visited you and Giles the other day.'

'Apparently,' said Mr Harrington, watching Devenish rather than Drusilla when he spoke, 'she disappeared on the afternoon of the day on which young Giles was attacked.'

'And nothing has been seen of her since,' asked Drusilla.

'Oh, doubtless Devenish knows more about that than I, the Jameses being his tenants.'

'Nothing,' said Devenish, wondering what game Mr Harrington was playing. 'So we have no notion whether she has run off, or whether, like Giles, she was the victim of some unknown assailant. The latter is the most likely since she left all her possessions at home—unlike Kate Hooby.'

'This is quite dreadful,' remarked Drusilla, trying not to show how agitated she was. 'Whatever is the world coming to that we may not walk abroad safely?'

'Oh, no,' said Mr Harrington in self-satisfied tones. 'It is not surprising at all when one considers all the poor fellows who have been turned away by soulless landlords since the war ended. No wonder that they seek vengeance on their oppressors who have treated them so heartlessly!'

Devenish drawled in his most cutting fashion, 'Since neither Giles Stone nor Mrs Faulkner are soulless landlords—indeed, I understand, they are quite the contrary—it seems a pity that they have to suffer for the sins of others.'

'But is not that the way of the world?' returned Mr Harrington eagerly. 'As the French aristocracy found during the late French Revolution when the poor peasantry—'

He got no further. Devenish cut in on him, saying, 'I am sure that we ought not to trouble Mrs Faulkner with the misdeeds or otherwise of the French peasantry when she must be sufficiently distressed already by the misdeeds of those who attacked her brother. And in any case, whoever attacked Betty James—if she were attacked—was not doing so to avenge themselves on a heartless landlord.'

'Well, no,' conceded Mr Harrington uncomfortably, 'and I did not mean to distress you, Mrs Faulkner, merely offer you an explanation.'

Drusilla inclined her head. She had not been in the least overset by Mr Harrington beginning a demagogue's sermon in her drawing room. On the contrary, the sight of Devenish elegantly putting down a man who constantly put down others was a pleasing one to her.

Whatever the reason, whether it was Devenish's put-downs, or something else, Mr Harrington had been rendered uneasy and shortly afterwards took his leave, begging Drusilla to remember that she had a true friend in him and he would do all in his power to track down the miscreants.

'Very nimble of him,' commented Devenish coolly when Mr Harrington was safely away, 'to turn the poor oppressed peasantry into miscreants in the course of a couple of sentences. His powers of logic may be poor, but his ability to stand on his mental head should be applauded, as you must agree.'

Drusilla began to laugh immoderately. She pulled out a small handkerchief, and said, her voice rendered weak by laughter, 'Oh, m'lord, you really shouldn't say such dreadful things, and I shouldn't laugh at them.'

'Why not?' he responded. 'We are a nation of hypocrites, to be sure, and the man who has just left is the biggest of them all. I wonder if he understands that, if he ever managed to secure his Revolution, his head would be among the first to roll when the guillotine was set up in Trafalgar Square. A man who is a traitor to his own interests would be adjudged to be a potential traitor to everyone else's.'

To Devenish's intense pleasure this set Drusilla off again: he was pleased to see that she had lost the Friday face which Mr Harrington's visit had given her.

'That's better,' he said approvingly. 'I like a female who laughs at my more learned jokes, and you looked as if you needed a good laugh.'

'So I did, but I wonder if I ought to enjoy one at Mr Harrington's expense.'

'All good jokes are made at someone's expense,' he told her. 'When I have finished this Madeira, will you allow me to visit Giles?'

'Certainly. And you know that we ought not to be enjoying ourselves when the poor Jameses must be grieving for Betty.'

'True, but our putting on a glum face will not bring her back. Tell me, Drusilla—you will allow me to call you Drusilla now that we have established that we share the same twisted sense of humour—do you see any similarity between what happened to Giles and to your late husband?'

'Only that they were both hidden in the undergrowth and were found at some distance from home, although Giles was not so far away. Otherwise nothing.'

'As I thought. Has Master Giles remembered anything more?'

'Nothing, and the doctor thinks that he never will.'

So Giles was still keeping his meeting with Betty a secret which, in view of the way in which Devenish's suspicions were mounting, was wise of him.

Drusilla might be putting a brave face on things but he thought that she was looking unwontedly pale. His care for her had him saying, 'Let me raise two points: first of all, do I understand that Miss Faulkner is not with you at the moment and, secondly, how long is it since you left the house?'

'As to Miss Faulkner,' Drusilla said slowly, 'she has gone to visit a friend. We have been thrown too much together over the last two years and I think that we both deserved a rest from the other. She would not leave until she was sure that Giles's recovery was certain. As to your second question, I have been indoors since Giles was attacked. Foolish of me, I know, but while his condition was uncertain I did not like to leave the house.'

'Your sense of duty reproaches me. Would you think it impertinent of me if I suggested that we took a turn outside? I should like to see the roses back in your cheeks, and there is no Miss Faulkner about to look at me as though such a proposal meant your instant seduction.'

'You are not to reproach her in her absence for worrying about me,' returned Drusilla. 'Like me, you may find it tedious, but it is surely better to be loved unwisely than not at all.' She was remembering with some sadness her own firm line with Miss Faulkner, and hoped that she had not driven her away for good.

Devenish was thinking of Rob, whose nannying of him he sometimes resented and to whom he had recently spoken sharply, and realised immediately the truth of what she had just said. How empty of affection would his world be if Rob was not in it. He must be more patient with him in future.

'You are my good angel,' he said, 'and I hope that my angel will consent to walk with me outside like a common-or-garden mortal since I am unable to fly with her.'

'I am not an angel, but I will walk with you. Nor are you the Devil, although you sometimes pretend to be. I, too, have been unkind to Miss Faulkner recently, and need to be forgiven.'

He held out his hand to help her to rise. 'Then let us take turns to forgive one another—and have done. Overmuch indulgence in repentance is nearly as soul-destroying as the original sin which caused it.'

They were standing face to face by now and Devenish began to ask himself whether he was going to be able to behave himself with her once they were alone outside, hidden from prying eyes. Perhaps this invitation was not a good idea for a man who was trying to behave himself with a woman who, all unaware, had become temptation itself.

For a diversion he tried to think of mundane things, saying, 'Do you need to ring for your maid to bring you a shawl? You look a little pale.'

'Indeed, no. The sun is shining and we shall walk briskly, I trust, and not dawdle. Do you know, I have never seen you dawdle.'

'Nor I, you. You are always busy. I am waiting for the day when I find you, like Lady Cheyne, draped over a sofa, surrounded by admirers, murmuring sweet nothings back at them.'

'Oh, I would not like that at all,' replied Drusilla entering into the spirit of the game, as they walked outside to stroll on the terrace and then to make their way down a twisting path to the lowest lawn, hidden from the house by the trees and shrubs on the slope of the hill on which it stood.

Devenish looked sideways at Drusilla in order to admire her perfect profile. He wondered how long it had been since he had known a truly good woman, one whose aim in life was to do her duty to those around her rather than avoid it. What surprised him most about her was that beneath her shy manner she possessed a keen intellect. She was well read and had a sly sense of humour which matched his own. There was nothing of the conventional Mrs Goody Twoshoes about her.

To prevent his mind—and his body—from dwelling too much on her many virtues, which included a beautiful face and a graceful body, he remarked casually, 'Have you had many visitors since Giles's accident?'

'Oh, half the neighbourhood. To begin with I was able to turn them away with a polite message saying that my first duty was to Giles in his sickroom. Later, when he began to recover, I invited them in—as I did Mr Harrington this morning. Lady Cheyne came two days ago and chattered non-stop about the black candles suddenly appearing in the church.

'She and Miss Faulkner had a long conversation about them. Miss Faulkner reminded Lady Cheyne that in one of the Tales of Terror which she had read—she couldn't remember which—black candles, not white ones, were used when the Black Mass was celebrated. I'm not quite sure what that had to do with our black candles.'

She paused and said, surprised, 'Why do you look at me like that?'

Hearing this news, for once Devenish had lost his perfect self-control. His shock at the possible explanation of the black candles was visible on his face. He was not a great reader of Tales of Terror, and although he conceded that he might once have heard of the Black Mass, he knew nothing of how it was celebrated.

He pulled himself together, thinking that perhaps it was not surprising that when he was with Drusilla he was not quite his usual self. 'Oh, I was visualising

Parson Williams officiating at a ceremony presided over by the Devil—horns and all. The mind boggles.'

'Indeed,' said Drusilla, laughing at the scene which Devenish had just created. 'Almost as much as the mind boggles at the notion of the Black Mass being celebrated in Surrey. But speaking of Parson Williams Lady Cheyne did say that the Black Mass had to be consecrated by someone who was—or had been—a real clergyman. Otherwise the Devil would not appear.'

Devenish tried to lighten matters. 'You know, I would never have thought that Lady Cheyne could have been conversant with such arcane matters.'

'No, nor Miss Faulkner either. But they vied with each other in supplying me with all the dreadful details. Why do people read such things?'

'Because their own lives are so dull and unexciting,' returned Devenish, wondering if that was why the Black Mass itself was celebrated. And had Lady Cheyne and Miss Faulkner, via Drusilla, presented him with the solution to his puzzle?

'Well, I wouldn't call my life in any way remarkable for excitement,' commented Drusilla, 'but I have little desire to read them. I much prefer Miss Jane Austen.'

'Ah, yes,' said Devenish, *Northanger Abbey,* for instance, where Catherine finds that the medieval chest contains nothing more terrible than old laundry bills!'

'Oh, never say that you like her novels, too. What good taste you have, m'lord!'

'Not m'lord,' muttered Devenish, taking her hand and kissing its palm in lieu of kissing anything else of hers, 'call me Devenish—or, better still, Hal. And judging by *Northanger Abbey* Jane Austen liked Tales of Terror too.'

His kiss startled Drusilla. Her palm burned where the kiss had lingered. He was so near to her now that she could see everything about him. His valet had nicked his chin a little when he had shaved him. Unlike Jeremy his beard was light in colour and he did not need to shave twice a day to keep himself in trim. For all his beauty, his jaw was stronger than Jeremy's had been—and warned her of his determination and the power of his will.

His blue eyes had flecks of silver in them. His eyelashes were longer than most women's. His teeth were excellent—unlike those of many gentlemen. The long mouth was tender when he looked at her so closely, not tight and hard as it often was in company.

His clothes—like the rest of him—were spotlessly clean, and the scent he gave off excited her. Jeremy had always smelled of horse and tobacco, but Devenish smelled of lemon soap and musk—the scent of the roused male which she had known with Jeremy only after he had taken a bath...which wasn't very often.

This ought to have frightened her, alone with him as she was, but didn't. On the contrary it served to rouse *her*. She was so roused, indeed, that she forgot her common sense which had been telling her that she must resist Devenish's advances because they were not, could not be, serious.

Tired after so many anxious days and nights worrying over Giles, she allowed herself to fall into his arms when he put them around her. Mixed with desire was a sense that she was finding refuge in someone else's strength, that she was not alone in a harsh world.

Her warm body against his and her scent, particularly that of her hair, which had recently been washed by a soap containing the lingering fragrance of verbena, both had a powerful effect on him. Devenish found himself stroking her, first almost chastely as one might stroke a tired child seeking comfort and then more boldly. His hands moulded her small, but perfect, breasts, his mouth found the hollows of her neck, and descended slowly towards the neckline of her dress.

And when, at last, he raised his head and his mouth found hers, passion, long suppressed, sprang forth like a tiger, ready to devour them both. They sank to the soft green of the lawn, beneath the spreading branches of a large oak which offered them both shade and secrecy from distant, prying eyes.

What recalled him to sanity, to the feeling which he had long entertained that he must not betray her in any way, Devenish never knew. Long continent himself, he was also aware that Drusilla had known the delights of the marriage bed and must herself be missing them, given that her reputation was that of a faithful widow as well as a faithful wife.

He must not, through his own selfishness, destroy that reputation. As gently as he could—even as his hands, of their own volition, had begun to pull down her dress so that he might see, as well as feel, what he was caressing—he lifted himself away from her to say, hoarsely, 'Not now, not yet.'

Passion had him in its grip so severely that he was in pain as his body screamed to him to continue and his intellect told him to behave himself lest he betray all that he believed in.

Drusilla gave a little moan of deprivation and despair, of paradise lost. To be in the arms of a man again, and a man whom she had come to love with an intensity which she had never felt for Jeremy, and then to have those arms snatched away, was to descend from heaven into a hell of loneliness.

Her loneliness since her husband's death, the sensation of having been abandoned, had been bearable until she had met Devenish and discovered that he was the man whom she might have dreamed of but could never hope to meet.

She sat up. Devenish was lying a little way away from her, prone, his right hand between his eyes and the ground. She leaned forward, touched his shoulder gently, and said, 'What is it? Is anything wrong?'

It was the only explanation which she could think of to explain his sudden change from passionate lover at the very moment when she thought that they were about to consummate their mutual attraction. Only attraction was too mild a word for what she was beginning to feel for him.

She had earlier offered him a neat definition for the difference between lust and love. It had been too simple. Whatever she felt for Devenish was now beyond that: it was nothing more than the most powerful urge to be one with him. She had thought that he felt the same—but perhaps not.

At the touch of her hand he rolled over, sat up and, breathing as though he had just run a race, said, 'Forgive me. I quite forgot myself. I had not meant to leap on you and try to ravish you so suddenly.'

Drusilla tried to offer him a light laugh—and failed. It sounded more like a sob.

'Ravish me, indeed! Any ravishment was mutual. If you were trying to tear my dress off then I was equally as urgent with your breeches flap! Or hadn't you noticed?'

He stared down, to find it hanging loose. He began to button himself up again.

'Oh, by God, so you were! A fine pair, are we not! I did not mean to demean your passion for me, when I broke off so suddenly. You must admit that I was its instigator even though I have been telling myself every time that I see you that I must behave myself. You are no lightskirt and I must not behave as though you are. Nor are you the sort of woman with whom I might enjoy a passing hour—and then never think of again.'

'What sort of woman am I, then?' asked Drusilla, whose whole body was aching as a result of fulfilment denied.

Devenish, his clothing decently rearranged, changed his posture again in order to kneel before her, his head slightly bent. 'A good woman whom I respect, and must not treat lightly.'

He wanted to say more but the words stuck in his throat. Was 'I love you' so hard to say that he could not come out with it? The habit of a lifetime's dedication to bachelorhood was keeping him silent.

'I am not to enjoy myself?'

This came out almost as a plea. Drusilla would not, for very shame, beg him to make love to her, even though in some odd way it irked that he respected her so much that he forgot that she had needs and passions to be satisfied, too.

She pulled her skirts primly down—in their abortive love-making they had somehow risen around her waist.

Devenish could not immediately answer her. He was watching her endow all her movements with a natural grace beyond that of any other woman he had ever met. Was that the truth? Or was it love speaking? He did not know.

'I would not ruin you,' he came out with at last. Later, alone in his room, he was to think what a fool he had been not to throw away his confounded principles and tell her that he loved her, come what may. Even if in honour, he must marry her after making love to her to save her reputation, not his own, for he had none.

Would marriage to Drusilla Faulkner be so very dreadful?

Might it not, on the contrary, be his salvation?

Reason, always strong in him, checked this suddenly tempting thought a little by reminding him that, whilst he was in the middle of what was turning out to be a dangerous enterprise he ought not to involve her with him more than was necessary—for her own sake.

Later—well, later might be different.

But at the time, 'I would not ruin you,' was all he could find to say to her.

'Well, that's a cold comfort,' returned Drusilla bitterly. 'It's enough to make me not want to be a good woman if being the other kind would have you in my arms!'

Devenish could not help himself. He began to laugh. It was very much the kind of thing he might have said himself if he had ever found himself in such a situation.

Momentarily Drusilla glared at him—and then joined him in his amusement. He moved over towards her and, defying temptation held her tenderly in his arms.

He pulled his handkerchief from his breeches pocket and wiped her streaming eyes. 'My dearest dear, I must not betray you, however powerfully we are drawn to one other. Let me help you to your feet and walk you back to the house. I was wrong to bring you out here alone, feeling for you as I do.'

It was the nearest he could get to saying, I love you, and would have to do for the moment.

Drusilla took comfort from him—as he had intended. She had often deplored Miss Faulkner's tendency to turn into a watering pot the moment life became difficult. She must not fall into the same trap herself.

It seemed strange to be walking back to the house so formally, as though nothing in the world had happened. Later, when, like Devenish, Drusilla thought of that afternoon's work, she came to a conclusion which she hoped was a correct one: that Devenish's holding off, far from proving that he did not love her, seemed, on the contrary, to prove that he did.

That being so, what was preventing him from declaring his love and marrying her?

It could not be that her birth was low, nor that she lacked wealth. Both the Stones and the Faulkners had been gentry families since Elizabethan times and might even consider themselves superior to the Devenishes, whose title and position only dated back to the end of the seventeenth century. She was well aware that the families of such as Devenish, although rich themselves, invariably wished to marry money and her own financial situation was more than comfortable.

So, what could it be? Reason said perhaps, after all, she was nothing but a passing fancy for him, something to combat rural boredom. Emotion said no, not at all, everything he says and does betrays the opposite.

In the end she came to the conclusion that it was useless to fret: time might tell in the end, even if it told her something which she did not wish to hear!

## Chapter Ten

The library at Tresham Hall was a large one. Devenish's grandfather had been a bibliophile who actually read his books and did not simply collect them. Since then the post of librarian had been an honoured and relatively well-paid one.

Devenish's first instinct was to consult the current occupier of the post, Dr Jonas Southwell, as to whether the library held any books on the occult in general, and the celebration of the Black Mass in particular.

On second thoughts he decided not to. The fewer who knew what he might suspect, the better. He remembered how surprised Rob Stammers had been when they were adventuring in Europe during the late war to discover exactly how cautious his romantic-looking friend was.

Always guard your back was Devenish's motto.

He left Drusilla with a chaste kiss on her cheek to return home to Tresham Hall and visit the library as though he were looking for casual reading matter. In reality he was looking for evidence to confirm his

202

growing belief that Marsham Abbey was being used to stage the Black Mass.

He roved around the shelves—a somewhat fruitless task since the books did not seem to be arranged in any order that he could discover. It was when he came to half a shelf devoted to the letters of Madame de Sévigné, a famous gossip of the court of Louis XIV, that something casual said to him long ago in this very room came to his aid.

When he had reached the age of sixteen his grandfather had provided him with a French tutor, 'French being the language of gentlemen and diplomats,' he had proclaimed. Devenish had had no intention of being a diplomat, but French fascinated him, and Monsieur de Castellane, a French *émigré* aristocrat trying to earn a living, had found him an apt pupil and encouraged him to read widely.

De Castellane had stood before this very shelf, had pulled one of the volumes of Madame de Sévigné's letters out and said, 'You will find them a mine of delectable French and equally delectable scandal. You are old enough, I think, to read her letters about the brouhaha around Louis XIV's mistress, Madame de Montespan, when she resorted to the Black Mass in secret to try to rekindle his interest in her. I will not say further, only that, as a result, half the aristocracy and a large number of the common people went to their deaths.

'Such,' he had added, 'has always been the consequence for those who practise it. Some of the French Radicals were reported to have done so in order to bring about the Revolution since legal and Christian methods had failed.'

For some reason which he could not recollect he had never read the letters—perhaps it was because Monsieur le Marquis de Castellane had left, suddenly and mysteriously, shortly afterwards, running off with the pretty youngest daughter of the then Lord Cheyne.

His departure had also coincided with Devenish's grandfather deciding that he was ready to go to University, where he had been sent with another tutor, Patrick MacAndrew, a harsh man who had orders to see that Henry Devenish should spend his time working and do nothing to disgrace the Devenish name—unlike his worthless father.

He pulled out the last volume to check the index for the name of Madame la Marquise de Montespan. Oh, she was there, her infamy waiting to be discovered over two hundred years after her death.

And so were all Madame de Sévigné's eagerly recorded details surrounding the scandal. Devenish read them at speed—another of his talents—and having done so, walked to the books on theology, to inspect them closely, much to the surprise of Dr Southwell who had emerged from his study to find m'lord's interest settled on something new.

'May I be of assistance, m'lord?'

'Perhaps,' returned Devenish. 'Much was spoken of the Devil at Mr Harrington's recent house party. I wondered what current theology made of him?' It was as near as he dare get to the subject which was occupying his mind.

'Current theology does not concern itself overmuch with him,' said Dr Southwell drily. 'Unlike our ancestors to whom he was as real as God, and as powerful. In a different way, of course,' he added, lest he be misunderstood.

'Of course, safer not to provoke him. After all, one might end up like Marlowe's Doctor Faustus—carried screaming off to Hell.'

'Best not to mock him, either,' said Dr Southwell, dourly.

'Just to be on the safe side?' replied Devenish as frivolously as he could, playing the idle nobleman to perfection.

'Exactly.'

'And did my grandfather, who, I believe, bought most of the books in the library, buy anything about the Devil?'

'I am not sure, m'lord. I don't think so. I could look about for you, but I don't offer much hope.'

Devenish not only minded his back: he guarded his front as well. After Dr Southwell had begun his search of the library he asked himself why he should have lied to him. For there, on the lowest shelf of all, which he had just been inspecting before the good doctor had left his study to join him, was a copy of the *Grimoire*, a book which concentrated on the occult and in which the Devil played a part.

To suppose that Dr Southwell was part of the conspiracy might make him like the man in Shakespeare who found it easy to suppose a bush to be a bear. On the other hand, he must be surrounded by conspirators who knew only too well what had happened to the girls and why.

Two difficulties confronted Devenish. The first being that he was in the dark about who the participants in the Mass were, and secondly, that he had absolutely no proof sufficiently convincing for any action to be taken by the authorities.

He could guess, but not prove, that many of the local nobility and gentry must be involved. He had no doubt, from what he had overheard at Marsham Abbey, that their leader, who probably played the part of the Satan who presided over the Mass, was Leander Harrington.

Parson Lawson was the minister who performed the Mass, and some of their senior servants, like Dr Southwell, who were themselves the children of gentry, might also be part of the congregation.

Had the whole thing begun as a kind of game, a perversion of the activities nearly fifty years ago of Sir Francis Dashwood's so-called Hell Fire Club? That, despite its name, had been little more than an aristocrats' drinking den, with a few of the willing local girls thrown in for their carnal pleasures.

Lord Byron, it was said, had organised something similar at his home, Newstead Abbey, but neither of these activities had resulted in the deaths of men and women.

Devenish thought again of Monsieur de Castellane of whom he had not thought these many years. Of his sudden disappearance—and that of a local young woman of good birth. Was that disappearance mysterious? Could it tell him anything that might be useful to him in his present dilemma?

He decided to visit Rob Stammers in his little office.

As usual, Rob was hard at work. He looked up when Devenish entered and said in his usual dry, but perceptive, manner. 'What is it, Hal? You look as though you have the cares of the world on your shoulders.'

'Not quite that. I was in the library and remembered a conversation I had with Monsieur de Castellane, years ago. What exactly happened to him, Rob? One moment he and I were enjoying the life of the mind together and then he was gone—without a word of explanation. When I asked Grandfather where he was, he roared at me for my impudence and told me it was no business of mine.

'Whose business was it, then? Do you know? Did your father, who was agent at the time, ever say anything about him to you?'

Rob put down his quill pen, leaned back and sighed. 'I only remember that about the time de Castellane left there was trouble at Tresham Hall. You knew nothing of it because...' He paused.

'Because I was confined to the attics and only let out once a day either to work in the library or be taught to ride... No need to tell me what I know. Tell me what I don't know.'

This was pure Hal, as bitter as acid. Rob ignored the slight, and continued. 'I remember your grandfather being closeted with my father, de Castellane and old Beaufort Harrington, Leander's father. They were shouting at each other.'

He smiled reminiscently. 'I was listening at the door, but I could hear very little. Finally my father threw the door open and strode off down the corridor, de Castellane following. They didn't see me, because I was behind the door when it was thrown open. I heard your grandfather raging at old Beaufort, and then I ran away in case my father came back and found me eavesdropping. The next day de Castellane left—I saw him enter your grandfather's coach and watched it all the way down the drive.

'They said that the youngest Cheyne girl ran away from home at the same time. I know that they were sweet on each other.'

'And that was all?'

'Not quite. Your grandfather and Beaufort Harrington, who had been extremely friendly, had little to do with one another after that.'

'Have you any idea where de Castellane went?'

Rob stared at him. 'Why, Hal? Why do you want to know now, so many years later?'

'Never mind that.' Hal was suddenly as autocratic as his late grandfather, no longer Rob's old friend to whom he usually spoke on equal terms. 'Just answer my question.'

'I'm not sure. From something my father once said I believe that they corresponded with one another for some time. If you want to know what his address was then, I have your grandfather's post book to hand. He was most meticulous in keeping his records. You would like me to inspect it?'

'Immediately.'

Rob rose and walked over to where shelves stacked with ledgers and papers rose from floor to ceiling. If the late Earl Devenish and Rob's father had been meticulous in the organisation and running of the estate, he and Hal were no less so.

He pulled down a shabby red leather-bound book with gilt trim and turned its pages rapidly.

'Ah, yes. Here we are. It was shortly before your grandfather died. He had been writing to de Castellane to offer him financial assistance in setting up an Academy. The Marquis wrote back from an address just off Piccadilly—4, St James's Court—to thank him for his help.

'I'm pretty certain that was the last time we at Tresham Hall corresponded with him. Certainly I've had no dealings with him in my time.'

Devenish picked up Rob's pen and a piece of paper and made a note of what he had just heard. 'Thanks, Rob. I'm sorry I was a little unmannerly towards you just now. Mrs Faulkner has reprimanded me more than once for my rudery to my fellows, and she is right to do so. You are always most helpful, and I ought not to snap at you.'

Rob shook his head. 'And I ought to remind you that that address is thirteen years old—he may no longer live there. Do you wish me to write to him?'

'I'll think about it. Let's leave it at that for the present.'

Now this was not honest of him, Devenish knew. What he wished to ask de Castellane could not easily be written in a letter which might go astray. It had to be said face to face.

He would go to London—ostensibly on other business—to see if he could find the man who had driven away from Tresham Hall so suddenly and so mysteriously.

Drusilla was playing backgammon with Giles on the day after Devenish's visit, but her mind was not on the game and he told her so.

'I'm sorry,' she said. 'I'll try to concentrate.' Which she did so determinedly that she ran out an easy winner.

'I wish I'd kept my mouth shut,' grumbled Giles, 'and beaten you. But you know, Dru, you're not quite A1 at Lloyd's these days. What's the matter?'

'Nothing,' she said—and knew that she lied. Devenish was the matter, and for two reasons. The first was that she was still not certain what his intentions towards her were. She had once read *Les Liaisons Dangereuses* and she could not help but wonder whether, like the wicked Vicomte de Valmont in the book, he was engaged in slowly and deviously seducing her whilst pretending to be in love with her.

That was how de Valmont had betrayed the virtuous Madame la Présidente de Tourvel, as part of a vile game which he and the even more vicious Madame de Merteuil were engaged in. She didn't think that Devenish was conspiring with the equivalent of Madame de Merteuil, but she did think that there was a chance that he was playing de Valmont's part.

And la Présidente had been in love with de Valmont as she, Drusilla, was in love with Devenish, but that had not saved her from him.

The second reason was quite different. She thought that Devenish was troubled about something, and that that something was, strangely enough, connected with her late husband. Entwined with this reason were her own misgivings about the strange occurrences in Tresham Magna church.

She had joked with Miss Faulkner and Lady Cheyne about the black candles and their possible connection with the Black Mass, but her amusement had not been genuine. And then she had seen Devenish's strange reaction when the Black Mass had been mentioned.

More, in their subsequent conversation, before they had begun to betray their feelings for one another, she had gained the impression that what had been said had disturbed him greatly—even though he had joked a little with her about it.

Once her game with Giles was over, Drusilla did something which she had been meaning to do for two years and that was to go again through Jeremy's desk. She had done so immediately after his death, on her lawyer's instructions, to see if he had any financial documents there of which he ought to know.

The rest had been a jumble of papers: letters never sent, and a commonplace book with most of its pages blank. Jeremy had been neither a great writer nor a great reader, and part of his admiration for Drusilla had come from the fact that she was both. Perhaps, among them, she might find something to explain why he had changed so much in his last days.

The desk stood where it had always stood, in the big drawing room under the window. It was a delicate piece of Chippendale, finely wrought. Drusilla opened it, and began to sort through its contents. Among memos about small matters on the estate there were notes on the building of a Folly in the grounds of which he had talked eagerly about a year before his death, but in which he had suddenly lost interest.

There were also letters, one half-written, to the architect about the Folly, and another to a landscape gardener about creating a lake on the lowest lawn—another project which he had suddenly dropped.

There seemed to be nothing in them which might help her. When she picked up the last scrap of paper but one she had almost given up hope of finding anything. Written on it in an agitated hand, quite unlike Jeremy's usual writing, were the words, 'Dru must never know.'

Drusilla stared at them. What must Dru never know? And now that Jeremy had gone, would she ever know what she mustn't know? To add to the mystery when she turned the paper over, the name and address of the Lord Lieutenant of the county were written on the back.

The commonplace book yielded nothing of value—other than the name, constantly repeated, of Apollyon.

Drusilla's hair stood on end. She remembered reading, years ago, Bunyan's *Pilgrim's Progress*, and being frightened by the Pilgrim's struggle with Apollyon, the

Devil. Why should Jeremy be writing down his name so urgently and so apparently frantically? Even as she thought this, Drusilla began to shiver.

The feeling of intense cold which she had experienced by the sundial at Marsham overwhelmed her again. Added to it was a terrible nameless fear which brought her to her knees before the desk, still clutching the commonplace book. Scarcely knowing what she did she cast the book from her—and the fear disappeared. But the memory of it did not, nor did the feeling of cold leave her quickly, so that minutes later she was still shivering.

The Devil, the black candles, the dead sheep on the altar, and her strange experience by the sundial, added to this most recent one, were all mixed together in her mind, telling her—what?

No one now believed in the Devil as people had done in Bunyan's time, but all the same she left the book on the carpet. Before she could stop him, Giles, who had been reading in the window seat and was plainly unaware of her distress, came over, picked up the commonplace book and placed it on the desk.

It was also quite apparent by his manner that handling it had had no effect on him. This made Drusilla feel colder than ever, and caused Giles to remark to her, 'You look ill, Dru—are you sickening for something?'

'Yes...no,' she replied distractedly. 'I had bad dreams last night and couldn't sleep.' This was not a total lie. Yes, the dreams had been bad, but she could not remember the detail of them. Only that Devenish had been in them—and now, she suddenly recalled, he had been in danger, and she had been unable to help him.

This is quite ridiculous, she told herself sternly, to start at shadows, and to imagine that I have been afflicted by a sudden chill. I am suffering from the megrims and must learn to control myself.

It was at this moment that Devenish was announced by the butler, fortunately before Giles could continue his tactless mothering of her. It had come to something that he should be worrying about her, instead of her worrying about him! On the other hand it proved that he was beginning to grow up at last, something which he demonstrated by bolting past Devenish as he walked through the door, exclaiming, 'I'm off to the stables—you two will want to be alone together.'

Both Devenish and Drusilla began to laugh together. 'Really,' Dru said apologetically, 'Giles's idea of tact is somewhat primitive.'

'He has the right of it, though,' commented Devenish. 'A few weeks ago he would have sat staring at us, content to make up a happy trio, without the slightest notion that we might wish to be tête-à-tête. It only goes to show that we mature without knowing it.'

Drusilla said, melancholy in her voice, 'There are times when I wonder whether I shall ever be mature.'

Devenish looked sharply at her. 'What's this? Does the most commonsensical person I have the pleasure to know doubt herself, and why?'

Should she confide in him? The last time they had met he had refrained from seducing her and had asked her to call him Hal. Did that mean she could trust him? Drusilla made her decision. She must trust someone and, whatever else, Devenish was a strong man, both physically and mentally.

She pointed to the book on the desk and the scrap of paper beside it and briefly described her recent experience with them both.

'And you must not laugh at me, Hal,' she told him, 'for seeing phantoms where none exist and feeling as though December had arrived in August.'

Devenish shook his head as he picked up the piece of paper and the book. 'I would never laugh at you, Drusilla, now that you have honoured me with my true name. I was Hal before I was ever Lord Devenish, and would always wish to be named so by my friends.'

After he had finished examining them both, he said, 'And you truly have no idea why Jeremy should have written these?'

'None at all. Oh, Hal, could this conceivably have something to do with his strange death? What could it be that he knew and I must not?'

Devenish could not answer her yet. He was beginning to think that he might know what it was that Jeremy had been engaged in which he was ashamed to reveal to his wife and had caused him to write down repeatedly one of the names of the Devil, but he still had no real proof.

Until then he must hold his tongue.

'I don't know anything definite yet, Drusilla. I wish I did. When I do I will tell you—although I fear that you might not like the answer.'

She knew that already—and told him so. Jeremy's note about her proved that there was something dreadfully wrong with him.

'And as a result of all this,' she exclaimed suddenly, 'I have become as mannerless as Giles. I have never asked you to sit down, but have plagued you with my worries.'

He took her hand and kissed it. 'You could never plague me, Drusilla. I am always at your service. Never forget that.'

She would not. His eyes told her that what he had just said was the truth. She nodded, near to tears.

'Thank you,' she said, and then was silent.

Her answer, he thought was simplicity itself without embroidery or qualifications or pretty simperings. She might look fragile but he had no doubt that she was as true as steel.

'I have come to tell you that I am on my way to London for a few days to perform a necessary errand. When I return I shall invite most of my neighbours to the house party which I promised them some weeks ago. You, of course, will be my most treasured guest. I may not stay long with you because I wish to leave later today.'

'Long or short, you are always welcome.'

'I know.'

There was nothing of his usual acerbic wit about him. He had become as simple as she was.

To prove it they sat silent for a time.

'You have a quality of restfulness,' Devenish said, 'which is rare. Your presence restores me.'

'You must not flatter me.' Drusilla was even a trifle
agitated as she spoke. It seemed to her that they had
been love-making by proxy, as it were, as though no
words, no actions, were needed, just a meeting of
minds in a quiet room.

'No flattery,' he said. 'And now I must go. I would
not wish to leave Tresham without telling you for I
would not have you think that I had abandoned you.'

If he were playing de Valmont's game then he was
doing so in such a masterly fashion that it was indis-
tinguishable from the truth, and for that reason Drusilla
did not think that he was.

They rose together to stand face to face, not touching. The passion between them was all the stronger for
not being directly expressed. It seemed to fill the very
air, resonating between them as it did.

'I will kiss your cheek before I leave,' he said. 'It
is all I dare to do.'

'I know—and I dare not respond...'

'...lest we are lost,' he ended.

The kiss was given and taken. Long after the door
had closed behind him Drusilla held her hand where
his mouth had blessed her as though doing so might
prevent the sweet sensation it had created from ever
dying.

Devenish was tired when he reached London. He
slept badly. In his dreams, or rather nightmares, he was
back again on yet another day when he had returned
to his attic home to yet another shock.

There was a carriage outside the door, a splendid one with a coat of arms on each door panel, two footmen at the back, and a coachman at the front. They stared at the ragged boy he had been as he rushed past them into the house.

He ran into the attic to discover that his mother was seated in the armchair by the empty hearth, instead of lying in bed. She looked more ill and shabby than ever beside the splendour of the old man who stood in front of her, leaning on his cane. Thirteen-year-old Hal Devenish knew little of the fashionable clothing worn by the great and mighty, but he knew at once that few men were ever as finely turned out as this old man was.

He was not the only strange person in the room. There was a large, fat man whom he later discovered to be a physician and a tall, thin one dressed as finely as the old man.

But it was the old man who dominated the attic room as he dominated every room he was ever in, and that by his manner as well as his appearance.

He raised a quizzing glass to stare at young Hal as though he were some insect which he had been unfortunate enough to encounter.

'Never say that this is the boy, Augustus's child.'

His mother said, 'Yes, this is Henry, your grandson. We call him Hal.'

'Henry. He shall be Henry in future. Make a note of that, Jarvis, I think nothing of the name Hal.'

His grandfather? Was this rich old man his grandfather? He could not be. He, Hal, would not have it so.

'Who are you?' he demanded, and although he was not then aware of it, he looked and sounded like a miniature version of the dominant old man who had arrived from nowhere to change his life forever.

'As your mother said, I am your grandfather. Has the boy been taught no manners, ma'am, that he speaks so rudely to me in the accents of a street Arab?'

'I have done my best,' his mother faltered. 'But after Augustus died we ran out of money. And I had to remove him from the grammar school and teach him myself.'

'And a remarkably poor fist you appear to have made of it, ma'am. Do not glare at me, boy. I'll not have it.'

'And I'll not have you speak to my mama like that. She says that you are rich—well, you may take your riches away and leave us alone. We don't need them. I can look after her. As I have done since long before you came here to insult us.'

His mother cried, 'Oh, Hal, do not speak so,' whilst the old man, turning to the thin man, said languidly, 'Take the boy downstairs to the carriage, Jarvis, whilst the doctor examines his mother to discover whether she is fit to travel.'

Jarvis seized him by the arm, saying firmly, 'Come, boy, do as you're told. It's all for the best. M'lord will look after you both.'

Hal wrenched his arm away. 'I can look after her, I can. Master Gabriel, the magician, is teaching me his magic tricks and I shall be his boy when he travels

South and he has promised that my mother will go with us, now that she's a little better.'

The old man, who was looking indifferently out of the grimy attic window, his back to them, said, without looking at either Hal or Jarvis, 'Have you not rid us of him yet, Jarvis? Must I always repeat myself? Do as I say, lest I rid myself of you as well.'

Hal tore himself from Jarvis's detaining arm to run to his mother, shouting defiantly, 'I don't want to go with him. Say I needn't.'

His mother looked at him earnestly, her eyes, the only remnant of a once remarkable beauty, filling with tears. 'It's for the best for both of us, Hal. His last remaining son has died without an heir and, although your father was the youngest son, you are now the only heir and will one day be Lord Devenish yourself. We shall be looked after and never be poor again.'

It was too much to take in. He had conceived an instant aversion to the old man who was strolling towards him brandishing his cane. Even to learn that, from being a poor brat who ran around the streets doing odd jobs and some minor thieving to keep himself and his mother, he was now to become one of the great men who ruled England, was of no comfort to him.

He stared defiantly at his grandfather, unaware that the very sight of him was anathema to someone who had lost his gifted, last remaining son and his beautiful grandson in a carriage accident and was doomed to have the misbegotten brat of his worthless youngest son in their place.

'You,' he said cuttingly, 'will be taught to behave as my heir should, if I have to beat you senseless daily,' and he caught Hal by the shoulders and used his cane to begin to do exactly that.

His mother screamed and Jarvis, daringly, caught the old man by the arm.

'Not now, m'lord, not now. The boy is upset and his mother is dying. You may discipline him later.'

His mother was dying. The man had said what Hal had been denying to himself for weeks. He ran to her and that dream ended—as it always did—as he collapsed sobbing at her feet before Jarvis dragged him away from the old man's wrath and down to the waiting carriage...

Devenish sat up in bed, sweating and trembling. His mother had died a month later in the comfort of Tresham Hall. Her rescuers had, ironically, come too late to save her. She had, without telling him, defied her late husband, and written to her husband's father many times, telling him of their plight and asking him for help, but until his son and grandson had died so tragically, he had never answered her.

Devenish's father, Augustus, was a handsome wastrel who had seduced a parson's daughter, made her pregnant, run off with her, and then, remarkably, had married her. Devenish never knew what belated chivalry had made Augustus act as he did, since she was by no means the first young woman he had ruined.

He had been an officer in the cavalry, but had been cashiered for drinking on duty and cheating at cards.

His father had hated him because in several generations he had been the only Devenish to be a black sheep. Consequently he also hated Augustus's son for becoming his heir. Devenish later came to understand that in punishing him, the unwanted grandson, he was punishing the son whom he had never been able to control.

Devenish cursed the frailty which made him occasionally relive his unhappy past in dreams. He knew that he was plagued by them only when he was troubled as he was now, not only over the problems at Tresham Magna, but also over his relationship with Drusilla Faulkner.

He turned over and tried to sleep. Tomorrow he would visit the address which Rob had found for him and hope to learn something from Monsieur de Castellane—if he still lived there, that was.

Morning found him in Piccadilly. He left his carriage there and walked on foot the rest of the way to St James's Court. He had brought no servants with him other than the coachman and one footman to hold the horses. He found Number 4 easily enough. It was a large house with a brass plate on the door. St James's Academy for Young Gentlemen, it announced in tasteful lettering.

He rapped a door-knocker in the shape of a laurel wreath and a stately butler opened the door. He could hear boys' voices in the distance, and the sound of a piano being played, badly.

'If Monsieur le Marquis de Castellane resides here I would like to speak with him.'

The butler stared at him and said, 'No one of that name here, sir,' and then added, as though inspiration had struck him, 'But the Academy's Principal is Mr Castle—perhaps it's him you seek, sir.'

Mr. Castle. Yes, he could well be the man he was looking for.

'Perhaps you would inform him that Lord Devenish would like to speak to him if he could spare the time.'

On hearing his title the butler's manner perked up amazingly.

'Oh, indeed, m'lord, I'm sure he would wish to speak to you at once. Pray enter, and I shall inform him immediately of your arrival.'

He ushered Devenish into a pretty little sitting room where a portrait of a handsome woman hung over the hearth, and pointed him at a large armchair. A few minutes later Devenish heard voices, the door opened, and a middle-aged man walked into the room.

Despite the years which had passed since Devenish had last seen him, the man who entered, was plainly the Marquis de Castellane. As for de Castellane, he stared at Devenish and said, 'Hal? *Mon Dieu*, who would have thought it? You were a midget when I last saw you. And now you are the m'lord of m'lords! What brings you here? And to the point, how did you find me?'

His slight accent had disappeared along with much of his hair, but his friendly manner, which had comforted the friendless and neglected boy whom Devenish had once been, had not changed.

'Oh, as you might guess, I have come to you for a favour. Is that not what we always require from our old acquaintances, when after years of neglect, we seek them out? But to excuse myself for never having approached you before, I was informed, years ago, that you were lost or dead. I only discovered in the last forty-eight hours that you are very much alive.'

De Castellane began to laugh. 'Oh, you will not like to hear this, but you are your grandfather to the life when he was your age, and I was a boy admiring his amazing sang-froid.'

Devenish replied drily, 'Yes, I know. I dislike it, and myself, intensely for resembling him—but nature will have its way. My favour may not be to your taste, but I hope you will grant it. First of all...'

'More than one favour, then,' returned de Castellane, smiling.

'Oh, I recognise my old tutor's insistence on exactitude,' was Devenish's riposte. 'First, then, I hope you will agree to inform me of the reason for your sudden departure from Tresham Hall.'

'Only if you will do me a favour. Why do you wish to know?'

'I see that we are at *point non plus*, here,' sighed Devenish, 'for I have no mind to oblige you, other than to say that I wish to solve a series of what I suspect to be great crimes, and you once spoke to me of something which leads me to believe that you might be able to help me.'

It was plain that Monsieur de Castellane, or Mr Castle as he now called himself, was extremely reluctant to oblige him.

He hesitated. Devenish said swiftly, 'I believe that the Black Mass is being celebrated again at Marsham Abbey and that this time it is not the idle joke it may once have been.'

De Castellane's whole manner changed. 'Ah, you merely wish me to confirm what you already suspect...'

'Yes. I have reason to believe that something similar took place all those years ago and that you left as a consequence of it. I would like you to tell me the truth—with the proviso that, if it incriminates you in any way, that knowledge will go no further.'

De Castellane leaned forward and rang a small bell. 'Only when we are seated over a glass of port and some ratafia biscuits. You are even more like your grandfather than I first thought, even more intimidating. When I last saw you—'

He was interrupted by the butler. 'Pray bring me a bottle of the best port and some ratafia biscuits—and then leave us alone. M'lord and I have many years talking to catch up.'

After the butler had gone, he steepled his hands under his chin after a fashion which Devenish remembered. 'Before we speak of the Black Mass, when did the change occur? I remember you as a surly, unwashed cub, confined to the attics of Tresham Hall and regularly thrashed for disobedience. You had only two aims in mind. One was to defy your grandfather by refusing to become the fine gentleman which he wished you to be, and the other to learn as much as you could about everything.'

Devenish laughed a little ruefully. 'You may remember that shortly after you arrived to be my tutor I ran away to join the magician at the Fair which arrived at Tresham Magna. He was my old teacher, and before my grandfather arrived to tell me I was his heir, he had promised to take me on as his apprentice. Imagine my horror when, after I had spent a happy evening with him, he returned me to my grandfather. I saw it as yet another piece of treachery practised on me.

'My old master told me that I had a powerful destiny before me as the future Lord Devenish, and that I should remember that the magician's greatest trick was to deceive people by offering them what they wished to see—or thought that they wished to see. The two things are not the same, he said. I asked him what he meant. He shook his head and told me to work it out for myself.

'It was only later that I understood that my old teacher was doing me a great service. I suddenly grasped that by becoming what my grandfather thought that he wanted me to be was to trick and disappoint him, because what he *really* wanted was for me to confirm that Augustus Devenish's only son was as worthless as his father. To turn myself into a fine and educated gentleman meant that I had won a victory over him. Alas, I succeeded only too well—by turning myself into him, a man I despised.'

He fell silent, staring into the empty hearth. Monsieur de Castellane said gently, 'I think not. Your grandfather had no self-knowledge. He was a ruthless man who took himself for granted. You, on the contrary, do not. The child you were still lives in you, I think.'

This piece of insight startled Devenish as he remembered his dreams of the previous night.

'Perhaps,' he said slowly, thinking of Drusilla—and realising, at last, that she might be his salvation. She would prevent him from turning into the old man in the attic.

'Tell me,' said de Castellane, watching, 'can you still do your magic tricks? You used to amuse me with them when learning palled.'

Devenish smiled. After a moment he leaned forward and pulled a golden guinea from de Castellane's ear, and another from the pocket where he kept his watch. He tossed them at his old teacher. 'As you see, I keep in practice. It amuses me.'

'And me. You were always an inventive lad—as your grandfather often complained.' The port had arrived and they began to drink it.

'Excellent,' murmured Devenish, 'but then your taste always was—and now, the Black Mass.'

'Like many things,' de Castellane said, 'it began as a joke and ended as something different. Beaufort Harrington was the instigator. He said that he wanted to form a drinking circle like Sir Francis Dashwood's Hell Fire Club which would meet in the crypt. To give it spice we would also perform a parody of the Black

Mass which is itself a parody of the Catholic church service. We were deceived. He had a deeper cause in mind.

'Like his son, Leander, who was then a young man, he believed in a new order—never mind that the ending of the old one in France had been so bloody, as I could testify. England would be different, he thought, and since being a devout Christian and believing in God was not bringing a new world order about, then why not invoke the Devil and see if he would be more obliging.'

De Castellane sighed. 'He was not to know that many of the French aristocrats and gentry had believed the same thing—my maternal uncle for one. Some practised the Black Mass, some became Freemasons. Whether or not the Devil brought about the Revolution they desired is a matter for conjecture—but if he did, then the price that was paid for it by his aristocratic worshippers was their heads, as my maternal uncle discovered when he mounted the guillotine.

'But in our early days at Marsham we knew nothing of this. Many of the local nobility and gentry met in the crypt when the moon was full, dressed up and drank, including your grandfather and me.'

He paused. Devenish, his fine brows arched, said, 'My grandfather joined in this simple mummery?'

'Yes, and simple mummery it was, at first. Your grandfather soon grew bored and ceased to attend the meetings. He said that he was too old. I, however, continued. Remember I was young and needed some amusement in life to keep me happy—but, alas, the meetings slowly began to change, and I was the only one who understood what was happening. Beaufort Harrington was gradually introducing the real Black Mass, and was corrupting his followers as he did so.

'Black candles appeared, the cross was placed upside down on a desecrated altar, and the Mass was said backwards by the local priest. And then one month I attended to find that the final abomination had been introduced. A village maiden was stretched across the altar and the Communion cup was placed upon her naked body. Beaufort Harrington wore a Devil's mask with the horns of a goat and young Leander acted as acolyte and swung the censer. At the end of the ceremony Harrington Senior pledged us all to secrecy on pain of death. Surprisingly most of his audience were far gone enough to go along with him.

'I was horrified, for by the next moon I was sure that there would be blood sacrifices to the Devil, and what had started in play was going to end in death. On reaching Tresham Hall I went straight to your grandfather and told him what had begun to happen—and what I feared the end might be. He was horrified. You must understand that he was a stern ruthless man, cruel even, as you well knew, but he was not a wicked one. Murder was something which he would not tolerate.

'He sent for Beaufort Harrington and told him that the club must be disbanded. That he was Deputy Lieutenant of the county and would not hesitate to use his powers if Harrington defied him. The result might even mean that some of the leading actors in the Club would swing for blasphemy.

'Beaufort Harrington swore at him, and at me. He shouted that m'lord might stop him, but the day of reckoning would arrive for us both. M'lord would perish on the guillotine which would be set up in London, and he would have his revenge on me for informing on him to m'lord. But m'lord prevailed—as he always did. He told Beaufort Harrington that this way the matter could be settled without scandal and ruin besmirching us all. But Beaufort Harrington stuck his face in mine as he left and told me that the Devil would come for me before long to punish me for my treachery. M'lord took him seriously and said that, much though it grieved him, I must leave Tresham Hall at once, for he was sure that by hook or by crook, Beaufort Harrington would have me killed.

'M'lord knew that I wished to found an Academy and he advanced the money for me to do so, and sent me off immediately to London, giving me enough to start me off. He lent me more later. He even helped me to carry off my future wife who was unhappy at home—that is her portrait over the mantelpiece—and that was the last I saw or heard of Tresham Hall and Tresham Magna, or anyone from them after m'lord wrote me his last letter, until you arrived today.

'I changed my name to Castle for I have been happy in England and have no wish to return to a few barren acres in Northern France.' He paused again before adding slowly, 'I have told you everything. I trust that it has been of assistance to you because the telling of it has disturbed me more than I would have thought possible.'

'And me,' returned Devenish. 'For matters are as I thought. Leander Harrington has revived the meetings in the crypt, is practising the Black Mass and this time there has been no one to prevent the inevitable ending. Sacrifices to the devil are being made: a number of local girls have disappeared, and I have reason to believe that one, possibly two, men may have been murdered to prevent them from informing the authorities of the Club's activities. A local lad was assaulted and left for dead—presumably because it was thought that he might have heard something incriminating.'

De Castellane sighed and said heavily, 'As Shakespeare might have said of your grandfather and me, ''We have scotched the snake, not killed it.'''

'You were not to know that it would revive again so many years later.'

'True. What made you to think of me in this connection?'

'Oh, I was browsing in the Library and came across Madame de Sévigné's *Letters*. You may or may not remember that you spoke to me of the great scandal involving Madame de Montespan, the poisons and the Black Mass. And then I remembered that you had disappeared mysteriously, too. I spoke to Rob Stammers and he told me that you had left after a grand brouhaha involving you, my grandfather and Beaufort Harrington. I wanted to meet you again, and some instinct told me that you might know something useful.'

'Some instinct, eh? Another talent you share with your grandfather. Perhaps you disliked each other so much because you were so alike. Are you married, yet?'

'No,' and then abruptly, without further thought, 'but I hope to be, soon. When I've decided what to do with the knowledge you have given me.'

'For the sake of you and your future wife, go carefully. You are in danger, m'lord.'

'Hal, call me Hal. You used to. I have been in danger before—and have survived.'

'Do not underrate the wicked powers of those who believe in the Devil, Hal. They will stop at nothing. And if they have murdered...'

'Oh, I am sure they have committed murder,' and he told his old friend and tutor of Jeremy Faulkner and where he had found the murdered man's ring. He said nothing of Drusilla for he did not want to tempt fate further by suggesting to de Castellane that she might consent to marry him.

They finished the bottle of port between them, and then de Castellane demanded that he stay to dinner, to which he agreed. There he met the Cheyne girl, now a mature woman and the mother of three children who sat quietly at table with them and made Devenish dream a little of the children Drusilla might give them and how he would try to ensure that their childhood was happier than his had been.

And yet he knew that it had given him steel—too much kindness might have meant that he ended up like his worthless father! Truly to do the right thing by one's self and everyone else required the most delicate of balancing acts—something which he must not forget when he returned to Tresham Magna armed with what de Castellane had told him.

His first target would be that amiable fool, Sir Toby Claridge, who was bidding fair to follow his late friend, Jeremy Faulkner, to an unhappy end unless someone rescued him first.

But to rescue him might mean Sir Toby swallowing some bitter pills first.

## Chapter Eleven

Lord Devenish's great house party was the talk of the district. This was partly because no one had ever expected him to return to Tresham Hall after such a long absence, and partly because everyone of any note had been invited.

It was rumoured that he hated the place: older people spoke of the cruelty with which his grandfather had treated him, and that on the very day of the funeral the young Lord had walked out of the front door, vowing never to return. Yet here he was, and prepared to stay for some time—if his staff could be believed.

The whole house had been made ready for the guests. State rooms had been re-opened and cleaned, chandeliers had been taken from their bags, as had pictures and statues, most of them not seen since the old Lord's funeral. Wagons, carriages and workmen streamed up the drive, bringing with them food, new linen, and the means of repairing what had been neglected. Devenish had given orders immediately after his grandfather's death that only the living quarters of the staff were to be kept up.

'Oh, it's just like the old days when his grandfather was alive,' twittered Miss Faulkner, as she made ready to travel the short distance from Lyford House to Tresham Hall. She had returned from visiting her friend refreshed, and determined not to annoy Drusilla—although she still suspected Lord Devenish's motives.

He had visited Lyford House on the very afternoon of his return, shortly before Miss Faulkner was expected to arrive—which was fortunate because he needed to speak urgently and privately to Drusilla. He found her on the lawn, drinking tea with a much-restored Giles, who said brightly, 'Oh, shall I leave you now? I have a book indoors which I am longing to return to, and you will not mind me going, I'm sure.'

Devenish's mouth twitched. This was a little more tactful than Giles's last excuse—by a slight margin.

'Not yet,' he said. 'Stay for a time and tell me how you are faring.'

'Oh, I am quite recovered,' returned Giles eagerly. 'Drusilla allowed me to ride again yesterday, but she is making a frightful pother about me going out on my own. It's a great trial being followed everywhere by two hulking footmen, I can tell you. I feel about six again.'

'Very wise of your sister,' drawled Devenish at his most provoking. '*I'm* sure that she thinks one attack on you is quite enough.'

True to his word, tea and small talk over, Giles left them alone.

'He was right,' said Devenish. 'I do wish to be alone with you, but not for the reason which you and he might suppose. I have a favour to ask of you, of which neither he, nor anyone else, must know.'

He took from the inner pocket of his beautiful coat a letter and handed it to her. Drusilla accepted it, saying nothing, although her eyes were questioning him.

'You will see that it is addressed to Lord Sidmouth, the Home Secretary. If anything untoward should happen to me I must ask you to forward it to him immediately by your most trusted messenger.'

He fell silent. Drusilla spoke at last. She did not gasp at him, hold up her hands and exclaim hysterically, 'Oh, m'lord, whatever can you mean?'

Instead she said quietly, 'Of course I will do as you ask. But you spoke of something untoward happening to you. May I know what that could be and why? Are you truly in any danger?'

He leaned forward, and as always, took her hand in his, clasping it round the wrist so that he could feel the steady beat of her pulse.

'Most admirable of women,' he told her, 'not to bombard me excitedly with frantic questions—but, instead, to go calmly straight to the heart of the matter. Which is most apropos of you for I do not feel, that at the moment, I can answer other than to say, I might be in danger, but I may not tell you why, for your own safety. I can only ask you to trust me and forward the letter if, unfortunately, it becomes necessary.'

'And does this strange request—for it *is* strange—arise out of the real reason why you returned to

Tresham—and does it have anything to do with the attacks on Jeremy and Giles?' she asked him, still quite composed.

Her shrewdness surprised as well as pleased him. 'I see that you have guessed at least one of the reasons why I returned to Tresham Hall. And now, you must trust me,' he said urgently, 'although I may not, for your own safety, answer your question. Are you able to do that, Drusilla? Trust me, without needing to know more? Because if you cannot, then you must return my letter to me and I must find someone who will do as I ask—though God knows who that might be—for I know no one else whom I can trust.'

He was so strange and serious that Drusilla said softly, making no effort to remove her hand from his, 'Since, Hal, you are so insistent I shall, of course, agree to carry out your request and question you no further.'

She did not say, May you not even trust your very good friend, Rob Stammers? She knew that they were very good friends by their manner with each other— but it was not for her to question him after she had promised him that she would not.

Had she done so Devenish would have told her that in this matter he dare trust no one—not even Rob. The conspiracy was wide-ranging, and considering the seriousness of the crimes which had been committed, the members of it must be desperate men. And they would undoubtedly form a large number of his male guests at Tresham Hall.

He released her hand, and watched her slip his letter into her embroidery bag. She saw his eyes follow her action, and said softly, 'Do not trouble yourself, Hal. I shall take good care of it and see that it is stowed away in my portable writing desk of which only I possess the key. God grant that I may never have to send it on.'

'Oh, I second that most fervently,' he told her, something of his usual, slightly mocking, manner returning. 'Now let us talk of pleasant things. I look forward to seeing you at Tresham. And Miss Faulkner, of course. Giles said earlier that she is due to return this afternoon.'

'Yes, and it is good of you to ask her, knowing how much she disapproves of you.'

'Oh, I am used to being disapproved of—what I would object to is being disposed of.'

This rather grim joke did disturb Drusilla's calm. 'Oh, how can you jest so if you are really in danger?'

'Well, weeping about it won't help. Cheer up, my love. I have been in danger before and I have survived—as I hope I shall survive this.'

Drusilla could not prevent herself from saying, 'Has it anything to do with the Black Mass?'

Now what had made her say such a thing? He answered her question with another. 'Why, Drusilla? Do you know something of which you ought to tell me?'

'Not really—only what I told you on your last visit—and because I keep having strange dreams about Jeremy in which he is pursued by something evil. Forgive me, I vowed that I would not question you, and here I am breaking my word. You will think me a ninnyhammer.'

'No, indeed. You will have me breaking my word, too, and making love to you instanter, here in the open, on the lawn, if you look at me like that.'

'Like what, Hal? Whatever can you mean?' This came out demurely, but her expression was both naughty and provoking.

It provoked him.

'You know. You do not need me to tell you. As though you could eat me whole.'

'Well, that is not surprising since that is how you look at me—when we are alone, that is.'

'Vixen,' Devenish said, and made to embrace her passionately, but, for safety's sake, he changed his mind at the very last moment and all that Drusilla received was the usual chaste kiss on her cheek.

He recognised her disappointment even though she tried to mask it. 'No, not now,' he said, 'but later...ah, yes, later will be a different thing. For the present we must behave ourselves. For your safety—and for mine—we must not appear to be too involved. I alone must be their target, and you must not be a hostage to fortune through whom they might strike at me, destroying you in the process.'

Drusilla wanted to ask him who *they* were, but desisted. He had become grave again. Miss Faulkner had once told her that when he looked so he was very like his formidable grandfather whose stern severity had been legendary in the district.

So she said no more, but after he had taken her hand to kiss it, she would not let it go, but clutched at it desperately, saying, 'Oh, you will take care, Hal. Promise me that you will take no unnecessary risks.'

'Dearest girl,' he whispered, taking her hand and placing it against his heart, so that she might feel its steady beat—as he had earlier felt her pulse. 'All risks, I fear, are unnecessary, or they would not be risks. I will be as careful as events will allow me to be, and you must promise me that you will never walk abroad without one of Giles's hulking footmen accompanying you. And that applies even if Miss Faulkner is with you.'

'I promise,' she whispered.

'That, at least, relieves me a little, and when you visit Tresham I shall make sure that you are safe. And now I must leave you, for there is much to do at Tresham before it is ready to receive my guests.'

He paused, and turned his head away from her for a moment, before saying quietly, 'It is a beautiful place and it grieves me a little that I have allowed it to be neglected. It was childish of me to punish a building in order to hit back at a dead old man. I have told Rob that it is our duty not only to restore it, but to embellish it to make up for its lost years.'

There was no one else but Drusilla to whom he could explain this and be understood. 'I must not drench you in remorse,' he said, 'it's a childish passion for it mends nothing. The thing to do is to behave better in future.'

Drusilla said, again without willing it as she so frequently did when with him, 'Oh, I know that feeling; after Jeremy died I thought of all the things I might have said to him and did not. I even blamed myself that he must have died so far from home, which was foolish, I know.'

'But human,' he said, giving her hand one last kiss, before releasing it and saying, '*Adieu*, my heart.' And so he left her, striding across the lawn towards the house as though he were setting off for battle.

Which in a way he was, and Drusilla wished, too late, that she had given him some favour to take with him such as ladies used to bestow on knights of old.

The weather, which earlier that summer had been both cold and wet, had improved as August ran towards September and, on the day the guests assembled at Tresham Hall, was almost Mediterranean with a brilliant sky of Wedgwood blue.

The harvest, Rob had told Hal earlier that day, whilst not good, would be better than they might have expected, which would have the advantage of allaying some of the discontent which the two previous bad summers and consequent poor harvests had created.

Not that most of the guests allowed such mundane considerations to distract them from their pleasures. They arrived in their fine carriages to be met by bowing servants who showed them to their rooms, where everything had been arranged for their comfort.

Drusilla found herself in a suite at the side, away from the bustle of the stables and possible noise from those using the front doors. From what Devenish had told her she had thought that she would find the house a little shabby, but there was no sign of this. Quite the contrary, its magnificence seemed to be undimmed.

She remarked on it when she met Leander Harrington in the large drawing room where portraits of earlier members of the Devenish family covered the walls above glass-fronted cabinets filled with the finest China.

'Oh, he must have spent a fortune over the past few weeks in order to achieve its present splendour,' Mr Harrington assured her. 'It was in a parlous state the last time young Stammers allowed me in so that I might use the library. That room, at least, was kept up, and stocked with all the latest books, Devenish being a bibliophile, as you doubtless know.'

No, Drusilla did not know, but the news did not surprise her. Nothing about Devenish would ever surprise her, she thought. He was such a strange mixture of contrarinesses and paradoxes, but she was becoming convinced that a good heart lay beneath them.

Their host arrived while they were talking and said, 'Did I hear the word library spoken? Knowing you, Mrs Faulkner, I cannot believe that it would be long before you discovered its whereabouts. Harrington I believe, already knows them—or so Rob Stammers tells me.'

'Indeed,' replied Mr Harrington smoothly, 'he has been kindness itself in allowing me to consult some of your rarer texts, although he has never allowed me to borrow them.'

'And quite right, too,' smiled Devenish. 'You know the old saying: ''A book lent is a book lost''—is not that so, Mrs Faulkner? I understand that you are something of a bibliophile yourself.'

It doubtless amused him to speak to her so formally in front of others, and added a touch of innocent conspiracy to their relationship.

She responded in kind by saying, 'Oh, no, m'lord, I dare make no such excessive claim. Books fascinate me, but I doubt that I have the right to be described as a bibliophile. I am, of course, very willing to learn from both of you.'

Devenish looked around the room, noting that the company were talking gaily among themselves over the tea-boards which had been set out on every flat surface and which were being presided over by a bevy of sturdy footmen.

'I don't think that we shall be missed, Harrington, if the three of us repair to the library so that we may show Mrs Faulkner some of our rarer treasures. Tresham boasts a Caxton—one of the earliest of printed books—and a Shakespeare First Folio among others, not so old but equally as fine.'

After he had been introduced to Drusilla, Dr Southwell duly fetched out the First Folio. He laid it carefully out on the big library table to be admired. He extolled the beauty of the binding and the print before adding to it the promised Caxton. 'A miracle of black letter' he called it. He told her that she was very welcome to use the library as often as she wished whilst she was staying at the Hall.

'We have, of course, other treasures,' he said enthusiastically. 'I am not sure, m'lord, whether you are

aware that your late grandfather possessed a remarkable collection of works on the occult. They are not on
the public shelves, being kept in a locked cupboard in
my study. Mr Harrington, I know, has frequently found
them of interest, although for my part, I look on this
whole business as being one of black superstition rather
than black magic—if you will forgive my little joke,
sir,' he said, bowing to Mr Harrington.

'Indeed, I was not aware of any such thing,' returned
Devenish a trifle drily. He did not point out to Dr
Southwell that he seemed to have forgotten that he had
specifically informed him recently that the library possessed no such volumes! He tried to avoid Mr
Harrington's eye and to appear totally uninterested in
any thing black.

'Being a convinced sceptic in such matters,' he continued, 'I have no desire to waste my time inspecting
them. I agree with you, Dr Southwell, that they belong
to the ages of superstition which, I am happy to say,
are long behind us.

'I trust, sir,' he said turning towards Mr Harrington,
'that I do not offend you by being so frank if they are
an interest of yours, but that is my honest opinion.'

Mr Harrington's response was to bow greasily in the
direction of both the good doctor and Devenish.

'Not at all, m'lord. My interest was purely superfi-
cial, I assure you, a matter of simple curiosity. Like
you, I am a devout son of the Age of Reason—if I may
use the word devout in that connection.'

To say that Devenish did not believe a word of this
charmingly spoken explanation would be an under-

statement. He knew that Mr Harrington must be lying in his teeth if what de Castellane had told him was true.

Drusilla, who had remained silent whilst the gentlemen indulged themselves, said, 'It may be simple-minded of me, but is there not some danger attached to studying such arcane and evil matters? Might it not be possible that we could be unwittingly corrupted?'

Mr Harrington metaphorically patted her hand. 'Now, now, my dear, the strong-minded among us are perfectly able to resist such temptation if we approach them in the theoretical sense only.'

His tone suggested that only weak-minded women were liable to be affected. Dr Southwell said hastily, 'I am sure that the late Lord Devenish's interests in such matters were purely theoretical—and he was very strong-minded, m'lord, as you well know.'

'Indeed,' replied Devenish grimly, for who should know better than he how strong-minded his grandfather had been! He also knew that the late Lord's interest in the occult was more than purely theoretical, something which he shared with Mr Harrington. He would not have wished to discuss with him anything which bore on his secret practices, but now that the matter had been raised in conversation he was not averse to continuing the discussion. Mr Harrington might yet say something incriminating which could be helpful to him.

If Dr Southwell appeared only dimly aware that there were strong and strange undercurrents in this innocent-seeming conversation, Drusilla, knowing him, was sure that Devenish was speaking with a double tongue and she thought that Leander Harrington might be doing the same.

She was beginning to suspect that this discussion might have something to do with the letter which he had given her for Lord Sidmouth—although how, she could not yet guess.

Dr Southwell hastily changed the conversation by pulling an old atlas from the shelves in order to show them its beautiful plates. At this point tea, ordered by Devenish before they had adjourned to the library, arrived. It was laid out on a beautiful marquetry-topped table which stood in a giant bay window near to the library's entrance which overlooked the elegancies of Tresham Hall's park.

'I had not known that Tresham and its grounds were so beautiful,' Drusilla said, admiring the romantic-seeming lawn, bordered by cypresses, with a small gazebo on its two far corners.

'That is my fault,' Devenish told her. 'I gave orders when I succeeded that the Hall should be shut up and no visitors allowed. I spared the grounds because they are so beautiful and I used to admire them from my bedroom window.' He did not tell them that his bedroom had been in the attics, and was more sparsely furnished than any in the servants' quarters.

It was Leander Harrington who revived the discussion on the occult, by remarking as he replaced his tea cup in its saucer. 'I am surprised, m'lord, that you are not interested in the occult. You have the reputation of a many-sided man who judges matters only after great consideration. If you are not prepared to study the occult, how can you make a just decision as to its merits—or lack of them?'

'Oh, there are many matters on which I have an opinion, and which I have not studied. Life is too short. The laws of chance, for example, which could be useful when one gambles, I am told. I prefer to trust my instincts.'

Now this was a thundering lie, but it was a bait put forward to tempt Leander Harrington and his possible fellow conspirators—principally Toby Claridge—to the gaming tables.

'I had heard that you were a great gambler, m'lord, a heavy plunger, but that you did not, unlike many, often play, and that when you did, you invariably won. Is that true?'

'Ah, that is a question which should not be put, and which I shall not answer, other than to say that if many of the gentlemen present would care to join me at the tables tonight, I shall be pleased to arrange for them to do so.'

He turned to Drusilla and added, 'Lest the ladies of the party should feel themselves neglected, I have arranged for the largest State Room to be cleared so that we may have a ball tomorrow evening. A party of musicians from London has already arrived to do the honours.'

Drusilla was not pleased to hear that gaming was being proposed, and was surprised that Devenish should suggest it. 'I have one proviso to make,' she told him, 'and that is that you will not allow Giles to form one of the party.'

'No, indeed. The gambling fever, if caught early, can be a dangerous one. The circumstances of my life meant that I came to the tables late. The later the better.'

'And if one never arrives there, the best of all,' murmured Drusilla provokingly.

'Perhaps,' he said, smiling at her to show that he was not offended, 'but gambling lends spice to otherwise dull lives.' He could scarcely tell her that the only reason he was suggesting that the party should indulge in play was because it was part of his plans to corner Leander Harrington and his murderous fellows.

And so it was arranged. Harrington had provided him with an opportunity, and he had taken it. So far he was certain that his prey had no notion that he had become prey, and from a quarter which he could not have suspected.

If the women—most of whom had never shared in the life of the *ton*—had mixed feelings about an evening of gaming, the men were delighted. Their only complaint was that their host had only decreed one, in deference to the wishes of the ladies. Or so he said. In truth it was because he valued the opinion of one lady, Mrs Drusilla Faulkner.

If he had not planned the gaming evening specifically to further his aim of trapping Leander Harrington and his associates, he would not have proposed it at all.

In the event the ladies of the party had to be content to leave the men first to their port—as was customary—and then to the card tables which had been set up in Tresham Hall's Venetian room—the creation of Devenish's great-grandfather.

He had come back from his Grand Tour of Europe loaded with loot to adorn his noble house and to demonstrate to the world his wealth and power as well as his taste. On the room's walls hung Canalettos and Guardis showing Venice before its fall to Napoleon had finally deprived the city of its centuries-old power. Below them stood glass-fronted cabinets filled with precious porcelain and *objets d'art*. His grandson's guests were gaming the night away in a treasure house.

Dawn was gleaming through the gaps in the brocade curtains when Devenish, who had won constantly throughout the night, finally broke Sir Toby Claridge whose IOUs stood in a great pile before him.

Toby was the last left in the game and, having drunk heavily, had rashly gambled that Devenish's run of luck could not last. He was wrong. At half past three on a fine morning in late summer he had lost all he possessed.

He sat there, surrounded by those who had won a little and lost a little, and did not fully understand that he was up the River Tick without a paddle. In his fuddled state he had thought that he might overcome Devenish at the gaming tables even if he had to give him best in the lists of love so far as Drusilla was concerned. Doing so would also solve his dire problems—or at least postpone the day of reckoning with his duns.

He said nothing for the moment as, the game over, the other players began to yawn and make for bed, leaving Devenish and Toby alone together, the pile of IOUs between them. Only Devenish knew that where Toby was concerned luck had played no part in his defeat.

Devenish had cold-bloodedly cheated him—and no one else—to bring about a situation where the man before him was at his mercy. He defended his conduct by arguing that it was the only ploy he could think of which would supply him with the information which he needed to bring Harrington to justice.

Toby said, slowly and hesitantly, 'I'm ruined, Devenish. I can't honour my debts.'

He pointed at the IOUs on the table, and added mournfully, 'I've no money to back them with. My father lost heavily on the Stock Exchange in the late wars, and after I inherited I spent my inheritance foolishly. My only destination is Calais where you, and the rest of my creditors, will be unable to dun me. You will let me go, won't you? You're rich enough without needing to persecute me for what I can't give you.'

Devenish said coldly, 'I have not the slightest desire to allow you to escape without payment.'

'But dammit, I've just told you, I can't pay you.'

'Oh, I don't want money,' Devenish told him, as Toby dropped his head into his hands and began to wail gently into them, quite unmanned. 'I want information which only you can give me. Oblige me by doing that and I will burn your IOUs before your eyes.'

Toby lifted his head and stared at him. 'Information? What information can I possibly give you which was worth this night's work?'

'Come,' said Devenish, rising and leaning forward across the table. 'You know better than that, Claridge. I want you to tell me all that you know about the infamous goings-on of your friend Leander Harrington and the circle of his fellows who celebrate the Black Mass at Marsham Abbey. Principally those matters relating to the murder of Jeremy Faulkner and the strange disappearance of a number of village girls over the past two years.'

Toby paled. He said hoarsely, 'You don't know what you're asking!'

'Indeed, I do. You are frightened of what Leander Harrington might do to you if you inform on him. I assure you that if you tell me the whole truth I shall not only burn your IOUs, but I shall never reveal to anyone that you were my informer. They must put that down to my so-called devilish powers!'

His victim gave a short mirthless laugh. 'Well, you've certainly behaved like the devil in ruining me, and that's flat! I suppose I must do as you wish—so long as you keep your promise and say nothing to anyone. I'm a dead man else. On the other hand I'll be a dead man if Harrington finds out what I've done.'

Devenish did not allow his exasperation with the fool before him to show.

Instead he said, as harshly as he could, 'You and the rest of your black-hearted brotherhood will be gallows' meat soon if I corner Harrington without your help—

as I surely will. So, you have your choice. Help me and, when the day of reckoning comes, that you have done so will save you from swinging. Refuse, and you'll share your companions' fate. Which shall it be?'

'You don't leave a fellow much choice,' moaned Toby, sinking his head in his hands again.

'Oh, I never do that—it's a damned bad habit I've no wish to acquire. Choose and have done with it. Refuse me and it's financial ruin and an ultimately dreadful death. Oblige me and you may survive. Nothing could be simpler.'

'What do you want to know?' There was a note of desperation in Toby's voice which Devenish ignored. This was no time for misplaced pity.

'Everything. Where you met, how many of you there were, their names, and how and why the young women and Jeremy Faulkner died will do to begin with.'

His face working, Toby Claridge looked away—anything rather than see the stern, unforgiving face before him, bent on stripping everything from him, on making him reveal what he had always hoped to keep secret.

His voice low and unsteady, he began his sorry story. 'It started as a joke, a drinking club with a bit of spice in it. Once a month when the moon was full we dressed up, wore masks and played about in the crypt, half-cut. We usually began the evening in the Abbey before dressing up in monks' robes and moving on to the crypt. Gradually it became more serious with less drinking and increased ceremony. Leander Harrington was the instigator and at first we called him our President. Later he took the name of Apollyon—another word for the Devil.

'And then he told us that in the genuine Black Mass a woman's body was used as an altar and he suggested that we arrange for one of the village girls to take part by bribing her with a little present.'

Toby swallowed. 'I remember that we all thought this a great joke, and so it was at first. George Lawson took the part of the officiating priest at the religious ceremony... And then, one evening, after we had all drunk heavily...'

He stopped and muttered, looking at the floor as he spoke so that his voice was scarcely audible, 'I can't tell you the details, but the upshot was that after coupling with the girl Harrington sacrificed her.

'We were all shocked, I remember—except that somehow it didn't seem quite real. It was like being at Drury Lane Theatre where the actors are only pretending to die. None of us protested at the time. Only, when we met at the next full moon, Jeremy got up and said that we ought to pass a resolution that we revert back to the club's original form. We were not to use the word Apollyon, but call Harrington our President again and drop most of the ceremonial.

'He said that he could only condone the murder of the girl if we agreed to his proposal. Leander Harrington said that we could not go back. The die was cast, he said, we were brothers in blood, and the ceremony would go on. Everyone seemed to agree with him. Jeremy told him that in that case he would go to the Lord Lieutenant and inform him of what had been taking place: he would not be a party to any further murders.

'It was a dam' fool thing for him to threaten knowing that Harrington had already committed murder—but then, Jeremy was always a bit stupid. Harrington told him that no one present would dare to betray him because of their own involvement. Jeremy refused to change his mind and Harrington said in that case Jeremy would be the next blood sacrifice and he called on the brotherhood to deal with him.

'At the last Jeremy realised what was about to happen. He shouted something at us all and tried to escape by running through the French windows into the garden with Harrington and most of the rest hallooing after him as though he were a fox. They caught him up at the sundial...'

Toby shuddered. Devenish sat silent, remembering the fit of horror which Drusilla had suffered there when in his company, and later the second fit when she had touched Parson Lawson. Her intuition of evil had been right there, as it always was.

'Go on,' he said coldly, determined to spare Toby nothing. 'Finish what you have begun.'

'I don't know exactly what happened to him. I was his friend. I couldn't look, and, God forgive me, neither did I help him. I only know that they joined together in killing him.'

He shuddered again. 'It was as though everyone had gone mad. They had executed him for treason, Harrington called it. He was carried to the crypt, half-stripped, his possessions taken from him, and then his body was removed to where it would later be found. I left for France soon afterwards. I wanted nothing more to do with it. Besides, I might have been the next to die, seeing that I was Jeremy's best friend. I suppose the girls who disappeared were those who took part after his death.'

So that was how Jeremy Faulkner's ring had come to be found in the crypt. It must have been dropped there when the frightened conspirators frantically and hastily tried to make it appear that when—and if—his body was discovered it would be assumed that he had been attacked and killed by robbers.

Devenish said nothing of this, but asked instead, 'Tell me, Claridge, knowing what you did, what induced you to return?'

Toby looked at him as though he were simple minded. 'Why, Dru, of course. Two years had gone by since Jeremy's death and I had always loved her. I hoped to make her my wife. And I knew that no one suspected what had happened and was probably still happening at Marsham Abbey. The coast was clear.'

Devenish closed his eyes. For a moment he could not speak. Of all the moral idiots he had ever encountered, Toby Claridge took the prize for insensitivity. If he had not murdered young Faulkner himself, he had stood by whilst it was done, had connived at his disappearance and then taken himself off to France to escape any consequences for him which might ensue.

And then, as he had said, when the coast was clear, he had cheerfully returned to court his dead friend's widow and, bearing in mind the conversation which

Devenish had overheard at Marsham Abbey, he had also rejoined the brotherhood as a fully fledged member!

Devenish did not reproach him, however, for he wanted to use his present ascendancy over the creature before him to try to end Leander Harrington's evil grip on what he could only conceive of as a brotherhood of blood bound together by their participation in a series of brutal murders.

Toby Claridge had been corrupted and now must pay for that by assisting in the brotherhood's destruction. His head hanging, he was waiting for what Devenish might have to say to him next.

He did not need to wait long. Devenish leaned forward, and said sternly, 'Look me in the eye, Claridge. This is what I want you to do for me.' Numbly, all his usual cheerful confidence leached away, Sir Toby Claridge agreed to try to make amends for the death of his friend.

After Toby had gone to bed, stumbling as he went, Devenish rose and leaned his forehead on the cold marble of the mantelpiece. What he had heard was worse than he might have expected. The thought of a pack of country gentlemen killing one of their company as cheerfully as they might have killed a fox or shot a pheasant, combined with the rape and murder of a few helpless country girls who had been bribed to their death, was almost too much to bear.

Worse, he was sure of one thing—that this appalling scandal must never become public because of the damage it would do to the society in which it had taken place. This was no simple matter for the local Lord Lieutenant to deal with.

He must try to end it in such a fashion that no one would ever know the dreadful truth and still ensure that Leander Harrington at least might be punished for his dreadful crimes. Remove him from the scene and it was likely that the conspiracy would collapse for lack of a powerful leader.

What troubled him about this solution—even if it could be achieved—was the thought that the deaths of Jeremy Faulkner and the poor wenches caught in Harrington's toils would never be publicly avenged and their families would never know what had happened to them. Best perhaps, if the dead girls' parents never knew the truth but believed that they had fled to London.

He thought of Drusilla, deprived so dreadfully of her young husband, and of the agony which she would suffer if she knew how and why he had died. He also remembered Jeremy Faulkner's last message from beyond the grave—'Dru must never know.'

There are some problems, he knew, which admit of no solution, and this was one. He prayed that he might be able to think of a way in which scandal could be avoided and justice could still be done—but for the moment a possible outcome still eluded him.

In the meantime he had to trust that the weak man he had suborned might not betray him to his evil master. It was a risk which had been forced upon him if he were to succeed in his object for he had not been able to think of any other way of penetrating the Brotherhood.

And now he must go to his bed, for morning was here, the servants were stirring, and soon he must be up and about as though nothing had occurred to add to the nightmares which he already suffered.

# Chapter Twelve

Drusilla was becoming aware that Giles was worried about something. Twice he had muttered at her, 'I say, Dru...' and then he had fallen silent, his young face sad.

She found this strange new mood of his surprising because until this morning he had been enjoying himself hugely at Tresham Hall. Devenish had included some of the other young hopefuls of the district in his party, and Giles had got on famously with them.

That afternoon she came upon him sitting alone on a bench which overlooked the lake, a neglected book open on his knee.

'What is it, Giles?' she asked him. 'Does your leg hurt that you are avoiding the others? Or are they avoiding you?'

His face shuttered, he shook his head. 'No, it's not that. The other fellows have been kind. It's...' and he fell silent.

Drusilla sat down beside him. 'I don't want to nag, Giles, but until today you seemed to be having a famous time. What's gone wrong?'

From being shuttered his face became tortured. 'Oh, I suppose I may as well tell you—though I know that you won't like it. It's Devenish. You and I have never believed the *on dits* about his wickedness, but there's a really unpleasant one going the rounds this morning. You're aware, of course, that Devenish arranged a gaming party for the men last night. It went on until the small hours and ended with Devenish ruining poor Toby. Those who took part said that he lost everything. I said that I didn't believe it, but Jack Clifton told me that his father was there and swore that that was the upshot.'

Her face white, Drusilla said, 'No, I don't...I can't...believe that Devenish would do such a thing. Surely if it were true Mr Clifton and the others would have left Tresham today rather than remain where their host had done something as dreadful as ruining one of his guests.'

Giles shook his head glumly. 'No such thing, Dru. They think it's rather clever of Devenish, you see. Gaming is what gentlemen do for fun, Jack says, and they must never crow if they win, or complain if they lose. He says it's to do with honour—though that seems very odd to me, and so I told him. He scoffed at me then and told me it was plain that I had been brought up by women if I didn't understand that.'

'Did he, indeed! Nothing would induce me to believe that such behaviour is other than wicked—as well as stupid. I hope, Giles, that you don't think that there is something clever in gambling—particularly if it's likely to result in ruin—either yours, or anyone else's.'

'Of course not, Dru. On the other hand—'

'There is no other hand, Giles.' Drusilla rose to her feet. That Devenish—she could not think of him as Hal any more—should do such a thing made her feel quite faint. Poor Toby—what must he be feeling on this bright and sunny morning?

She walked rapidly back into the Hall after reading Giles another short sermon on the evils of play because she feared that he might prefer Jack Clifton's verdict on the matter. By chance she met Devenish in the entrance hall. He didn't look as though he had spent the night in play, ruining one of her oldest friends in the process.

He looked, in fact, just as he always did, and his smile when he saw her was a warm one.

'Ah, there you are, Drusilla. I gather the ladies are arranging an archery contest today and I thought that you might like to take part.'

Still in shock, she could not immediately answer him. The empathy which had recently grown up between them had him saying, 'What is it, Drusilla? You look distressed.'

For some reason this echo of her own words to Giles disturbed her profoundly. She said, her voice shaking, 'Oh, m'lord, Giles says that a rumour is running round that you ruined Toby at play last night. Tell me it is not true.'

He might have known that such a rare piece of gossip would fly round the company at record speed. He could not, dare not tell her the truth, even though without doing so she would inevitably think the worst of him. He did not need to answer her for his hesitation told Drusilla everything.

'It is true, then? Oh, I can scarcely believe it of you, m'lord. I had not thought—'

He caught at her hand urgently. 'Drusilla, look at me, and do not judge me. Instead, I ask you to trust me. To trust Hal and forget Devenish.'

Drusilla tried to pull her hand away from his. 'Trust you! I believed that you were not the man that gossip said you were—but what am I to think now?'

He would not release her hand, but gripped it ever more tightly. 'Drusilla, I believe that you love me. Everything that you say and do to me betrays that one fact. If your love is true, then you must trust me unquestioningly in this matter—and not believe the worst of me—however wicked last night's work must seem to you. I cannot explain to you why I behaved as I did.'

Her eyes, he saw, were full of tears. 'Oh, Hal, I want to trust you, I do, and yes, I love you—and want to believe you.'

There, she had said it aloud.

He stood transfixed.

So did she.

At last she spoke, her voice faltering. 'My reason tells me not to trust you. That inside me, which is beyond reason, tells me that I must, against all the evidence, do so. I have already trusted you once over the matter of your letter by refusing to question you further about the reason for it. But oh, Hal, don't lie to me over this, for I do not think that I could easily survive another such agony as adding your falsity to Jeremy's death would create in me.'

Devenish was in nearly as great a torment as she was, but his face showed no sign of it. 'Believe me,' he said passionately. 'And trust me. I ask nothing more and nothing less than that.'

She could not speak, but nodded agreement.

He released her hand.

They stood face to face and Henry Devenish said at last what he had always thought he would never be able to say to any woman.

'Oh, Drusilla, I love you. I love you because you are the woman I feared I would never be lucky enough to meet. A woman I do not deserve. I hope never to let you down, and that one day soon I can come to you with clean hands as well as a loving heart. For the present that is all that I can say to you.'

He bowed to her as she stood there, shaking a little with the silent passion which, once again, was passing between them.

'And now I must leave you. I have duties to fulfil, and work to do, but rest assured that you are the one person in the whole wide world whom I love and trust as much as I hope that you love and trust me.'

He was gone, and Drusilla held to her heart the words which she had never thought to hear him say. She would trust him and pray that her trust was not misplaced.

She walked slowly to her room. Her inward distress was such that she felt unequal to meeting and talking to any other of Tresham Hall's guests. But she had not gone further than the first landing on the great stairway when she met Sir Toby Claridge walking along it, his manner as carefree as though nothing in the whole wide world could trouble him.

He must have seen her distress for he stopped, his simple face worried, and said, 'What is it, Dru? Are you ill?'

For the moment she was almost unable to speak, and then words gushed from her lips in a torrent, for she must know, she must, and surely he would give her a plain answer. 'No, I'm not ill, but tell me, Toby, is it really true that you lost everything at play last night to Lord Devenish?'

He gave a short, nervous laugh. 'Oh, is that the tale that's going round, Dru? No wonder you've a Friday face. Of course, it's not true. It is true that when the others left us alone I was in a bad way, but Devenish agreed to go on playing and after a short time I had recouped most of my losses, and so we called it a night—or rather day—for the sun was already up.'

It was the tale which he and Devenish had agreed on to explain away why he was not, after all, ruined.

Relief swept over Drusilla coupled with a feeling of bewilderment that Devenish had not explained this to her. But, of course, he would not justify himself to anyone. It was not his way.

More, he had been right to say that if she loved him she would trust him unreservedly. Joy ran through her—a joy which Toby saw and recognised for what it was.

'It's him you care for,' he said sadly. 'It's Devenish, isn't it? I've never had a hope of winning you, had I? Oh, Dru, are you being wise? He's a ruthless devil, I know, but—' and something suddenly struck him '—you're a strong woman, aren't you? The way that you coped and arranged things after Jeremy's death should have told me. Most women would have had hysterics and needed rescuing themselves, but not you. All the same, don't let him hurt you.'

'Oh, Toby,' Drusilla said, sad in her turn. 'I like you as a friend—and you're right, he's ruthless—but perhaps that's what I admire about him.'

He leaned forward and kissed her gently on the brow. 'I shan't say anything more, Dru. I've lost the right to do other than wish you happy.'

Tonight, he promised himself as he walked slowly down stairs, the day having lost its savour for him, I shall get drunk—and then I'll think about tomorrow.

The gossip about the result of the previous night's gaming was not confined to the great and mighty. The servants' hall was enjoying it, too. Leander Harrington's valet, Ashton, twitted Toby's valet, Grayson, on his losses.

'Not so bad as at first thought, though,' retorted Grayson. 'After the night was supposed to be over, they played again and my master recouped most of his losses, isn't that so, Erridge?'

Erridge was Devenish's man, a silent creature, given mostly to nodding his head and looking wise. 'So it seems,' he said at last, grudgingly.

'Well, either he did or he didn't,' retorted Ashton.

'There was something odd about it, though,' said Grayson slowly. 'When I helped him into his night rail Sir T allowed as how Devenish was a tricky swine who never gave you something for nothing. When I asked him how so, he swore at me and said, "Never mind."'

'That's true enough, he is a tricky swine,' nodded Erridge. 'He did a deal with that young fellow Allinson who lost everything to him just afore we left London. He let him off his losses after he promised to stop gambling.'

'Wonder if he did a similar deal with Sir T?' pondered Grayson.

Ashton said, 'For sure, your master's an odd creature, Erridge. Winning—and then throwing his gains away.'

He thought that this might be a useful titbit to pass on to his own master when he dressed him for dinner. He knew that Leander Harrington considered all gossip as grist to his mill—it helped him to control people, he had once said. Always tell me anything you think I ought to know—I shan't reproach you if it's useless.

He had obviously heard something useful this time. Mr Harrington regarded his handsome reflection in the mirror. 'Say that again, Ashton,' he instructed.

Ashton duly obliged him.

Mr Harrington thought a moment before summing up, 'So Erridge said that it was a habit of his master's to let his victims off if they obliged him in some way?'

'Not quite, sir,' said Ashton scrupulously. 'In young Allinson's case it was simply a promise to stop gambling—which you might say obliged Allinson, not Lord Devenish.'

'I wonder what Sir Toby promised him,' mused his master. 'Try to find out, if you would, Ashton. You'll not lose by it.'

After he had sent his valet away with a guinea in his hand, Leander Harrington sat down and thought for a moment of what he had just learned. Sir Toby, he knew, was a weak fool. He was also a friend of Drusilla Faulkner's, who seemed to be Devenish's latest female conquest. That being so, it was odd that Devenish should fix on Sir Toby to ruin. And having ruined him, odder still that he should give him a chance to recoup.

Could it be that he had not, but had simply returned Claridge's IOUs in exchange for something else? And if so, what could it be? It might be wise to lean on Claridge and try to find out the real truth behind this strange story.

Unease rode on his shoulders. He knew that he was playing a dangerous game of a different kind where failure might mean more than the simple loss of money. His life—and the lives of those he controlled—could be at risk.

Another thought struck him. What was the true reason why Devenish—who, gossip said, had always vowed never to set foot in Tresham Hall again—had returned to it this summer? Was it simply boredom, curiosity, or something more which had brought him back? A wise man always considered every option put before him—particularly where survival itself could be concerned.

He would not question Claridge here, at Tresham Hall, for the man was so light in the attic that he might immediately run to Devenish babbling about Harrington's curiosity over what had passed after the pair of them had been left alone once the night's play was supposedly over. No, he would wait until the house party had dispersed—and then find an opportunity to make Claridge drunk enough to loosen his tongue.

He would also warn the other conspirators to be careful what they said in front of Devenish. It was immaterial whether the man knew, or suspected, anything—caution could never be misplaced. If his early morning deal with Claridge was an innocent one having nothing to do with the secret activities at Marsham Abbey, a misplaced word might still serve to give them all away—with disastrous results.

Drusilla was thus not the only person for whom the end of the meeting at Tresham Hall to which she had so looked forward could not come soon enough. She needed time to think, away from Devenish and the fascination which he had for her.

They met little after that, and he made no attempt to single her out, and she reciprocated by avoiding him whenever she could whilst trying not to look overly cool towards him.

I am growing as devious as he is, she thought mournfully as she was driven home to Lyford House.

He had come to see her off, had bowed to her before handing her into her carriage, and had said under his breath, 'Soon, soon, I hope that we may be less circumspect. Until then, *adieu*. My heart travels with you.'

Full of a strange apprehension for which she could find no reason, Drusilla had bowed back and murmured so that none might hear her, 'Your wishes accord with mine, m'lord. I long for that day to come.'

'Hal,' he had murmured back, straightening up. 'Hal, remember. For you, m'lord and Devenish do not exist.'

She had not looked back. Giles, who was handed in after her, asked curiously, 'What did he say to you, Dru? Has he ever explained about that damn'd odd business over Sir Toby? First it was said that Devenish had ruined him, and then the *on dit* was that he had not—that it was all a misunderstanding.'

'It's none of our business what he does,' she told him quietly. 'I would rather that you did not speak of it further. We ought to ignore gossip, not perpetually chew it over. M'lord treated you very kindly while you were at Tresham, and that should be enough.'

'So he did,' remarked Giles, brightening. 'I had a really jolly time once the first rumours over Sir Toby proved false. Devenish let me ride that dear little mare of his. He told his head groom to lend it to our stables since she was just the thing for me to ride. Neither too lively, nor too sluggish, he said. He doesn't make a great *tohu bohu* either way over my game leg, you know. I like that.'

It was another mark of Devenish's kindness, Drusilla knew, and it comforted her. He was a man of such contrarieties that it was difficult to judge him easily.

Which was exactly what Toby Claridge was thinking of his late host as he drove home. Shortly before he had left Tresham Hall Leander Harrington had come up to him.

'We have enjoyed ourselves so much here,' he had said, 'that I should not like to wait until the next full moon to carry on the festivities. I have asked a few friends round to Marsham for an evening's drinking tonight. If I have a criticism to make of our host at Tresham, it is that he does not take his drinking seriously.'

'Doesn't take it at all, seriously or otherwise,' grinned Toby. 'Damn'd abstemious, ain't he?'

He didn't particularly relish spending an evening drinking with Harrington in view of what he had told Devenish about the Black Mass, but as he had never refused such an invitation before, it might look odd if he did so now.

'Do nothing out of the ordinary,' Devenish had warned him. 'Continue to live as you have always done. That way you avoid the kind of suspicion which suddenly changing your habits might provoke.'

'You will make up the party?' Harrington pressed him.

'Oh, certainly. Never miss an opportunity to join a few friends over a glass of something.'

'Excellent. You won't regret coming. I like to share the glories of my cellar with my friends. Unlike

Devenish. His grandfather must be turning over in his grave to see it so neglected.'

'So long as he don't come out of it,' laughed Toby, relieved. Harrington didn't appear to suspect anything, and a happy evening's drinking might dispel some of the qualms he felt over ratting on the Brotherhood as Harrington always called it.

Harrington watched Toby's carriage leave, a grim smile on his face. Claridge might not be so cheerful in a few hours' time if his suspicions proved to be well founded. If he had betrayed them his punishment might take some time in coming, for it would not do to have another mysterious death to explain away—particularly since Claridge had been a great friend of Jeremy Faulkner's...

His main problem would be what to do with Devenish if his suspicions over the real reason for his presence at Tresham proved to be true.

'Well, I suppose it was worth all the hard work,' remarked Rob Stammers to Devenish when the last guest had gone and the servants were setting the Hall to rights again.

'Indeed it was,' said Devenish. He was feeling weary unto death. Tomorrow he would ride to London with as little pomp and circumstance as possible, ask Sidmouth's advice, and then try to act upon it. He had no idea of what the Home Secretary might say—other than that he would wish an open scandal to be avoided. That he had been chosen to perform this mission at all was proof of that.

'What are you up to, Hal?' Rob asked, his tone conversational.

'Up to? I don't follow.'

'No? You have that face again. The one I haven't seen since the days when we worked behind the French lines in Spain and Portugal.'

Devenish sighed. 'Am I so transparent, then?'

'Only to me, I suspect. I have seen it before, others haven't.'

'I can't tell you, Rob. For your own sake.'

This was not strictly true. He had to consider that Rob *might* be one of the Brotherhood—and therefore ready to betray him. He thought not, but it was a risk he dare not take—unlike the one with Claridge.

'For my sake? You weren't so tender of my skin in the Peninsula.'

'Ah, but what I am "up to" now—mind, I admit nothing—is more dangerous than when we were working behind the lines in order to spy out the enemy's ground for Wellington. Then we were little more than careless boys; now we are grown men with responsibilities for others, so you must forgive me if I don't confide in you.'

Without meaning to Devenish knew that he sounded abrupt and forbidding: exactly like the grandfather whom he had hated.

Rob's face fell a little. 'You rarely pull the Earl on me, Hal. If you are about to do so permanently, then release me. I want my memories of you to be kind ones.'

'Oh, Goddamn,' said Devenish who rarely blasphemed. 'Believe me, I would tell you if I could. What I am ''up to'' will, I hope, soon be safely over—and then you will be one of the few with whom I may safely share what I have been ''up to''. Don't let us risk our friendship because I have taken what is virtually an oath of secrecy over this matter.'

Rob began to argue with him, but Devenish silenced him with a wave of his hand. 'Leave it, Rob. I have enough to worry about without having to take account of your hurt feelings. Forgive me—and let me go—and don't talk about wanting your release. You are not my prisoner—you may leave at any time if that is what you wish.'

He did not wait for an answer but strode off down the corridor, leaving Rob to ask himself whether, in some fashion not understandable, what troubled Hal had to do with Drusilla Faulkner, Toby Claridge and Leander Harrington.

For the life of him he could not imagine what strange connection could exist between the three of them which would cause Hal to act so uncharacteristically towards the one friend whom he had cherished since his boyhood had ended.

'Damn you, Grandfather,' muttered Devenish aloud as he strode up the stairs, 'you made me over in your image and I shall always hate you for that.'

He paused outside his room. 'On the other hand, you saved me from being like my father—for which I suppose, you ought to have my gratitude. So where does that leave me? An unlikely mixture of the two of you, I suppose!'

'I thought that this was goin' to be a drinking party, Harrington,' said Toby Claridge, looking round Marsham Abbey's small and comfortable drawing room which opened off the cavernous Great Hall with its Minstrels' Gallery, flambeaux holders and pointed Gothic windows, and finding it empty of guests other than himself.

'So it was,' smiled his host, motioning him to a chair before which stood a long low table covered in bottles and glasses, 'but my other guests seem to have mistaken the date. I can only assume that they thought that I was inviting them to come tomorrow and not today.'

Toby not being, as he frequently admitted to himself, great in the thinking line, did not question this somewhat dubious explanation.

'Want me to leave and come back tomorrow?' he asked a trifle mournfully.

'By no means. We can entertain one another by splitting a few bottles between us. The less of them, the more for us.' He handed Toby a glass of port. 'Drink up, Claridge.'

Toby duly obliged. He thought what a jolly good fellow Harrington was as they laughed and talked together—and drank heavily while doing so. Or at least Toby did. He was too busy enjoying himself to notice that Mr Harrington was actually drinking very little.

'And, of course, you'll be at the Brotherhood's next meeting.'

'Of course,' muttered Toby over the top of his glass. He was not drunk enough to be incapable, but was well on the way. Mr Harrington decided to hurl a few darts at him before he fell under the table.

'Not going to let Devenish persuade you otherwise, eh?'

'He said not—I was to go on as I always did,' proclaimed Toby wisely, congratulating himself on remembering so well what Devenish had told him. What he had forgotten in his drunken condition was that this advice was meant to be as secret as their previous conversation.

'Did he, indeed? Now why should he say that?'

Toby nodded importantly before answering. 'Oh, yes. I wasn't to tell anyone that I had informed him about the Brotherhood. It was to be a secret, he said...'

His voice trailed away, agonised, as he grasped that in his drunken state he must have given himself and Devenish away—and to the very man to whom he had sworn to Devenish he would say nothing!

'A secret.' Leander Harrington smiled. 'What secret was this, Claridge? Surely you can tell an old friend.'

'Nothing,' mumbled Toby. Far gone as he was he understood, if only dimly, that he had allowed himself to be cozened into betrayal. 'Can't say. Mustn't say.' He put a finger by his nose and tried to smile as though what he was babbling was of no importance.

Mr Harrington leaned forward and seized him by his cravat, thrusting his face into Toby's as he did so.

'Oh, no, Claridge. You've said both too much—and not enough. Tell me what the secret was which you shared with Devenish—or I'll do for you as Faulkner was done for. You understand me.'

'I can't,' gasped Toby, now so frightened that he was almost sober again. 'I promised that I wouldn't.'

'You promised that you wouldn't!' exclaimed Mr Harrington derisively. 'Have you forgotten the oath you swore to your great master, the one-time archangel, Apollyon? That surely takes precedence over a mere promise to a fellow mortal.'

'No,' gabbled Toby. 'It was made to you, not to the Devil.'

'Yes, but in my capacity as Apollyon's emissary on earth.' Mr Harrington used his not inconsiderable strength to bring his victim to his knees. 'Answer me, I command you.'

Choking and gasping, cursing his unwariness and his folly, Toby mumbled, 'He blackmailed me, I swear it. He said he'd cancel my IOUs if I told him all about the Brotherhood.'

'At last!' Mr Harrington released Toby who fell back into his chair, rubbing his damaged throat. 'You unmitigated ass, Claridge! Do you realise that you may have doomed us all to the hangman's rope since I take it that you told him about Faulkner and the girls.'

'He threatened me with ruin,' half-sobbed Toby. 'I might have known that I was doomed either way.'

'There was no need to drag us down with you,' sneered Mr Harrington. 'And now I will have to deal with Devenish before he hands us over to the authorities—as he surely will. And then...' he paused and smiled '...Apollyon will deal with *you*. And to make sure that you don't go whining to Devenish you'll not leave Marsham. You may send your groom home to report that you have drunk so heavily that you prefer to stay here overnight.'

He was left with no alternative. He was simply poor Sir Toby Claridge whom stronger-minded men and women manipulated for their own use. He had been caught between a rock and a hard place—which was as good a way as any to describe that unholy pair, Leander Harrington and Lord Devenish. He could only hope that he might not at some future date either share Jeremy Faulkner's fate or swing on the end of a rope at Tyburn.

Devenish had ordered horses for himself and an attendant groom to be ready to leave for London shortly before eight o'clock in the morning. He was not to know that Mr Harrington, with several of his most faithful servants who were as deep in the Brotherhood's doings as he was, were, from six o'clock onwards, keeping watch a couple of miles down the byway which led from Tresham to the road to London.

Mr Harrington had sat up a great part of the night debating with himself what Devenish's next move would be. He was now certain that his unexpected visit to Tresham Hall was connected with the authorities wishing to know exactly why there were so many strange deaths and disappearances in the district.

If he were right, then Devenish would not go to the Lord Lieutenant, he would go straight to the Home Secretary for advice and help—which was what Mr

Harrington would do if their positions were reversed. It would do no harm to keep watch on the byway from Tresham Hall and see whether or no Devenish was travelling on it—and by what means. He would then need to improvise.

Devenish, in fact, wished to travel light in order to travel quickly. He had debated setting out the previous evening, but there had been reports of highwaymen working the byway at night and it was a risk which he preferred not to take. Nor did he wish his journey to look other than casual and innocent—as his visit to de Castellane had done.

He had told Rob that he would be back within the day. The full moon was due by the weekend and it might be possible to arrange—with Sidmouth's permission—for the whole gang to be caught at their evil orisons in the crypt and dealt with. How, he was still not sure.

Rob walked with him to his horse, saying below his breath so that the other servants might not hear, 'What bee is buzzing in your bonnet that you must be off to London at such short notice? And so soon after the last time.'

Astride his horse Devenish looked down at his friend. 'I have a mind to visit an old acquaintance,' he drawled. 'Tresham is beginning to pall.' He still dare not tell Rob the truth of the matter.

Rob took this for the empty lie it was. 'Very well,' he said, resigned. 'I'll not question you further. Only, take care of yourself. Not all highway robbery is committed at night—and I wish that you might let me accompany you.'

'Oh, I'm armed,' Devenish told him. 'And so is Martin. I'll be back tonight.' He smiled a little provokingly. 'This reminds me of night rides in Spain. You were a deal more light-hearted about my riding off alone then—behind the French lines as I recall. This is England, Rob.'

He was not quite as airy as he sounded. He had no wish to alert Harrington in any way, make him suspicious. Neither could he be sure that none of the servants at Tresham was involved in the conspiracy of the Brotherhood. He had brought Martin with him from London and could be sure of his loyalty—which was why he had chosen him, and only him.

He was only sorry that he had not been able to leave the morning after he had winkled the truth out of Toby, but there was no plausible explanation which he could give his guests for such a sudden excursion.

Rob watched him ride down the drive, Martin following. Devenish was behaving in a manner which suggested that there was danger, and Rob thought that he might be taking too much for granted by travelling without a proper escort—but there was no moving him when his mind was made up.

He shrugged his shoulders and went back into the Hall. Surely Devenish must be right—this was England in peace time, not Spain during the war. Nevertheless, unease rode on his back for the rest of the day.

Devenish and his groom had travelled exactly two miles down the byway when Leander Harrington and his men rode out of the stand of trees where they had been hiding to confront the pair of them.

'Ah, Devenish, there you are. I have been expecting you ever since that broken reed Claridge babbled in his cups to me about your blackmail and coercion of him. I must ask you to accompany me to the Abbey so that we may debate on what to do with you.'

'Alas,' said Devenish, smiling as easily as though he had not a care in the world, 'I have urgent business elsewhere. Another time, perhaps.'

'Alas, not.' Mr Harrington was mocking him. 'I have no desire for you to go elsewhere. We may, I suspect, usefully debate why that should be at the Abbey.'

Devenish looked at the silent party of mounted men who were now surrounding him and Martin. 'You are determined not to allow me to travel on my way?'

'Quite so, Devenish. I always thought that you were sharper than many give you credit for.'

One of the mounted men sniggered. Martin called to his master, 'M'lord, we are not going to allow him to delay us, surely?' and before Devenish could stop him, he drove his horse between two of the men, shouting, 'Let me pass, sirrah,' and was on his way towards London again.

What followed next shocked even Devenish, who had always counted himself unshockable. Mr Harrington leaned forward negligently, pulled his horse pistol out of its holster and shot Martin in the back. He was flung from his mount to lie, broken, in the road.

'Catch his horse,' Mr Harrington shouted, 'don't let it escape. Now,' he added, turning to Devenish, his smile vicious, 'you know that I mean what I say. Try to imitate your lackey there and I shan't hesitate to shoot you in the back. It would be a pity for you to die before you have done me a few small services, but you must see that there is no question of my ever releasing you.'

'Oh, indeed,' drawled Devenish, nothing about him betraying his anger, both at Harrington for what he had done, and for himself for putting Martin in the way of his death. 'I can quite see that, having committed murder upon murder in the foul name of Apollyon, you will not be able to let me survive to be a potent witness against you.'

'Quite so. Now, you may either ride quietly back to the Abbey with us without trying anything so foolish as to escape, or I shall be compelled to ask my men to manhandle you sufficiently to ensure that you arrive there without having caused us unnecessary trouble. The choice is yours.'

Since it was futile to try to escape at this point it would be foolish to do anything other than surrender gracefully.

'Oh, I always submit to *force majeure*,' Devenish said coolly. 'I learned that lesson from my late beloved grandfather. The trick is to do it as gracefully as possible.'

Afterwards he was astonished at his own apparent cold-bloodedness in the face of his faithful servant's murder. He thanked his grandfather for a gift which he had unwittingly blessed him with: the ability to remain impassive while undergoing both mental and physical torture.

'What a sensible fellow you are, Devenish,' commented Mr Harrington approvingly as he turned his horse for home. 'Just like your grandfather. You resemble him greatly, you know.'

'Do I? I am not of that opinion, but you knew him better than I. Did he join in your fun and games when he was alive?'

'Now, now, Devenish, you know about that already. I had you followed to London before, and knew only that you had visited that mongrel de Castellane. It was only when our friend Claridge spilled his guts to me that I was certain why you had visited him.'

Oh, he had underestimated Harrington all along, had he not? And was about to play a bitter price for it. Although, to be fair to himself, he had not been certain of the elder Harrington's connection with the Black Mass and the Brotherhood before he had visited de Castellane.

'I always guard my back, you see,' Harrington continued. 'I was worried when you returned to Tresham Hall so suddenly after such a long absence, and when you spoke so lightly of the Devil—and behaved so oddly in the crypt—I became even more worried. Hence I had you followed.'

'I see,' said Devenish thoughtfully, rather as though Harrington and he were discussing a problem in logic instead of a problem involving murder and blasphemy. 'We have, I gather, been playing a game of chess in the dark—and now, it seems, have reached checkmate.'

He had, for no reason at all, a sudden brief and agonising vision of Drusilla smiling at him. Drusilla, who had in her possession his letter to Sidmouth detailing his suspicions about Leander Harrington. After Martin's death he dare not put her at risk by threatening Harrington with it. He was sure that if the jovial murderer riding beside him learned of its existence he would not hesitate to hunt down everyone connected in any way with Devenish in an effort to find it and destroy it.

So he said nothing, hoping against hope that they might meet someone on the way back to Marsham Abbey, but, as is always the way, the only people they saw were a few labourers in the fields who stared uncomprehendingly at them as they rode by.

There was no salvation there.

Nor at the Abbey, either. He thought again of Drusilla as though he were holding a talisman in his hand to keep the dark away. He wondered what she was doing—and Giles, too. If he ever managed to get himself out of this trap—which seemed increasingly improbable—he would ask her to marry him so that he might look after them both.

He gave a cynical inward laugh—what a vain hope from a man who could so palpably not look after himself!

Drusilla was having her usual busy day. She half-expected Devenish to visit her, but tried not to count too much on it. Giles, missing the jolly fun and camaraderie with his fellows which he had enjoyed at

Tresham Hall, pronounced himself dead bored and lounged about the house yawning.

In the afternoon he persuaded her to allow him to ride the little mare which had already arrived from Tresham. He set off with Vobster whilst Drusilla was sitting on the lawn with Miss Faulkner. They were embroidering kneelers for Tresham Church—which activity, of course, constantly kept Devenish at the forefront of her mind.

As always that mind circled around his contradictions, and to keep herself steady—and fair to him—she began to list her own contradictions, finding them more and various than she had supposed!

Miss Faulkner said, for once showing some insight, 'Are you thinking about him, Drusilla? Lord Devenish, I mean.'

'Yes,' which was the truth. The other truth was that she was remembering herself in his arms, remembering his whispered endearments and the last words which he had said to her as she left Tresham Hall.

'Perhaps I was wrong about Devenish,' conceded Miss Faulkner grudgingly. 'He's very kind to Giles and not many men are. When I remarked on it he told me that he had once had a little brother, and had never liked being an only child after his brother died. Mr Peter Clifton told me in confidence when we were at Tresham Hall that the rumour was that his grandfather was very harsh with him when he first arrived at Tresham. Perhaps that's why he's so stern.'

Was Devenish stern? Perhaps he was. Perhaps seemed to be a word associated with him.

Miss Faulkner had not quite finished. 'The late Earl's harshness apparently stemmed from the fact that when he found his grandson he was, in manners, speech and habits, little more than a street Arab, and he was determined to make him a person fit to inherit as soon as possible. He was, in fact, the only male heir left. It seems that after his father died he and his mother lived in extreme poverty.'

Drusilla's eyes filled with tears as she thought of the poor boy who had been handed over, friendless, to a cruel old man. His pride, his hauteur, and his apparent coldness stemmed from first his harsh life as a child, and afterwards from his determination to surround his shattered and betrayed self with a hard shell of indifference so that no one should ever come too near him again.

She remembered the tenderness with which Devenish had held little Jackie Milner in his arms, and the stark simplicity with which he had told her, 'I had a little brother once.'

'Why did Mr Clifton tell you this, Cordelia? And how did he come to know what is known to few, if any?'

Miss Faulkner flushed and looked away. 'I spoke to him because I could see that you were strongly attracted to Devenish—which worried me. I asked him for his advice—as you know he is reputed to be remarkable for his common sense—because I was fearful for you. He told me that he had reason to know that beneath his haughty exterior and cutting tongue Devenish had a kind heart.

'As to how he knew Lord Devenish's history, he became a friend and confidant of the late Earl in his old age, and shortly before he died he had spoken to Mr Clifton of his regret concerning his harsh treatment of his grandson after he had brought him to Tresham.'

Drusilla looked away. 'Thank you, Cordelia,' she said at last, 'for telling me this sad story. It explains so much about him, does it not? But who, looking at him now, would have thought that he had such an unhappy past?'

'Indeed,' agreed Miss Faulkner, whose tender heart was also bleeding for the poor lost child whom Devenish had been. 'So unlikely, is it not? It shows, however, that we must not judge people too hastily. One could never have guessed that m'lord had ever known real privation or suffering.'

Their embroidery forgotten, the two women sat silent, considering the wheel of fortune which, as the old poets said, raised some men high and brought some men low.

It was thus quite apposite that Vobster should come running on to the lawn, his honest face distressed. 'Oh, madam, I'm sorry to bring you sad news, but there's nothing for it. Through no fault of his own Master Giles has had a bad fall...'

'Not from his horse,' exclaimed Drusilla, jumping up, her face white.

'Alas, yes, madam. We were on the path by the brook when a stray dog, a great brute of a thing, ran at the mare so that she reared and unhorsed poor Master Giles in an instant. The mare was unhurt, but

Master Giles was knocked unconscious, and although we could not find that he had suffered any real injury he didn't recover, so we brought him home. He has been carried to his room—still unconscious. He has the worst luck, madam, no doubt of it. I have been riding these many years and have had none like it.'

Devenish and his childhood forgotten, Drusilla and Miss Faulkner hurried to Giles's room to find him lying there still and white. The doctor had been sent for and they could only hope that he might be able to diagnose the cause of his condition.

As Vobster had said, there was not a mark on him.

## Chapter Thirteen

By this time the same could not be said of Devenish. At first when they had arrived at the Abbey Mr Harrington had been everything that was civilised. He had produced a bottle of port, and asked Devenish, who had remained standing after he had been escorted to the little room off the Great Hall, to drink with him. They were not the only persons in the room: two of Mr Harrington's largest servants stood on each side of the door, their eyes firmly on Devenish, and ready to do Mr Harrington's bidding.

Devenish had refused the offered drink politely. He saw no point in ranting and raving at his captor.

'I must commend your common sense,' said Mr Harrington, smiling. 'Many men in your condition would be railing at me and demanding to be freed. Do try this port—it's excellent.'

'By no means,' retorted Devenish coolly, 'I never eat and drink with persons who are determined to kill me. I am, in fact, all agog to discover why I am still in the land of the living. It cannot be that you are merciful for you disposed of poor young Martin easily enough.'

'Oh, I had no further use for him,' replied Mr Harrington airily. 'Now you are different. First of all I must ask you whether you have informed anyone else of your suspicions concerning the Black Mass and the Brotherhood. Secondly, when you have been good enough to oblige me on that score I shall keep you here until our next service at the time of the full moon. I decided some time ago that offering the Devil a male human sacrifice might spur him to some action on my behalf. He has been singularly idle lately.

'I say my rather than our because the Brotherhood do not fully understand that the main purpose of our offerings to Apollyon is to bring about our long-delayed revolution in Britain. They believe that what we do is merely idle amusement—and see nothing serious in it.'

Devenish was fascinated. 'Idle amusement, indeed! The sacrifice of young women and the murders of your valet and of poor young Faulkner scarcely seem to come under that heading! And do I understand that I am to be added to the pantheon of your sacrifices? Are you quite sure that the Brotherhood will stomach the murder of a leading member of the aristocracy, the friend of Liverpool, Sidmouth and Canning!'

Mr Harrington smiled. 'I see that you underrate me again. They will, of course, not be aware of who is being sacrificed. You will be masked and dressed for this great occasion and Apollyon's emissary on earth, myself, will tell them that you are a traitor who tried to inform on them to the authorities. Bearing that in mind, they will enthusiastically endorse your death.'

'Will they, indeed? And shall I rest quiet while this delightful ceremony is going on?'

Mr Harrington frowned at the bitterly jesting tone Devenish was adopting. 'Your mockery is not fitting. You would not mock God in his church, so why should you mock the Devil in his? You will, of course, be gagged beneath the mask.'

'Your ingenuity fascinates me. Before I am served up to—Apollyon was it not?—perhaps you will inform me what figure the mask I shall wear will represent?'

'Why, Gabriel, of course, my leader's arch enemy.' Mr Harrington's voice was pitying. 'I am surprised that a man of your learning should need to ask.'

'A man of my learning is wondering what the Devil I am doing here at all,' riposted Devenish, 'participating in an act of mummery only fit for a puppet show at a fair rather than as an occupation for supposedly sane men...'

He got no further. Almost negligently Mr Harrington struck him in the face. 'You shall not mock my master, Devenish, or those who worship him.'

With difficulty Devenish kept himself erect and impassive. He saw one of the servants start forward in case he replied to Mr Harrington in kind.

'You may tell your bully boys,' he said coldly, 'that I have no intention of inviting their ministrations by trying to give you the thrashing which you deserve. Now I wish to get down to business with you, without further delay. Firstly, I have no intention of telling you whether or not I have informed anyone of your criminal activities, and secondly I have no intention of being served up on Apollyon's altar for the idle amusement of my more stupid neighbours.

'As to how I shall avoid that I have at present no notion, but I am an inventive man, and I shall have several days to make my plans. That is all.'

He turned his back on Mr Harrington, who deciding that nothing was to be gained by further action on his part, said in a bored voice, 'Wattie, see that Lord Devenish is removed to the Abbey's gaol and when you get him there, try to change his mind for him. Be careful how you treat him for I don't wish him to be visibly damaged. Also he must be able to walk to his doom and Apollyon's triumph.'

'Aye, aye, sir,' said the largest man of all, a great bruiser of a fellow who was rather disappointed that he wasn't going to be able to have a real go at a belted Earl.

'Come, you,' he grunted, 'do as my master bids,' and he seized Devenish by the arm.

Devenish wrenched himself free. 'You may take your dirty hands off me. I am not stupid enough to try to escape when I'm in the company of three felons all of whom are larger than I am. You may lead the way and I will follow.'

'You disappoint me, Devenish,' Mr Harrington called after him as he left, 'I had thought you had more spirit. I misjudged you. I see that you are a commonplace coward after all.'

'Oh, a coward perhaps,' Devenish called after him, 'but commonplace—never. You do misjudge me there.'

He wished that he felt as brave as he sounded. He wished it even more later on after the large man and one of his smaller fellows had worked him over without success and left him feeling sick and winded on the floor of the Abbey's gaol.

It was a tiny barred cell at the corner of what had, in earlier times, been a kind of guard room, reached only by going through the Great Hall and down a corridor which ended at the room so that a prisoner trying to escape had nowhere to hide.

His tormentor had yelled at him, 'You needn't think that you will defy me forever. I shall go to my master for permission to give you a real beating, and we'll see how brave you are then.'

Probably not brave at all, thought Devenish morosely. Whilst the bully boys had knocked him about he had tried to remember some of the tricks which the Master Magician had taught him to hold back pain. Tricks which had enabled him to defy his grandfather until he had decided to beat him at his own game.

One of them was to detach his mind from his body by slowing his breathing beforehand and thinking of something distant and far away and trying to hold that image even through inflicted pain.

'An old brown man taught me that trick,' Master Gabriel had said, 'he called it yoga. He said that you could sit in snow and keep warm if you did it properly.'

Maybe, thought Devenish wryly, but it was a trifle more difficult when trying to ignore what Harrington's bruisers were doing to him. But it had succeeded enough for him to hold his tongue and thwart his tormentors—for the time being.

To prevent himself from thinking about his present desperate situation he tried another trick. He called up Drusilla's face and her graceful figure—and then he sat beside her in the garden at Lyford House with the sun shining down on them, and the birds calling, so that when the disgruntled chief bruiser came to see how he was faring, he found him lying on the floor asleep, a smile on his face.

The bruiser was disgruntled because Mr Harrington had refused to let him work m'lord over seriously, saying that it was likely that he had, in truth, not told anyone of his suspicions, and for the time being he might be allowed to stay in the gaol unharmed.

He kicked m'lord awake, bade him stand up, and then he tied his hands behind his back—'No point in letting him be too comfortable,' Mr Harrington had said, 'pain might take the edge off that nasty tongue of his.'

What neither he nor his bruiser knew was that Devenish had immediately tried another trick to see whether he could still perform it. The ability to hold his hands in such a way that the person tying them was unaware that at any time his victim could free himself if he wanted to.

Devenish did not want to escape now, but it was pleasant to know that he could still work the trick. Who knew when it might come in useful?

And in the meantime he worried when and if Rob Stammers would realise that he was missing—and what he might then do—if he were not already lost to the Brotherhood...

Rob Stammers did not worry overmuch when Hal did not return at night as he said that he would. It was likely that his business had taken longer than he thought and that he would return on the next day.

When he did not, nor on the day after that, either, he began to worry. He worried even further when one of the stable lads came to tell him that the whip which Jack Martin, Hal's groom, had always carried with him, had been found on land about half a mile from the byway which Hal and Martin had taken.

'Two miles down the byway it were,' said the lad.

'How do you know it was Martin's whip?' asked Rob reasonably. 'After all, one whip is much like another.'

'Not that one,' said the lad positively. 'It had a chased silver handle with Jack's initials on it. M'lord gave it to him for faithful service. He treasured that whip, did Jack, he'd not be parted from it—so what was it doing there?'

He passed the whip over Rob's desk to prove that he was telling true, as he later said to the other lads when Rob sent him away.

Rob stared at the whip. 'Nothing else?' he asked. 'You found nothing else there?'

The lad shook his head. 'Oh, there'd been a party of men on horseback recently in the stand of trees by the byway, not far from where the whip was found. It's a queer do, master, that it is. Why would Jack leave his whip there?'

Why, indeed? Hal was missing, and Martin had been with him. And Hal had admitted that the business which he was engaged on was dangerous.

What was the business? Rob did not know.

Had Hal ever reached London?

He would send a messenger to Innescourt House to check whether Hal had arrived there, and if he had whether something had occurred which had caused him to delay his return. After that he would go to the spot where Martin's whip had been found and use the skills which he had learned in Spain to try to discover any clues which might offer an explanation as to how the whip came to be there.

On the way he would call at Lyford House to ask Mrs Faulkner whether Hal had said anything to her which might throw light on his mysterious journey to London.

Drusilla came down from Giles's bedside when Rob Stammers was announced. Giles was still unconscious. He was lying there so peacefully with no sign of injury on him that the doctor had just told her that it was almost as though he didn't want to wake up.

Which was very unlike Giles who, despite his crippled leg, was always lively and ready for anything, as he had once said.

Rob had been informed by the butler of Giles's sad condition and immediately offered her his commiserations. 'You must not lose hope,' he told her, 'when I was in Spain I heard more than once of soldiers who had suffered a head injury which left them unmarked but unconscious and who later recovered quite suddenly.'

He didn't tell her of the ones who hadn't recovered. He could only hope that Giles was one of the lucky ones.

Drusilla said wearily, 'He really is the most unfortunate boy. Vobster tells me that his accident was due to no foolish act of his—which is some comfort, but not much.'

She thought that Rob was looking as harried as she felt, and wondered why. She was soon to find out.

'I've come about Hal,' he began. 'I mean Lord Devenish. I know that you and he are great friends these days. He set off for London suddenly two evenings ago without giving me any information as to why his errand was so urgent. I wondered if he had let slip to you any hint of what he might be about.'

He was putting his question so tactfully that for a moment Drusilla was not quite sure of what he was asking her.

'Has he confided in me, you mean?'

'Exactly. For once, he has said nothing to me, and now I need to know what his business was.' Rob did not immediately wish to tell her that he thought that Devenish might be missing.

'He has said nothing of this recent visit, but...' and she hesitated '...he did ask me to do something for him not long ago. Before I tell you what it was I must ask you to be truthful with me. Do you suppose Lord Devenish to be in any danger?'

She had almost said Hal, but she remembered that Devenish had trusted her with the letter, and not Rob, so she must go warily.

'Now, why do you think that possible?' exclaimed Rob, a little surprised.

'You have not answered my question,' returned Drusilla.

'Yes. I will tell you more only when you have told me what Devenish said to you.'

'On the contrary, I shall tell you nothing until you tell me why you think that he is in danger.'

Rob stared at her. Behind her demure appearance she was one of the most strong-minded females whom he had ever met. Was that why Hal was attracted to her? Like calling to like. He gave in.

'Very well. The morning after the house party ended Hal set off for London with Martin, his most trusted groom. He said that he was on an urgent, and perhaps dangerous, errand and would be back the same day—even if he had to travel through the night. So far he has not returned—which is very unlike him. He is punctilious over such matters. This morning one of the stable lads found Martin's whip abandoned not far from the byway they would have followed en route for London.

'Martin's friends assure me that he would never willingly have been parted from his whip and I am bound to ask myself if some mischance has befallen them. I have sent a messenger to London to find out whether they ever reached Innescourt House. When I have left you I shall go to the place where the whip was found to see if I can discover anything more.'

Drusilla sat down—and motioned to Rob to do the same. She remembered how urgent Hal had been when he had given her his letter. She looked at stolid Rob sitting opposite to her, his face anxious, his fingers drumming lightly on his knee, a sure sign of distress in a man: she had seen Jeremy doing it.

She would trust him. Without more ado she told of Devenish having left the letter for Sidmouth with her, and her promise that she would forward it if any harm came to him.

'He did not tell me,' said Rob, a trifle bitterly. 'He did not trust me—God knows why he couldn't. We have been friends for so long.'

Drusilla leaned forward to put a hand on his. 'I am sorry to inform you that he told me that he could trust nobody and the reason that he gave the letter to me was because it was not possible for me to know anything of what he was about. Oh, he didn't say that directly, but it was the only meaning I could put on what he did say.'

'And you have the letter?'

'Yes. In a safe place.'

'And if everything points to him being in danger, or needing help, you will send it on to Lord Sidmouth.'

'Indeed.'

'And you have no notion of what is in it?'

'None. He implied that it would not be safe for me to know.'

'In God's name,' exclaimed Rob, exasperated, 'what can he be hiding—have you truly no idea?'

'Only that I think that it has something to do with Jeremy's murder, the disappearing girls and the attack on Giles. He never said so, it is simply what I am supposing.'

'Then we must open the letter before you send it on because I can think of no connection at all between them.'

'No, I promised that I would not.'

Rob struck his hands together. 'You will not reconsider?'

'I cannot,' she said simply. 'Only if you could tell me that his life is at stake if I don't.'

Rob groaned. 'I don't even know that he *is* missing, or that his life is at risk. I only feel that something is wrong.'

They stared at one another. Drusilla said, 'He told me that the letter is to go only to Sidmouth—it was too dangerous otherwise.'

'Because he didn't trust me,' exclaimed Rob violently. 'But now you know that you can.'

'No,' said Drusilla, 'I don't. For you might be pretending to be concerned about Hal in order to get the letter from me and read it. If he had wanted you to know what was in it, he would have told you.'

Her logic was impeccable—and, for a female, re-markable. Fortunately Rob did not tell her so or she would have been even firmer with him than she was already being.

'Until you tell me that you are sure that Hal is miss-ing, I shall not send the letter. If you are, then I shall forward it—unopened, as he wished.'

Rob rose. 'Very well. I shall go immediately to where Martin's whip was found. If I discover anything to suggest that Hal is in danger I shall return at once. Otherwise I must wait until my messenger returns from London—and in the meantime we are doing nothing for Hal.'

'It was his choice,' said Drusilla simply.

'Yes, the obstinate devil.' Rob was too annoyed to be polite. Oddly Drusilla thought that this did him credit and she was prepared to believe him honest, but she must still do what Hal had wished.

Rob rode away in a vile temper, the astonished stable lad who had found Martin's whip behind him. He had always known Mr Stammers to be the mildest of men but he had bellowed orders at him like a madman and ridden like the devil himself to the place where Martin's whip had been found.

Rob dismounted warily and walked around trying to disturb the undergrowth as little as possible. Not far from where the lad said the whip had been found were the marks of something heavy having been dragged along. Men on horseback had been there—and more than one of them. He tracked around and through the stand of trees where there were again, as the lad had said, evidence of horsemen, and then he examined the byway.

Unfortunately it had not rained recently and the ground was dry so Hal and Martin had left no hoof marks behind them. Other than the discovery of the whip, there was nothing to indicate that Hal or Martin had ever been there.

Rob swore. The whip in itself, without any other evidence, proved nothing. And who, in the smiling landscape around them could have a reason to attack someone as powerful as Devenish? As he had told Drusilla he could not, for the life of him, see any connection between young Faulkner's death, the disappearance of the girls and the attack on Giles.

There was no point in returning to Lyford House and Mrs Faulkner. The only thing left to him was to cut his losses for the moment and wait for his messenger to come back from London.

On the way home he met Leander Harrington, attended by one of the large fellows whom he favoured as servants. He took the opportunity to stop him, and say, 'We are well met. I wonder if Devenish said anything to you when you were at Tresham Hall to indicate why he might suddenly need to go to London. After all, you are a JP and I thought that he might have confided in you.'

For some reason—he had always been a cautious man who played his cards close to his chest—Rob did not mention his recent conversation with Drusilla, nor even that he had visited her.

Mr Harrington smiled easily at him. 'No, indeed, he said nothing to me. I was not aware that he was going to London—which explains why I have not seen him lately. Is the matter so urgent that it cannot wait until his return?'

Rob could not say, 'I have a strong feeling that something was wrong,' it might sound feeble. Nor did he wish to babble about whips, so he held his tongue over that, as he had done over visiting Drusilla.

He was not to know it, but it was just as well that he had remained silent.

Mr Harrington stared after him as he rode away and said casually to his attendant. 'It's a good thing that the full moon is tomorrow night. It doesn't leave very much time for Stammers to go running round after his absent patron. In forty-eight hours we shall be safe— and m'lord will no longer be a danger.'

He turned his horse for home, thinking happily of Devenish sitting half-starved and impotent in his prison cell at the Abbey.

He would not have been so cheerful had he known of the letter sitting quietly in a pigeon hole in Drusilla Faulkner's escritoire.

Drusilla returned to her vigil over Giles after Rob had left her. His nurse told her excitedly that 'Master Giles opened his eyes for a moment and looked at me. He closed them almost at once. I tried to talk to him but he cannot hear me.'

This was little enough in the way of good cheer over Giles's condition, but it was the first time that he had shown any sign of life which must offer them a little hope.

Drusilla sat by his bed and talked quietly to him, his lax hand in hers. She spoke of his dogs, of her promise that, taking Devenish's advice, she would arrange for him to study at Oxford.

'You can take Vobster,' she told him. 'He's such a steady fellow and he thinks the world of you.' She did not tell him that Devenish might be missing, but when Cordelia relieved her so that she might eat a little dinner, she wondered as she walked downstairs, whether bad news might revive him rather than good.

If he was ever going to revive again, that was. The oddest thing about his condition being that when he was lifted up and a cup of warm milk was put to his lips, he drank it eagerly. Which, no doubt, was why the doctor asserted that, for some reason, he did not wish to regain full consciousness.

And now she had two men to worry about, for the thought that Devenish might be in trouble was yet another burden for her sad heart. Rob Stammers had not returned, which was something of a relief, since it must mean that he had found nothing to indicate that Devenish might be in trouble.

Now there was nothing either of them could do: it was merely a question of waiting for Rob's messenger to return from London. She could only hope that his news might be good and that it would not be necessary to send Devenish's letter to Lord Sidmouth.

\*     \*     \*

Devenish, whose only hope was that Rob had remained true to him and was trying to discover why he had not returned to Tresham, was lying on the floor of his cell. He was waiting for one of his captors to bring him his meagre dinner. He had little idea of the time. All his possessions and most of his clothing had been stripped from him, leaving him wearing only his shirt and breeches.

Wattie, his largest gaoler, had been particularly pleased to inherit his gold watch and the signet ring which was the only gift which he had ever received from his grandfather. To his surprise the loss of that had grieved him even more than the privations he was suffering.

One reason for his ability to endure the long days of solitary confinement was that he had continued to practise the yoga which Master Gabriel had taught him—much to the disgust of Wattie and his henchman.

He refused to sit on the stool which was all the furniture allowed him and instead lay on the cell's floor, summoning up mental pictures of himself and Drusilla walking hand in hand in the most beautiful scenery which he could imagine.

Never once did he try to visualise the pair of them in bed, enjoying themselves, because Master Gabriel had told him that tranquillity and peace were essential. Images of battle and of sexual intercourse were to be avoided. His other occupation was to try to think up ways and means of escaping from his deadly predicament—and this involved reconstructing in his head the ground plan of Marsham Abbey.

The main problem he had to face was that the only way out of the Abbey from the cell in which he was confined was through the Great Hall and the main doorway—which would make any escape difficult.

Wattie's disgust was roused by his constantly discovering m'lord lying supine on the floor, staring at the ceiling. He had never made the slightest effort to defy him, or to rail at him, as most of those whom Wattie previously held prisoner had done.

'Why, he's no more spunk than a puling priest,' he had told Mr Harrington, a sneer on his face as well as in his voice.

Mr Harrington said, 'Are you sure? Such is not his reputation.'

'Ah, well, but he's allus been in charge afore, hasn't he? Not so clever now, is he?'

Mr Harrington remained uneasy. When Wattie took his next frugal meal to Devenish, he, and not the other large bruiser, accompanied him. As Wattie had said, they found Devenish lying peacefully on the floor, on his back, his eyes shut.

For some reason this irritated Mr Harrington mightily. He snarled through the bars as Wattie opened the door to push Devenish's dinner inside, 'Get up, man. I wish to speak to you.'

Devenish opened his eyes, and turning his head sideways without making any attempt to do as he was ordered, said mildly, 'Indeed not. I am quite comfortable as I am. My position is no bar to us having a pleasant chat, if that is what you want.'

He had always found that these tactics had infuriated his grandfather beyond belief. Mr Harrington was no different. He wished that he had brought Wattie's fellow with them, but Wattie would doubtless be able to make Devenish see reason on his own.

'Kick him to his feet,' he roared. 'I refuse to talk to him until he behaves sensibly.'

Wattie duly obliged by kicking Devenish in the ribs, hard. Devenish rolled away into a corner where he took up a position with his head between his knees which he had drawn up to his chin, so that he was now in the shape of a ball.

Furious, Wattie caught him under the armpits and tried to pull him to his feet. This proved difficult since Devenish refused to co-operate and hung, a dead weight, from Wattie's paws.

'Should have brought Jem with us,' panted Wattie as Mr Harrington roared.

'Let the fool drop, Wattie. What game are you playing with us, Devenish?'

'No game,' returned Devenish pleasantly, rolling on to his face so that his voice was muffled. 'I much prefer the view of the floor to the view of you and friend Wattie. Say what you have to say—and go.'

Prisoner he might be, dishevelled and barefoot, his civilised hauteur stripped from him, but in some odd way he still managed to hold the whip hand in a situation where he ought to have been a humiliated victim.

Devenish could have told them that he had been taught by two masters how to conduct himself in a tight corner. Master Gabriel and his grandfather could not have been less alike, but both of them had done their share in making him the man he was. Master Gabriel because he had helped him, his grandfather because he had not.

'Shall I do him over, sir?' ground out Wattie. 'He needs a sharp lesson.'

'No, leave him alone and take his dinner away. If all he does is lie on the floor he doesn't need to eat. I wonder at you, Devenish, I really do. Where is your dignity, man?'

Devenish did not answer him. Before Wattie could bend down to remove his dinner, he rolled over again, seized the plate, and began to cram into his mouth as much as possible of the meagre fare on it before it disappeared.

'Too hungry to be dignified,' he said, his mouth full. 'Do go away, Harrington. Your conversation was never your best point, and any virtue it once had seems to have disappeared.'

Wattie wrestled the tin plate away from him and kicked him for good measure before leaving the cell. He turned at the door and roared, 'You'll sing another tune tomorrow night when we tie you to the altar.'

Mr Harrington nodded agreement, and added briskly, dwelling lovingly on each sadistic word, 'Indeed he will. Remember the girls, Wattie, how they screamed at the end—and that pair of traitors, Jeremy Faulkner and my valet. They didn't relish their punishment overmuch, either. Nor will you, Devenish, you'll be no different from the rest when the devil claims you.'

'Exactly, and now you know why I'm lying on the floor. I'm rehearsing for the pantomime Harrington here is going to put on tomorrow. Wouldn't want to let him down. Must get my screams out in the right order.'

He grinned infuriatingly up at Mr Harrington who turned away and, without speaking to Devenish again, ordered Wattie to lock him up and give him nothing more to eat or drink until the morning.

'He's not a puling priest,' he informed Wattie crossly as they made their way back to the Abbey's living quarters. 'Far from it. He made fools of the pair of us. It will be a pleasure to cut his throat for him tomorrow.'

'What I don't understand,' Wattie whined at his master, 'is why you won't let me duff him up. That would change his tune, for sure.'

'I've told you, I don't want him disfigured, because after we have sacrificed him we shall unmask him so that all the Brotherhood will see and know that the strongest power of all belongs to our master Apollyon if even such as Devenish cannot stand against him.'

The other reason, of which he did not inform Wattie, was he thought that, by involving all of the Brotherhood in Devenish's murder, not only had he made them accessories to it but none would dare stand against him in case they, too, ended on Apollyon's altar. Nor would they dare to inform on him to the authorities if, by doing so, they chanced sharing his punishment...

\* \* \*

And that little scene, Devenish said to himself somewhat morosely when his tormentors had departed, was all very fine and clever tonight, but, God help me, unless I can think up something tricky between now and tomorrow night which will get me out of this confounded pickle, I shall be cat's meat for all my haughty lordship.

He lay down again and contemplated the price of failure, before going on to try to plan success. His plans of necessity were vague. He would need to improvise—something which he had often done in Spain—and he could only trust that the talent had not left him. After that he dreamed of Drusilla and before he knew it Master Gabriel's magic had worked again and he was asleep.

## Chapter Fourteen

Drusilla started up from sleep in the night, suddenly wide awake. She had been dreaming of Hal—she rarely thought of him now as Devenish—and some nameless fear drove her out of her bed and into the little study which opened off her bedroom. The moon was almost full, which normally would have cheered her, for she did not care for the dark, but tonight the moon offered her no solace.

She drew the study curtains, used her tinder box to light a candle and opened her escritoire; a charming, graceful piece which had been a present from her dead father. She then pulled from its pigeon hole the letter which Hal had given her. For a moment she held it in her hand like a talisman before laying it down on the desk.

Was Rob Stammers right? Ought she to open it? Was it her duty to Hal to do exactly as he had asked, or did a higher duty require her to disobey him, if by doing so, she could help him immediately in whatever danger he might be in.

Moved again by instinct rather than reason she picked up the letter and the candle and returned to her bedroom. She climbed into bed, tucked the letter under her pillow—it was as near as she could get to him in his absence—blew out the candle and tried to sleep.

He was in her dreams again. She was promenading with him in a city which she had never visited, but had once seen in a coloured print. It was Venice. They were walking by the Grand Canal—and how did she know that?—and then they were in a gondola drifting past noble palazzos and under delicately pretty bridges. He had an arm around her and was speaking to her—only she could not hear what he was saying. She only knew that they were together and that they were happy.

The sun was up and shone on the water. Then, without warning, it disappeared, and she was in a dark, strangely suffocating place. From being pleasantly warm she was icy cold. There were bars in the room. She knew that although she could not see them.

And then that vision was gone, and she was back in Venice, but only for a moment for the shock of these sudden changes woke her up again, shivering this time. Hal had been trying to tell her something—but what? She pulled the letter from under her pillow and held it in her hand.

Drusilla was sure of one thing, and one thing only. Hal was in danger. She was certain of that, if of nothing else. She had no notion of where he might be, nor of how she might help him. She would give Rob Stammers one more day, and if, by then, he had no more news, she would open the letter herself.

*     *     *

In his cell Devenish lay shivering. He had been lying awake and had conjured up Drusilla. Remembering his dreams he had taken her to Venice and had told her that he loved her and wished to marry her. Only, she had not answered him, but looked at him with great wondering eyes. He had tried so hard to make her hear what he was saying that he forgot what Master Gabriel had taught him. The vision had vanished and he was back in his cell once more.

After a short time, when he had composed himself again, he tried to revisit Venice, but for some reason the vision would not hold for more than a few seconds, so he let it go.

He was bound to Drusilla now by such deep emotional ties that their very existence destroyed his ability to recall her without breaking the calm which Master Gabriel had told him was necessary if he were to be successful in removing his essential self from any place where he might be suffering.

Instead, he thought himself back into the gardens at Tresham where as a boy he had taken his book in order to avoid his grandfather. He lay on a bench again, in a late spring afternoon, and sleep came at last, shortly before the dawn of the day which Leander Harrington had promised him would be his last.

It was the longest day of his life. Wattie brought him black bread and water for his breakfast. Luncheon never came. What he thought must be an early dinner was gruel. In between them he tried to rest, and, using the neck strings which he had ripped from his shirt, he practised a few more of Master Gabriel's tricks.

When Wattie finally came into the outer room his henchman, Bart, trailed behind him. He was a stocky man with a woebegone face—Devenish thought that he looked like the second murderer in a Shakespearean play. He was carrying black monk's robes, rope and what appeared to be masks.

Devenish could hear a great bustle outside. Men were shouting, and Leander Harrington's voice could be heard. Then Wattie shut the heavy door, which cut off the noise, and impatiently ordered Bart to lay down the robes before he unlocked the door of Devenish's cell.

'Stand up,' he ordered, 'or it will be the worse for you.'

'Such originality,' mocked Devenish as he did as he was told—somewhat to Wattie's surprise.

'Decided to be reasonable, have you?'

'Depends what you mean by reasonable,' drawled Devenish, 'but I think a man ought to go to his death with a little dignity, don't you?'

Wattie sniggered, 'Going to miss my fun with you, am I?'

'Not exactly,' returned Devenish. 'I'm sure that, like the rest of the audience, you'll enjoy watching me sacrificed in the crypt.'

Wattie, disappointed at being deprived of a chance to do his victim over, shouted, 'Bart, help me to tie his hands behind his back. I'll hold him for you. And as for you,' he added, turning on Devenish, 'you're wrong about the crypt. Seeing as how you're such an important fellow my master has chosen the Great Hall for our ceremony tonight. We've spent all day transforming it—you should be honoured.'

He stopped taunting his victim long enough to grab him by the shoulders and swing him round. 'Put your hands behind your back, sirrah, so we can truss our goose.'

Devenish duly obliged. He felt Bart fumble with the rope behind him and smiled to himself. Master Gabriel's tuition had not been lost on him. He offered Bart no resistance—indeed, he appeared to be helping him.

Wattie stood back, his hands on his hips, watching Bart at work and grinning at Devenish's apparent subservience. 'Not so noisy now, are we, m'lord? Have you nothing clever left to say?'

'Only that I am quite aware of the honour that you are doing me. I trust that my mask *is* different from yours. I wouldn't like Apollyon to become confused and sacrifice the wrong victim.'

Wattie began to laugh. 'Oh, he thinks of everything, does Apollyon. As he told you, you've the mask of the archangel Gabriel, and we've the masks of Apollyon's attendant devils. I wanted a pitchfork to carry wi' me, but he said we weren't at Drury Lane.'

'Indeed, not,' said Devenish, who was busy working his hands free of Bart's knots, and blessing the man who had taught him how to do it. 'Much better organised and real life, too. Hurry up and bring on the mummery. I can't wait to see what Gabriel looks like. I rather fancy meeting my maker looking like an arch-angel.'

'Fetch the masks and robes, Bart,' ordered Wattie importantly. He kicked the cell door open and turned back to face Devenish who was now sitting on the stool which he had previously rejected.

For the first time Wattie felt some compunction over what he was doing. 'You're taking this mighty cool. You won't suffer much, you know. He's a rare hand with the knife is Apollyon.'

'Charmed to know that,' murmured Devenish feel-ingly, 'it makes me feel much better.'

'Aye, there is that,' agreed Wattie. He shouted through the open door, 'What's taking you so long, Bart?'

Bart glumly held out the robes and the masks. 'There's only two on 'em here, not three. I've left one behind.'

'Oh, hellfire and damnation,' returned Wattie, an ex-clamation which seemed highly appropriate given the circumstances, thought Devenish. 'You great fool, can you never do anything right! Here, come and guard our man, I'll have to fetch them myself.'

'I can't really count,' said Bart apologetically to Devenish as he entered the cell after Wattie had roared impatiently away. 'Me mam couldn't afford to send me to the Dame's school.'

'A pity, that,' agreed Devenish sympathetically, ris-ing from his stool and walking towards Bart. A horri-fied expression crossed his face. 'For God's sake, man, there's a rat over there!'

'There is? Where?' shouted Bart, his face more hangdog than ever.

'Over there,' cried Devenish, motioning with his head in the direction of the outer door. 'I hate the damn'd things, always have.'

'Me, too,' agreed Bart. 'I'll kill it.' He swung round, offering Devenish a splendid view of his back.

Without further ado Devenish sprang. He flung the rope with which Bart had tied him up—and which he had straight away undone—around Bart's neck and pulled. Gasping and gurgling, Bart fell against him, his hands rising uselessly to try to save himself from strangulation.

Devenish bore him to the floor, took off one of Bart's heavy shoes and knocked him out with it. He then used the rope to tie Bart's hands behind his back.

Praying that Wattie would not return too soon he darted through the door, picked up the two robes and masks—one of which he was happy to see was Gabriel's—and wrestled the unconscious Bart into one of the robes before tying the Gabriel mask on to him.

Next he dragged him on his back into the middle of the floor to lie there as he had done since he had been captured. He then put on the other robe and the devil's mask himself. Finally he pulled out of his breeches pocket his two shirt strings which he had twisted together to strengthen them—and waited for Wattie.

Fortune had been with him for Wattie returned almost immediately carrying the third robe and the second devil's mask.

'Good work,' he said approvingly at the sight of Bart apparently dressed ready for the ceremony. 'And quick work. The Mass has already begun and we shall be sent for soon.'

He stared at the supposed Devenish. 'What the devil is he doing lying on the floor again?'

'Got cold feet,' grunted Devenish hoarsely. 'Swooned.' He thanked God that Bart was a man of few words and those barely understandable.

'Has he, now? Not so brave after all.'

He kicked the supposed Devenish hard in the ribs and when that did not answer, bent down, and grunted angrily 'Come on, man, wake up…'

He got no further. He had presented Devenish with a perfect target, allowing him to do to Wattie with his shirt strings what he had done to Bart with the rope. When Wattie's struggles had subsided he pulled him into the corner and flung the third monk's robe over him.

He had neither the time nor the need to dress him up.

Panting slightly, for he had not eaten properly since he had been captured, and exhaustion was beginning to claim him, Devenish pondered on what he might do next.

He decided that there was nothing for it but to try to escape through the Great Hall. Chance had aided him so far. He had to pray that chance would aid him again.

\*   \*   \*

Wattie had been telling the truth. Leander Harrington had been determined that sacrificing someone as important as Devenish to His Satanic Majesty should be done in as splendid a style as possible. This night's work would begin a new era. There would be no more skulking in crypts.

The altar had been set up at the far end of the room between the door which led to the kitchens and the door which led to the small Entrance Hall. It was covered in a black velvet cloth trimmed with silver. Mr Harrington himself stood directly behind it, clad in his robes as Apollyon. They, too, were of black velvet. He wore the traditional devil's mask which had the face and horns of a goat. Parson Lawson stood before the altar ready to begin the ceremony. He was wearing a mask similar to those which Wattie and Bart were to have worn.

On the altar was an upside-down cross and a silver chalice which contained red wine. In front of the altar, as in church, benches for the Mass's congregation had been set out with a wide aisle between them. Light was provided by flambeaux: giant fiery torches which were fixed in the metal holders which had been part of the Great Hall since medieval times.

At the far end of the room was the heavy door which led to the living quarters of the Abbey, including the room containing the cell in which Devenish had been held prisoner. Flambeaux were fixed, head high, on either side of it. Devenish had to pass through this crowded room before finding freedom.

Difficult though it would be he concluded that it might be easier to escape from it than it would have been to free himself from the crypt. All the same, he had no real idea of how he was going to accomplish this. Chance, he told himself, as he ran towards the Great Hall, chance must be my guide.

It had, however, already helped him when Bart had left one of the robes behind. Successfully working Gabriel's trick with the confining ropes and then escaping would have been much more difficult if he had had both Bart and Wattie to deal with at the same time, instead of being left alone with Bart. He could not really hope that chance might favour him twice in the same night.

Perhaps he could sneak in and hide among the congregation in the Great Hall, and then slink away in the confusion which would surely follow when Bart and Wattie failed to arrive with the sacrificial victim. Thinking so, he pushed the door to the Hall open—and found himself in a splendidly lighted room.

He paused, for he had expected gloom. He must change his plan. In any case, simply to sneak away would still leave Harrington unscathed and himself without any real evidence of his villainy. Once Harrington discovered that he had escaped the only sensible thing for him to do was to disband the Brotherhood, destroy any evidence, and deny all of Devenish's accusations, claiming that he had lost his reason.

Devenish looked at the twin flambeaux and he looked at Mr Harrington standing, arms uplifted, behind the altar. Parson Lawson was droning away in a mockery of the real Mass. The expectant congregation must be all agog waiting for yet another human sacrifice.

And as Devenish did so, inspiration struck.

Praying that when Harrington saw him he would believe he was either Wattie or Bart come betimes for some unknown reason, he snatched up the flambeaux, one in each hand, and walked up the aisle towards the altar.

He was halfway up it when Mr Harrington at last noticed him.

'Begone,' he cried dramatically, pointing in Devenish's direction, seeing him as only one of his henchmen in his ceremonial robes. 'Put down the lights. Your time is not yet. The messenger has not been sent to fetch you.'

Devenish took no note of him and continued to advance.

Mr Harrington roared, 'Brothers, I bid you seize this man so that I may deal with him as he deserves.'

No one so much as moved. They stared at Devenish, many of them suspecting that this mysterious stranger might be an emissary from the Pit itself. They had called on the Devil often enough—and now they seemed to have been successful. Fearful, they watched him advance until he stood immediately before the altar, the flambeaux now extended before him.

'I am not your messenger, nor am I Man, either,' cried Devenish in as deep and hollow a voice as he could assume. 'I am the Devil, the Great Lord Sathanas himself, come from Hell to reproach you for troubling him with your piddling concerns. Damnation and hell-fire await you, but you may have a taste of it now.'

So saying, and remembering how Mr Harrington had boasted of slowly murdering the poor dead girls, and his ordering of the deaths of Jeremy Faulkner and his own valet, he threw one flambeau straight at him, and the other on to the altar. The first set Mr Harrington's goat's mask and robes on fire, the second burst open, pitch and flames flowing from it. It rapidly began to consume the altar cloth and the robes of Parson Lawson.

Confusion followed as the flames flowed in the direction of a congregation which feared that it had succeeded only too well in its repeated invocations of the forces of evil. Panicking, some of them began to shout 'Fire' as they made for the nearest doorway which might lead them to safety.

Devenish, who was ahead of them, turned right to run through the door to the Entrance Hall. Behind him the congregation, stumbling and stamping, scuttled towards the door, knocking one another over in their haste. Others, braver or more stupid, whichever way you cared to look at it, tried to extinguish the blaze…to no avail.

The flames which had engulfed Leander Harrington next attacked the hangings behind the altar. The fire was rapidly running out of control; smoke and burning soot filled the air. Those unfortunates at the back of the panic rush towards salvation began beating out the hot flames which were now leaping on to their clothing, before they reached the open air where they rolled on the grass to try to put out the murderous and unforgiving fire. Toby Claridge was among them.

The servants in their quarters above the stables at the back of the house—the Abbey had no attics—came running to help them, alerted by the light of the fire and the noise made by the survivors.

No one dared to enter the Abbey itself, although some brave souls fetched pails of water from the stables and threw them—unavailingly—on to the outskirts of what was now a major conflagration.

Fearful that what had been engaged in might yet be revealed, the survivors made for their horses and began to gallop down the drive towards home, safety and anonymity.

Devenish knew nothing of this. He tore, barefoot, through the gardens, flinging off his robes and mask as he ran by a devious route towards the main gates of the Abbey. He was sure that they would have been left open ready for the return of the congregation to the homes which they had desecrated by taking part in Mr Harrington's fatal mummery.

It had been a conspiracy of brutal murder, and he was sure not only that he had ended it, but also that he had done so in such a way that open scandal would be avoided. All that remained was to try to return secretly to Tresham Hall to ensure that he could not be suspected of having any connection with what had occurred at Marsham on this fatal night.

Devenish could not regret what he had done for both Harrington and the Brotherhood deserved to be punished for their wickedness. They had corrupted not just one another but the poor girls whom they had exploited and whose families would fortunately never know what their daughters had been engaged in—but neither would they ever know that those who had used them so ruthlessly had been punished for their wickedness.

He hid himself in the trees just short of the gates and watched the remnants of the Brotherhood stream by before he set out for home himself.

A mile down the road he began to stagger as exhaustion claimed him—just as the flames from the burning Abbey were bursting upwards into the night sky. The only thing which kept him going was the thought of Drusilla and the future which he hoped to share with her.

'Are you quite well, my dear?'

Drusilla looked up from the book which she was not reading, and said pleasantly, 'Oh, yes. I'm a little low because I'm very worried about Giles.'

She was, of course, not being entirely truthful. She had spent a quiet day worrying not only over Giles, but where her duty to Hal lay. She had hoped against hope that Rob Stammers would reappear with good news, or, better still, that Hal would come riding along the sweep to the front door, ready to be wryly amused by their joint concern about him.

No such luck. Giles still lay in his semi-coma. Hal's whereabouts remained dubious. She knew that her manner had been so subdued that Miss Faulkner thought that she might be sickening for something.

After an early dinner Miss Faulkner proposed a game of backgammon which, contrary to her usual habit, Drusilla lost. Miss Faulkner decided to retire early, leaving Drusilla alone. She discarded the book she was too distracted to read, deciding that she would follow Miss Faulkner's example when the door opened and Giles's nurse burst in.

'Oh, mum, you must come at once. Master Giles has recovered and is calling for you. I wonder that you could not hear him downstairs. He says that he must see you immediately.'

Drusilla gathered up her skirts and ran full pelt upstairs, the nurse thundering behind her. She could hear Giles shouting, and entered the bedroom to find him sitting up. His eyes were huge in a face, which had been thinned by illness, and instead of being pale his cheeks were red again. His hands were plucking nervously at the bedclothes.

'What is it, Giles? What's the matter?'

He said, almost incoherent in his haste, 'Alone, Dru. I must speak to you alone. I must, I must, and now.'

She went to sit by him to take his hands in hers. 'Gently, Giles, have you been having nightmares that you are so distressed?'

'No nightmare, Dru—or not of the kind you think.'

He was shaking so violently that Drusilla sent the protesting nurse from the room.

'Now you may speak freely, Giles. But slowly, so I may understand what you are trying to tell me.'

He passed his hand over his eyes and sank back against his pillows. 'Oh, Dru, when I woke up I remembered what poor Betty was trying to tell me when I last saw her!'

It all came tumbling out of him. 'She told me that she had taken part in secret meetings at Marsham Abbey which had been organised by Mr Harrington and in which some of the local gentry took part. They were masked, she said, so that she couldn't name them. At first she and the other girls thought it was all a bit of fun, just the gentry enjoying themselves. Only one of the girls ever took part in a ceremony in the crypt. The others were given good food in the house while they waited until it was over. The gentlemen then joined them in the house, ate and drank and...enjoyed the girls.'

Gradually Giles began to grow less agitated and to speak more slowly and coherently, his hands still in Drusilla's.

'She said that all the girls who took part had been given money and a special necklace. When the girls began to disappear, one by one, those who were left were told by a man called Wattie that they had been given money to go to London where, because they had been so obliging, well-paid work waited for them—and that the same would be done for them when their turn came.

'Betty quite looked forward to going to London herself until her friend, Kate Hooby, came to her one day and told her a dreadful tale. One of the footmen, who later disappeared, had told her that it was all a tale: the gentlemen, he said, had been worshipping the Devil. The girls had never gone to London. Instead, those who had taken part in the ceremony itself had been murdered, sacrificed on an altar, he said. He also told her that Mr Jeremy Faulkner and Mr Harrington's valet had been killed because they had threatened to report Mr Harrington and his friends to the authorities.

'Betty and Kate thought it must be a story, because no one would ever do such terrible things—until Kate disappeared. Kate's father told Betty that she had left her clothing behind and that he had found money and a necklace in her room. Betty knew that Kate would never have gone anywhere without them, so she decided to tell me what she suspected so that I could ask Devenish whom she knew to be my friend to look into the matter. Only...just as she finished...and I was assuring her that I would tell Devenish...nothing.'

He stopped. 'I remember nothing after. I suppose that she talked too much, someone became suspicious, followed her and found her with me. They must have killed her on Mr Harrington's orders, and left me for dead, too, so that we should not inform on them. Oh, Dru, we must tell Devenish immediately.'

He was so agitated that Drusilla did not dare to tell him that Devenish might also be missing.

Instead she said, as calmly as she could after hearing such a shocking tale, 'I'll see that a message goes to Tresham Hall immediately. Now, lie down and try to sleep. You've done your duty by poor Betty. But you must promise me one thing. Speak to no one about this, no one at all. Not Cordelia nor any of the Cliftons. Not only for your own safety but because you won't want to put anyone else at risk.'

Giles nodded, and slid down into the bed. 'I feel so much better now I've told you, Dru. It was queer. When I woke up it was as though it had happened only a moment ago. I was trying to comfort Betty, and then—nothing—until I found myself in my own bed. How long have I been asleep?'

Drusilla told him. He shook his head. 'I can scarcely believe you. But I must.'

'Lie down,' she said tenderly, 'and try to sleep.'

He did as she bade him, leaving her to stand there, shocked beyond belief by his dreadful tale. Could Betty's story possibly be true? If it were not, then she would have to believe that Betty had invented it—and that was not possible. An uneducated country girl could not have known of or imagined such a thing as devil worship and human sacrifice. Her story had the ring of truth.

Drusilla remembered as she ran to her room that the doctor had said that it was possible that Giles didn't want to wake up—which now seemed highly likely. She went straight to her escritoire and tore open Hal's letter—in the light of what Giles had just told her he might already be dead or dying if the letter confirmed that he had discovered the truth about the poor girls, Jeremy and the valet.

Dreadfully the letter confirmed all—and more—of Giles's story. It must be sent to Lord Sidmouth as soon as possible, but she—and Rob Stammers when she told him the news—dare not wait for him to take action if

Hal were to be found alive. She rang for her maid, told her to lay out the breeches, shirt, jacket and boots which she had worn to ride in before she had married Jeremy, and to send word to Vobster that he was to have two horses saddled immediately.

Her maid stared at her. 'It's gone nine of the clock, ma'am. Are you sure you wish to go riding now?'

'Of course I'm sure,' she snapped. 'Do as you are bid.' Every moment lost might put Hal in further danger if—dreadful thought—he were not already dead.

Vobster was equally argumentative. 'At this time of night, ma'am? To Tresham Hall? In the dark?'

'At once,' she shouted at him for the first time in her life. 'Immediately. There's a full moon and a clear sky—we shall be able to see our way without any difficulty. We have no time to lose. And Vobster, tell no one where we are going, and make as little fuss as possible. And saddle Pegasus with Giles's harness. I don't want a side saddle—it will slow me down too much.'

He eyed her resignedly. Either the mistress had run mad or he had. He could not be sure that he was hearing her aright.

Ten minutes later they were thundering out of the main gates to Lyford House as though the Devil himself were after them.


Devenish was finding his long walk back to Tresham Hall growing harder and harder. He had not eaten properly since he had been captured. His body was covered in bruises from Wattie's mistreatment. He even thought that Wattie might have cracked two of his ribs.

His feet had begun to bleed and only the thought that he must reach Tresham before the news of the fire at Marsham Abbey had the whole county in a furore kept him going. Above all he must try to sneak into Tresham before anyone saw him in his present condition. Which, he conceded wryly, was going to be nearly as difficult as escaping from Marsham Abbey had been.

He was almost at the end of his strength and was trying to prevent his tired body from lying down of its own volition, when he heard horsemen approaching behind him, riding fast and furiously.

He dodged into the shadow of the hedge in case someone at Marsham Abbey might have guessed who the unknown Sathanas might have been. Perhaps, by some mischance, Leander Harrington had survived and guessed that he had escaped from his prison cell. It was scarcely likely even though stranger things had happened. But his body would not obey him, he was beginning to sway as he stood.

The horsemen stopped when they reached him. One of them said, 'There's a beggar in the road. What's he doing at this hour of night?'

Devenish recognised the voice. It was Vobster, Drusilla's most trusted man. He had Master Giles with him. Where could they be going at this time of night? He thought that it might be safe to speak to them. He had no real suspicion that any of Drusilla's staff might

be involved in Leander Harrington's mischief—and besides, Giles's presence would probably protect him.

'Vobster,' he said. And then, without him willing it,
he muttered hoarsely, 'Help me.'

It was Drusilla who recognised his voice, changed
though it was. Joy ran through her. The supposed beggar was Hal. A Hal who was barefoot and dressed in
rags. He was alive, but hurt, and even from a distance
he smelled of fire. Her relief on seeing him was so
strong that she almost fainted. Common sense kept her
steady, for her first duty was to help him.

'Hal!' she exclaimed—and for Vobster's benefit,
'Lord Devenish!' She slipped from her horse, throwing
the reins to the astonished Vobster, who, turning in his
saddle, exclaimed, even as Drusilla embraced Hal, 'By
God, the Abbey's on fire. I wondered why the night
was so light!'

Neither Drusilla nor Devenish heard him. Devenish
muttered, 'For God's sake, Giles, don't kiss me. It ain't
proper. You're too old.'

'It's not Giles, it's me,' said Drusilla incoherently.
'Giles is at home in bed. Oh, Hal, what in the world
has happened to you? Where have you been?'

'Nothing, nowhere,' he mumbled, passing a hand
over her face and then down her body. 'Yes, it is you,
Drusilla. What are you doing out at this hour?'

She stood back from him, 'I might ask you the same
question. I'll answer yours later when we have seen
you safely home. Vobster, dismount and help Lord
Devenish on to your horse. We must get him to

Tresham Hall as quickly as possible. He's at the end of his tether.'

She might have guessed that distressed as he was, Hal's tongue would still be as sharp as ever. 'No, I'm not,' he told her, 'I slipped my tether some time ago. Thank you, Vobster, don't coddle me. I'm not yet dead.'

'Nor yet truly alive, either,' retorted Vobster, noting how m'lord swayed after he had hoisted him into the saddle. 'Good God, what have you done to your feet, m'lord?'

'Walked on them,' Devenish riposted as though he were back in his drawing room, sharpening his wits on others. 'That's what feet are for. It's just that they prefer shoes—especially on rough ground.'

Only he knew of the effort he was having to make to stay conscious and coherent—although his two helpers were aware that staying on horseback was draining him of his remaining strength.

'Walk his horse for him, Vobster,' Drusilla ordered sharply, 'and watch that he doesn't fall off. We were on our way to Tresham Hall to give Rob Stammers some information which might help him to discover where you had disappeared to. He and I have been worrying over your whereabouts for the last few days.'

She did not ask him about poor Martin. He would tell her of that later, and in the light of everything she feared that the news must be bad. For the moment they must concentrate on getting him safely back home so that they might decide what action to take against Leander Harrington and his fellows.

Back on Pegasus again, Drusilla rode alongside Hal to keep watch over him. He turned his head, and said, his voice a little clearer. 'I thank you for your consideration for me—and Rob's too. By the by, I like you in boy's clothes, but I prefer you in dresses. Why the get-up?'

'Riding at night,' she told him briefly, 'best if rogues think that Vobster has a boy with him and not a woman. Now save your strength for riding.'

'Shrew,' he threw at her with something of his old sharpness, but his smile was gentle, and his eyes told her of his pleasure at seeing her.

Slowly, the three of them set off for Tresham Hall. Both of them wondered how much the man riding alongside Drusilla had to do with the fire at Marsham Abbey which was turning night into day.

## Chapter Fifteen

Seen in the brighter light of the drawing room at Tresham Hall and not under the lesser glow of the full moon, Devenish's condition was parlous.

When he had told Vobster that he wished to enter the Hall without anyone seeing him, Vobster put his finger beside his nose and winked at him.

'Easy, m'lord, easy,' he said. 'No names, no pack drill, though.'

Despite his exhaustion Devenish grinned at him. 'Oh, I know the tricks the servants get up to in order to sneak in and out the house. I'll look the other way.'

Vobster shinned up a drain pipe, reached a window above one of the side doors to the hall, did some intricate manoeuvring with his hands, and had the window opened in a trice. Some moments later he opened the back door to let them in.

After that he left Devenish and Drusilla alone in the drawing room whilst, following Devenish's instructions, he slunk up to Rob Stammers's suite of rooms to tell him that m'lord had returned.

Oddly it was Rob who was most distressed at the sight of Devenish's fire-blackened face, his light growth of beard, his badly bruised torso, glimpsed through his tattered shirt, and his torn and bleeding feet. Drusilla had been so relieved to find him still alive that his battered and unkempt state scarcely mattered to her. Hal was with her and she was with Hal, and she knew instinctively that the last thing which he wished was to be fussed over.

Devenish's relief that Rob had never formed part of the Brotherhood was great—even when he could not persuade him that he did not wish to be treated like a year-old babe about to snuff it at any minute.

'Sit down, sit down,' Rob ordered him distractedly. 'For God's sake let me get a doctor to you—and your valet. You should be in bed. And what is Giles Faulkner doing here at this hour—and Vobster?'

'For God's sake, no,' retorted Devenish. 'I came home late, you understand, and did not wish the whole house woken up to accommodate me. I got myself to bed alone often enough when my grandfather was alive, that I have not forgotten the trick of it. As for Giles Faulkner, he is in his own bed, and if you are so flustered by my fortunate return that you don't recognise his sister, you are scarce fit to hear my sad tale.'

'*You* didn't recognise me, Hal,' said Drusilla pertly.

'Ah, but I was only half-conscious in the moonlight. By the by, before I enlighten you all as to my adventures I should prefer to go to my room in order to assume the appearance of a civilised man and not a savage. While I am doing that you might order some food and drink, not just for the pair of us, but for Master Giles and Vobster, who are only here because they rode out to see the fire at Marsham and, by great good fortune, met me on the way and saw me safely home.'

'Master Giles?' queried Rob, 'I thought that you said that Giles was Drusilla. And to what fire are you referring?'

'Indeed, so she is. For our purposes, though, Mrs Faulkner is safely in bed at Lyford, not Giles. I am in fine fettle or shall be when I am dressed and Vobster is the splendid fellow he always is. Truth has many faces.'

These Hal-like jokes set Drusilla laughing if no one else.

Rob said impatiently. 'What fire?'

'Oh, the fire is at Marsham Abbey. I should be surprised if any of it is left standing by morning. Forgive me, I must make my lies truth. And creep quietly—and alone—to my room to do so.'

Rob groaned when he had gone.

'Can either of you tell me where he has been and what he has been doing? He really ought not to go upstairs on his own but in this mood there is no gainsaying him.'

Only Drusilla understood that there was an undercurrent of something very like hysteria beneath Devenish's determined jollity. She said, 'We know nothing. He will tell us everything when he returns, I am sure.'

'Oh, you may be sure of one thing only,' said Rob, full of gloom. 'He will not do that, he never does. I will go and arrange some food and drink for us all—and tell whoever is about that m'lord is back.' He paused. 'Did he say anything about Martin?'

'He said nothing about anything,' returned Drusilla. 'He was near to collapsing. How can he be so lively now?' Vobster nodded his head vigorously in agreement with her before taking himself off to the kitchen for his own meal.

The food and drink arrived for the three of them before Devenish did. When he walked in he looked, except for his golden beard, as though he had been riding in Hyde Park. He had met a footman on his way downstairs who had stared at him and had asked if m'lord wished for his valet to help him to change out of the clothes which he had travelled in.

'I told him I might need him later,' Devenish said. His high spirits seemed to have deserted him along with his rags. He sat carefully down and drank a glass of wine before eating a little of the food—a large beef sandwich and a chicken leg. He felt weary unto death, wanted his bed and oblivion, but he owed Rob and Drusilla some sort of explanation.

'Harrington kidnapped me as we rode down the by-way the day I went to London. He killed poor Martin so as to silence him and intimidate me. He took me to the Abbey because he had blackmailed Toby Claridge into telling him that he had informed me that he—and what he called the Brotherhood—were celebrating the Black Mass there. He was fearful that I would tell the authorities of his many murderous crimes. And Drusilla, my love, you should know that your poor husband behaved honourably—and that was why he was killed, as was Harrington's brave valet.'

Drusilla said impulsively, 'Which agrees with what Giles told me not two hours ago. I had thought that he might be dreaming.'

'Giles? How did Giles come to know of this?'

'Oh, I forgot. While you were missing Giles had a bad fall, was brought home unconscious and remained like that for several days. This evening he came out of his coma and straight away remembered that Betty had been telling him about Mr Harrington and the Black Mass at Marsham Abbey when they were attacked. I thought that Mr Stammers, who had come to me because he was worried about your apparent disappearance, ought to know immediately—even though it was possible that Giles might have been dreaming.'

'So that was why you were on the road with Vobster, dressed in your brother's clothes. What a resourceful creature you are, Mrs Faulkner. You quite saved my life when you suddenly appeared out of nowhere just as I feared I was about to fall into a coma myself!'

He became silent and leaned back in his chair, his eyes closed. He opened them again to say softly, 'Remind me to thank you. Where was I? Yes, Harrington kidnapped me, imprisoned me and decided to sacrifice me to the Devil tonight, instead of one of the girls. I should simply disappear or—like your husband, whose death he had brought about—be found dead, far from home, murdered by thieves on the way to London.

'Fortunately I managed to escape from the prison in which he held me, shortly after the ceremony began. I had to escape through the Hall, something which provided me, I thought, with a major problem. Happily, when I reached it, it seemed that one of the flambeaux which illuminated the Hall had fallen from its moorings on to the altar and started the fire. In the confusion I was able to escape unseen. And then Drusilla and Vobster found me.'

He smiled at them as he finished telling this lying tale. 'Fortune was truly with me.'

Rob and Drusilla stared at him.

'And that,' said Rob at last, 'is exactly what happened? You just walked out?'

'Oh, yes,' he stared back at them unblinkingly, 'I certainly walked out—remember my poor feet.'

'And you're sticking to that?'

'Only to you. No one else will know other than that I visited London, sent poor Martin to work for me on one of my estates in the north and then came home. It would benefit no one to know the truth.'

'I'm exceedingly happy to learn that you are so wedded to the truth, Hal,' said Drusilla sweetly. 'I would never have thought it of you.'

The look that Devenish flashed her for this quip was so loving that it quite shocked Rob.

'How well you know me,' he murmured.

'What story will the Brotherhood tell?' asked Rob anxiously.

'What story can they tell? There they were, having a jolly little drinking party—just like old Dashwood's

Hell Fire Club—when, lo and behold, by pure mischance they were suddenly engulfed in fire.'

'I don't believe a word of it,' announced Rob gloomily, 'but I suppose that come hell or high water—your pardon, Mrs Faulkner, I keep forgetting that you're not Giles—you'll stick to it. A pity that the Abbey had to burn down, though.'

'*Fiat justitia, ruat coelum.* Let justice be done, though the heavens fall,' was Devenish's response to that.

He gave a great yawn, behind a discreetly placed and beautiful hand. Food and drink were having their way with him.

'Bed for you,' announced Drusilla briskly, as though he were even younger than Giles. 'Even liars deserve a good night's rest.'

'Particularly liars,' agreed Devenish. 'It's such hard work. You and Vobster will spend the night here, I trust.'

'Certainly not. To make our lies convincing I must return home before anyone knows that I am not Giles.'

'Only if you allow Rob and one of the grooms to accompany you. There will be such a fine old commotion over the fire that I doubt whether robbers will be out in force tonight.'

His eyes closed again. He looked, Drusilla thought, tired unto death. Regardless of Rob's presence she leaned forward and kissed him on the cheek. 'Be off with you,' she murmured softly, 'before your lies catch up with you.'

He nodded sleepily. 'Off with *you*, then. I shall call on you as soon as I am a civilised man again. You promise to receive me?'

'Ever and always.'

Rob accompanied her to the stables. 'What an unlikely tale,' he said gloomily. 'I'd stake my life that Hal was the prime cause of the fire.'

Drusilla shook her head at him before she mounted Pegasus. 'No, indeed. We must believe what he told us. Him being so truthful always—and Lord of All Around into the bargain.'

It was her turn to be looked at in wonder by Rob. He said slowly, 'Why, I do declare that you are as bad as he is. You'll make a fine pair.'

'You anticipate,' said Drusilla severely. 'For tonight it is enough for him to get some rest and for me to go home.'

Which she did.

Lord Sidmouth read Devenish's two letters. The first one, which Drusilla had forwarded to him, and the second one, which Devenish wrote on the morning of his return, telling him the same tale as he had told Rob and Drusilla about his escape and Mr Harrington's fortunate death. Like Rob and Drusilla he did not believe a word of it, but scandal had been avoided and that must suffice.

He put them both in the fire and then wrote m'lord Devenish a letter of thanks—'...which must, I fear, be your only reward. I was sorry to learn that the Abbey had been destroyed, but it's a small price to pay, given the circumstances of its destruction.'

In his London home Mr Castle, late a French nobleman, read in his paper that 'news has come to us of a sad tragedy which has occurred in Surrey. Marsham Abbey has been burned down, as a consequence of a footman's carelessness in affixing flambeaux, it is said. The owner, Mr Harrington, had been entertaining a gentleman's club in his Great Hall, and by great good fortune only four persons had perished in the flames.

They were Mr Leander Harrington, the owner of the Abbey, long known for his good works and high principles and Parson Lawson, a young theologian of great promise, confidently expected to become a Bishop. Two of Mr Harrington's most faithful servants had also perished in the flames. Some few gentlemen had suffered burns, but were all reported to be on the mend.'

Mr Castle put his newspaper down and thought of the resolute man whom he had so recently entertained. 'A likely tale,' he told himself as he lit his pipe. 'But it will do. Like grandfather, like grandson.'

Devenish had said that he would visit her when he was civilised again, and Drusilla hoped that she had interpreted his last burning glance at her correctly. Yet two days had passed, the third had now arrived and neither he nor any word came from Tresham.

Giles, now up, and as rampant as ever, said reproachfully, 'I'm surprised that Devenish hasn't visited us since he came back from London. I would dearly love to talk to him about the fire at Marsham. There's the oddest rumour going about. Jack Clifton said that when Sir Toby Claridge was visited by the apothecary to be treated for his burns on the night the Abbey was destroyed, he was not himself and babbled about the Devil suddenly appearing and setting fire to the Great Hall. When the constables asked him about it yesterday he claimed that he had said no such thing. That the apothecary was light in the attic through over-excitement.

'And Dr Southwell, Devenish's librarian, who was also there and was slightly burned, said it was all a nonsense. Just someone's carelessness with the flambeaux.'

I wonder, Drusilla began to think, and then stopped herself sternly. I will not speculate, it's not fair to Hal. If he had wanted us to know anything, he would have told us.

She had not informed Giles of her late-night journey in his clothes and the faithful Vobster had been sworn to silence about the night's events by Hal and Rob Stammers before he had escorted her home.

'I say, Dru,' Giles had begun again. 'How would it be if I rode over to Tresham Hall? I'm sure Devenish will know a great deal about how Marsham Abbey came to burn down. He is a local JP, you know.'

'I don't think so,' she said as her butler entered with the welcome news that Lord Devenish had arrived and wished to know whether madam would receive him.

'What luck,' exclaimed Giles eagerly. 'Of course she will. Send him in at once. He's sure to have news about the fire. What a pity I was stuck in bed that night and couldn't ride out to see it. Jack Clifton did...'

'Hush, Giles, don't pester him about it when he comes in.'

The butler coughed. 'Ahem, madam. M'lord wishes to speak to you alone—to begin with, he said.'

Giles's face fell. 'What can he have to say to you that I can't hear? Oh, well, if that is what he wishes. But don't forget to ask him about the fire, Dru, before he goes.'

Drusilla rose and waited for Hal to come in, her heart beating furiously. He had not forgotten her, and by asking to speak to her alone she could guess what he was about to say to her.

Apart from his face showing the lines of recent strain he was his usual immaculate and calm self. No one seeing him could have thought that he could ever resemble the ragged vagabond she had met on the road to Tresham.

She would not have thought him either calm or immaculate if she had seen him arguing with Rob and the doctor earlier that day. He had collapsed on rising the morning after his return home and Rob had sent for the doctor, overruling all of his protestations.

The doctor had condemned him to remain in bed, and, again, over his protests, Rob had kept him there by the simple expedient of locking him in his room for the next two days.

He had felt too weak to do more than grumble at them both, but on the third day he felt himself recovered and announced his intention of rising and going to Lyford House as soon as he had finished breakfast.

'That you won't!' Rob was downright. 'Some light exercise today and perhaps an outing tomorrow...'

He got no further. Devenish walked over to him, caught his right arm in a painful wrestler's lock, and announced civilly, 'Say that again, Rob, and I'll do you a mischief.'

The doctor threw up his hands. 'Pray do not over-exert yourself, m'lord. You might harm yourself severely.'

'Oh, I'll not do that,' Devenish assured him cheerfully. 'No over-exertion is ever needed with this grip. And the harm will be all Rob's and not mine.'

'I see that you are quite recovered,' Rob ground out. 'Have it your way, and don't blame me if you fall off your horse before you reach Lyford.'

'Be sure the groom will pick me up if I do, so no need for you to worry.'

He released Rob and said, 'Now send my valet to me. For once I would value his assistance in dressing me.'

None of this showed as he bowed to Drusilla—other than a self-satisfied gleam in his eye which puzzled her a little.

'You are in looks, Mrs Faulkner. Night riding in boy's clothes obviously suits you.'

'Thank you, m'lord. And spending a few days in Marsham Abbey's gaol before undertaking a long walk home has done wonders for you, too.'

They both began to laugh together. 'Why did I never meet you before, Drusilla? You are quite unlike any of the women I have encountered since I reached my majority.'

'May I again return the compliment, m'lord. You are quite unlike all of the men I had ever been acquainted with before you arrived at Tresham Hall.'

'Ah, madam, you relieve me, and make my task easier. Proposing is something I have never done before and I have no wish to make a botch of it. Pray sit, so that I may kneel before you and take your hand while I do so. I believe that is the proper form.'

Eyes alight, Drusilla did as he bid her. She spread the narrow skirts of her dress about her, placed her hands demurely in her lap—and looked up at him worshipfully.

His lips twitched. 'Minx,' he told her as he went down on one knee, regardless of his tight white breeches. 'How can I be serious when you look at me like that. Stop it at once or I shall fall upon you—you are temptation itself in this mood.'

She closed her eyes, lifted her head, opened them again and said, 'Better?'

'No, not at all. I preferred you the other way, but unfortunately, it deprived me of sense. Now we must both be serious. My dear Mrs Faulkner, Drusilla if I may so call you, it is my dearest wish that you will accept my hand in marriage and make me the happiest man in England. Pray, will you marry me, your most faithful and humble servant?'

'Yes,' she said simply.

'Yes, simply yes, after all my eloquence? Drusilla, my heart's delight, cease to tease me. I can scarcely hope that you love me as much as I love you...have loved you almost from the moment that we met...'

She put a gentle hand over his mouth to silence him. 'Oh, Hal, I love you so much I can scarcely speak, let alone compose a serenade to my happiness in accepting you. Rest assured that to be with you deprives me of sense. I had not known that I could feel so much for another being. My feelings for poor Jeremy were on quite another plane. When Rob told me that he thought that some calamity had overcome you, I nearly ran mad.

'That is the truth—does it satisfy you, sir?'

He kissed the palm of the hand she had placed over his mouth before saying hoarsely. 'Promise that you will always tease me and bring me down to earth. You have taught me to love again. My grandfather taught me only how to hate and to dominate. Until I met you I had forgotten how to love as I once loved my mother and my little brother who, because I could not earn enough to feed my mother, died of starvation when her milk dried up.

'I have been raging against heaven ever since, but no more, I promise you. That is over—and if I backslide you must stop me. Whilst I was a prisoner at Marsham I could only think and dream of you, and what we would do together when I escaped. It was always when, never if. I took you to Venice in my dreams and will take you there in reality. And Tresham shall be our home, for it is a fine place to bring up children...and for you to teach me to be kind.'

Drusilla leaned forward and kissed him on the cheek. Truly, for the moment that would have to suffice, but the desire to be one with him was stronger than ever since he had told her a little of himself.

'How strange,' she said, as he rose to sit by her, and take her in his arms. 'In my dreams while you were captive I was in Venice with you. I have never been there, only seen engravings of it, but in my dream it was coloured, and...'

'And I was loving you—like this,' he said.

They were lost to the world, only knowing one another when Giles came in.

'So that's what you're at,' he exclaimed as they sprang apart, Drusilla rosy-cheeked and Devenish with colour in his face for the first time since he had escaped from Marsham. 'I might have guessed. You *are* going to make an honest woman of her, Devenish, I trust, for I should hate to call you out. You'd be sure to shoot me, or run me through—or something—and I shouldn't like that at all. Oh, and by the by, can you tell me anything about the fire?'

'Giles!' exclaimed Drusilla.

And, 'Dear boy, I shall tell you anything you wish— if you will only go away—immediately,' drawled Devenish.

'Certainly—but I shall hold you to that promise.'

'And now to work, or rather play,' Devenish said when the door had closed behind Giles. He took Drusilla into his arms again where she fitted so sweetly that it was a good thing, she afterwards said, that she was there for life.

The Devil never visited Surrey again. Hal took Drusilla to Venice for their honeymoon and they walked hand in hand by the Grand Canal. Later the kind grass grew over the ruins of Marsham Abbey and Hal and Drusilla watched their children playing around them in the gardens of Tresham Hall. At night, safe in Drusilla's loving arms, Hal's unhappy dreams of the past were banished forever.

\*     \*     \*     \*     \*

# LADY KNIGHTLEY'S SECRET
### *Anne Ashley*

Miss Elizabeth Beresford had become an heiress on her grandmother's death. Her sister Evadne thought she was very clever when she engineered that Elizabeth would be trapped overnight in the cellars with Evadne's brother-in-law. Except that the plot misfired and it was Sir Richard Knightley who became entrapped with Elizabeth! Richard was not unwilling to marry, for Elizabeth had changed beautifully from the young girl he remembered. It was Elizabeth who was reluctant, for she loved him and there was something she couldn't tell him…

# A GENTLEMAN'S MASQUERADE
### *Sally Blake*

After her father's death in 1912, Lauri Hartman decided to use her legacy to visit her English relatives in Devon, but she always intended to return to Boston, and had no inclination for a husband. So her attraction to neighbour Steven Connor, a *very* different man from his twin Robert, took her by surprise! When her aunt fell ill, Lauri decided to stay, cancelling her passage on the *Titanic*. That tragic voyage upset Lauri tremendously, and she and Steven became very close. In daily expectation of a proposal, Lauri began to wonder just what was holding him back…

### *Available in July 1999*

MILLS & BOON®

*Makes any time special*™

# THE LARKSWOOD LEGACY
### *Nicola Cornick*

Widowed Mrs Annabella St Auby's situation was uncomfortable, but meeting Sir William Weston was *wonderful*! He made his interest *very* clear, and she was hugely drawn to him.

But when her father's tangled affairs were finally sorted out, she found her sole inheritance, Larkswood, was of prime importance to Sir William, for *he* said the purchase from his father had not been above board. And Annabella began to wonder—was Sir William's pursuit for herself …or her legacy?

# GALLANT WAIF
### *Anne Gracie*

Miss Kate Farleigh was virtually kidnapped by Lady Cahill, after refusing that lady's 'charity'. But she saw her purpose when included in a visit to Jack Carstairs, Lady Cahill's grandson. Wounded in the Peninsular War, he'd returned home to find his fiancée had ended their engagement. He'd retreated to his country estate, but Kate had no patience with Jack's forcefully uttered requests to be left alone! Her brisk attempts to manage him both amused and enraged Jack, until he saw behind the gallant courage and fell in love…

***Available in August 1999***

# MISTRESS OF MADDERLEA
## *Mary Nichols*

Miss Sophie Roswell wanted to marry, but as an heiress she felt her money would attract the wrong suitor. A chance came to switch places with cousin Charlotte for the Season, and she took it with glee. But when she met Richard, Viscount Braybrooke, she knew she'd made a mistake. For it was clear that while Richard was looking for a wife, and the pair were falling in love, as heir to the dukedom he couldn't follow the dictates of his heart, and Sophie was apparently ineligible…

# BLACKWOOD'S LADY
## *Gail Whitiker*

David, Marquis of Blackwood, needs an heir, but his requirements in a wife are precise. Lady Nicola Wyndham appears to fit the bill—she's older, likes country living, has managed her father's household for some time, and nothing detrimental is known about her.

But when he coolly proposes Nicola's brief look of hurt prompts him to a sudden show of warmth. It gives Nicola hope that they might have a good marriage and she accepts. *But* she has a secret—which he is bound to find out—and which goes against *every* idea David has of his future wife…

*Available in September 1999*

MILLS & BOON®

*Makes any time special*™

# HISTORICAL ROMANCE™

## LARGE PRINT

## THE WOLFE'S MATE
### *Paula Marshall*

Unknown to Miss Susanna Beverly, her stepfather had cheated her out of her rightful inheritance, resulting in her becoming the companion of Miss Amelia Western, who was betrothed to Viscount Darlington. That set of facts resulted in Susanna being mistaken for Amelia and kidnapped by Mr Ben Wolfe's henchmen! Ben's intentions were honourable, he did at least intend to *marry* Amelia, but his aim was revenge upon Darlington's family.

Kidnapping the wrong woman upset all his plans, but as Ben got to know the forthright Susanna, he couldn't *really* admit to being sorry…

## THE ADMIRAL'S DAUGHTER
### *Francesca Shaw*

A freak accident with an ancient rowboat launched Miss Helena Wyatt into the ocean, until a timely rescue by Lord Adam Darvell. But Adam knew, if Helena did not, that he would have to marry her. Helena's quick wit and vivid little face appealed enormously, so it was a tremendous shock when his proposal was turned down flat!

No one knew Helena had been with him, so she saw no reason to accept a duty marriage, particularly one to a man she found so utterly fascinating…

*Available in October 1999*

MILLS & BOON®

*Makes any time special*™